Praise for PUCK

"Full of mischief and romance, this book is everything you'd want in a Shakespearean retelling. A joyful, riotous romp!"
—Ashley Herring Blake, award-winning author of *Delilah Green Doesn't Care*

"*Puck* is pure chaos, a madcap speed-run that pushes the boundaries of the rom-com genre in the best way. An insanely funny read, perfect for gender neutral goblins and the people who love them."
—TJ Alexander, *USA Today* bestselling author of *A Gentleman's Gentleman*

"So much fun! Unique and heartfelt, *Puck* by Samantha Allen balances humor and swoony spice with a thought-provoking story about Puck coming to terms with the person they've become since college. I loved the well-crafted cast of characters, the friendships, and the wedding setting in the book, but what really stood out was Puck's emotional growth as they learn how their actions can affect the people they care about."
—Farah Heron, author of *Accidentally Engaged*

"Hilariously messy and charmingly honest."
—Natasha Bishop, author of *Only for the Week*

"A masterful adaptation of the bard's most riotous play with the perfect combination of humor, heart, and wit. This book is a must read for Shakespeare nerds everywhere."
—Nisha Sharma, award-winning author of the If Shakespeare Were an Auntie series

Also by Samantha Allen

Roland Rogers Isn't Dead Yet
Patricia Wants to Cuddle
Real Queer America

Puck

A NOVEL

SAMANTHA ALLEN

zando
NEW YORK

zandoprojects.com

First Edition: June 2026

Text design by Kevin Ullrich
Cover design by Joanne O'Neill and Christopher Brian King
Title page images via Adobe Stock: (couple) YuliaShlyahova; (film set and crew) ssstocker

Library of Congress Control Number: 2026932438

978-1-63893-341-0 (trade paperback)
978-1-63893-342-7 (ebook)

10 9 8 7 6 5 4 3 2 1
Manufactured in the United States of America
LBK

For the brave one

"Reason and love keep little company together nowadays."

—William Shakespeare, *A Midsummer Night's Dream*

Saturday

Chapter 1

Puck has a date with a croissant. It's not a long one. They only have five minutes before they have to go back to filming interviews with *Homewreckers* contestants, and they've ignored a flurry of pings on their walkie already. A stale pastry swiped off the craft services table will have to pass for lunch today.

But just as they're about to take their first bite, a production assistant with a worried look on his face approaches Puck's perch on the veranda.

"You're, uh, Puck, aren't you?" the PA asks.

"Right you are!" Puck chirps back condescendingly. This kid will have to toughen up if he wants to survive here; he's already sweating through his shirt, probably from nervousness as much as the summer heat. One of the first lessons Puck learned when they started seven years ago was to never wear white at work.

This guy—awkward, maybe about twenty-three, hair hidden in a red beanie except for the hint of a beard he's scratching—must have just started because anyone who's worked at the *Homewreckers* mansion longer than a day could pick Puck out of a lineup while blackout drunk. It doesn't take long for new hires to hear legends about the lead producer's prowess, and almost everyone gets the talk about Puck's pronouns on day one.

Only a few have ever dared disrespect them. Why risk one of the best jobs in Atlanta TV production by insulting the show's second-in-command?

No, amid a turbulent ocean of reality concepts that briefly bob above the surface before sinking just as quickly, *Homewreckers* is solid earth, a long-running series with a surefire premise: Bring in five couples for a "relationship retreat," only to reveal that the sexy singles who once threatened to break up those pairings are going to live with them, too. The show crams the faithful partners, the cheaters, and the tempting free agents all into one house, with the goal of inflicting as much emotional damage as human rights legislation permits. And viewers can't get enough.

For ten years now, couples have come on *Homewreckers* to "put their love to the ultimate test," as the promos put it—and for most of that decade, they have met their match in the form of a nonbinary English major with a buzz cut.

On Puck's first season in 2018, back when they were a lowly PA themself, they broke up all five couples on the same night with their idea to hook the cheaters up to heart rate monitors during a cocktail party. At first, Puck's predecessor resisted the idea based solely on its provenance, telling them that they should be "sorting props somewhere" instead of offering input. But Ron overheard the exchange, backed Puck's idea, and the rest was history. The numbers didn't lie. Once the faithful partners saw the cheaters' pulses rise as the paramours walked in, even the most committed relationships crumbled.

Since that first stroke of genius, it's been nothing but promotions, perks, and pay raises for Puck. And while they haven't managed to replicate their 100 percent success rate since season five, their decision to add hidden cash incentives has more than paid for itself in streaming ratings. Break up a couple? The temptress receives a thousand dollars. It's shocking how much the contestants will do for so little money. The diehard fans who populate the *Homewreckers* subreddit have started to catch wind of Puck's payment scheme, despite all the NDAs the contestants have to sign, but most viewers will never interrogate how the show is made so long as the result is the same: chaos.

"Ron sent me to get you," the PA tells Puck. "He told me to say that you need to come work your magic."

Puck rolls their eyes. They take their time pulling apart a piece of croissant, popping it in their mouth, and chewing, knowing they might not get to eat again until the night crew takes over. Ron could actually try to do some showrunning once in a while, but why bother when Puck's around? That'd be like hiring a Michelin-rated chef to watch *you* make a turkey sandwich. God, Puck would kill for a turkey sandwich right now.

"Will I find the king on his throne?" they ask, folding up the half-eaten pastry in its wax paper before shoving it into their pants pocket.

"Um . . ." The PA looks confused, and more than a little grossed out by Puck's slovenliness.

"The boss," Puck clarifies. "Is he in his trailer?"

"Oh, no, he's at the video village by the pool. Monica and Jason aren't reacting to Erica sunbathing right next to them, and I think he's freaking out."

This is the kind of communication that will get this kid somewhere. You don't tell Puck what Ron *said*; you tell Puck what Ron is *thinking*, and you know what Ron is thinking because you can read his face like a book. Now Puck can spend the forty-second walk around the *Homewreckers* house coming up with a solution to Ron's problem—and that's all the time they need.

Jason is scared of his girlfriend, and rightly so: Monica, one of the most faithful women to ever come on the show, shoots lasers out of her eyes whenever Erica, the woman Jason cheated with last year, so much as blinks in his direction. A sufficiently cowed Jason has largely behaved himself for the first two weeks of filming. He even kept his composure when Erica recreated the whipped cream bikini scene from *Varsity Blues* at Ron's urging. Puck's reminder that none of the contestants was old enough to remember that movie had gone unheard. Hell, Puck was only four when it came out, and at thirty, they are far from the youngest person on the crew anymore.

Puck had already been cooking something up for the Jason-Monica-Erica storyline, but if the head honcho wants to press the panic button now, they know exactly what to do. There are simpler and more sanitary ways to a man's heart besides putting dairy near someone's vagina. Also, Jason is probably wearing swimming trunks right now, which makes this impromptu scheme especially delicious.

After gliding up next to Ron in the tented video village set up on the back lawn, Puck quickly assesses the situation. Over by the pool, one camera crew is capturing footage of Erica suntanning on her stomach, while a smaller crew remains trained firmly on Monica and Jason as they lie on adjacent chaise lounges, determinedly holding hands across the gap between them. How sweet. Alas, the lovefest won't last long.

"Let's get Jess out here, please," Puck orders to no one in particular, knowing one of the underlings will scurry off and fetch the contestant for them.

"Hello to you too," Ron says, adjusting the bill of the Dodgers ballcap he never seems to remove, still clinging to his Angeleno allegiances even after all these years in Georgia. "You are aware Jason cheated on Monica with *Erica*, right? Not with Jess. We're dying out here, Puck. We need some action."

You'd think Ron would have learned by now not to second-guess his own salvation. Besides, when is he ever out here in the middle of the day? Isn't it about time for his afternoon wind-down? A Scotch and a nap would do him some good.

"You wanted magic?" Puck says. "Then let me pull a rabbit out of my hat."

Only they can get away with talking back to the top brass like this; anyone else would get thrown off set for insubordination. Ron obediently hushes up and pretends to consult a clipboard that probably has nothing but doodles on it.

While Puck waits for Jess to be delivered, they scan various monitors set up around the video village. Jason isn't even glancing in Erica's direction, even though the sunlight is kissing her skin just right. Little beads of sweat are forming on the back of her thighs. The string of her swimsuit bottom is so thin it almost looks like she's bare-assed. And still, Jason is clinging to Monica's hand like he'd float off into space if he let go.

"What's the ETA on Jess?" Puck asks, only to find that Red Beanie Boy has reappeared with the missing piece: Jess Sandusky, twenty-four, a physical therapist from Akron, Ohio, and most importantly for Puck's purposes, an absolute babe, even by absurdly high television standards. Sadly, Jess has ascertained that she's the hottest girl on her cast—and she acts like it.

"Did you need me for something?" she huffs.

"Oh, hi!" Puck greets her with an enthusiasm that should be suspicious. "Thanks for coming."

"It's not like I have a choice."

Contestants like Jess sometimes get cute about their contracts, acting like they're being held captive even though they're free to leave at any point—so long as they can afford to fend off life-ruining litigation from Hollywood's meanest lawyers.

"You always have a choice," Puck lies, then adds, "Hang on just a second—"

Jess looks annoyed while Puck pulls the new PA aside. *Good.* Let her fume. It's important to reinforce the power dynamic once in a while, and Puck does, in fact, need to whisper a few urgent instructions to the gofer. There are a lot of delicate components in this hastily formed plan of theirs, but Puck is in the mood to show off. Ron doesn't get to interrupt croissant time without suffering the consequences.

After the PA nods and scurries away, Puck turns back to Jess, ready to level with her. "So, listen," they begin. "Erica over there mentioned to me that her back was feeling a little tight . . ."

Puck knows the ulterior motive here will be immediately obvious to someone as savvy as Jess, so there's no point trying to be subtle.

"And let me guess: You think it'd be a good idea for me to give her a massage right in front of Jason?" she asks, already catching wise.

"Bingo."

Jess says nothing, but Puck doesn't rush to fill the silence. Never let the inherent desperation of your profession show—it's a principle all good producers learn early on. Puck knows they'll have to make a sales pitch eventually, but Jess should get the objections out of her system first. The more headstrong *Homewreckers* contestants often need to rage against the machine for a minute before accepting their role as dutiful cogs within it.

"Isn't that a little un-feminist of you?" Jess asks, after a moment's consideration. "I mean, aren't you . . ."

The girl's eyes dart up and down Puck's outfit: a tank top with a rip down one side, black Dickies, and a beat-up pair of Doc Martens they've been dutifully re-soling since Pride of 2015. Their bare arms are covered in blackwork tattoos. The only way they could be more of a stereotype is if they had a carabiner or a septum piercing, and they've been considering the latter.

"Super gay?" Puck says, taking Jess's thought to its extreme. It's fine. They didn't get to be an openly queer producer on a major reality show by having thin skin. This is among the least offensive suppositions they've withstood at *Homewreckers*. Puck once made the mistake of bringing a now ex-girlfriend to set one day and a particularly crude lighting tech asked "who the man was" in the relationship. He was promptly fired. But for the record, the man was definitely Puck.

Jess hedges when put on the spot. She wasn't prepared for Puck to make her implication explicit, and it shows in the panic on her face. "I mean, I wouldn't put it like that . . . but yeah."

Is she trying to imply that Puck should be above appealing to the lowest common denominator just because they're queer?

Principles are nice to ponder when you don't have to entertain anyone. If Puck were back at Emory, then sure, they could churn out a term paper about heteronormativity, reality TV, and the limitations of the "male gaze" as a mode of analysis, but this is no time for theory. Every second the *Homewreckers* crew spends filming the contestants being idle, the production burns money. This isn't *Love Island,* as Ron often reiterates. They need something big to happen every episode.

"Look, I'm gay but I'm not stupid," Puck tells Jess. "And because I'm not stupid, I know what you getting on top of Erica would do to Jason. And I know that it would make amazing television."

Jess crosses her arms in front of her chest. "And how does that benefit *me*?"

Puck hopes the PA has had enough time to handle their first request by now, because for their next trick, they want to pull off a flawless no-look assist, just like Sue Bird used to do before she retired from the Seattle Storm. OK, they were being sarcastic before but maybe they *are* super gay.

"Look at the upstairs bathroom window, Jess," they instruct.

Puck follows the girl's eyes up to the second story, and sure enough, Micah is there looking out over the backyard. "Think about what it would do to *him*," they emphasize.

Jess has spent her time on *Homewreckers* so far trying to ensnare Micah, a douchey Buckhead bro she used to meet up with for secret trysts at the W. But Micah's girlfriend Alexa has been stuck to his hip, only separating when the junior producers pull them apart like cinnamon rolls. In that way, Jess and Erica have similar problems, and they haven't yet realized that the solution might be for them to join forces. The sad thing about Jess, though, is that, unlike Erica, she doesn't want any prize money—she actually thinks Micah is her one true love. It's tragic, but then again, so is heterosexuality.

"Where's Alexa?" Jess asks, correctly intuiting that her window of opportunity will be short by design.

"Oh, she was needed out front for an 'in the moment' interview. She'll be back in a few minutes, though," Puck says, knowingly. "And Micah just got a text letting him know he might see 'something interesting' if he 'went upstairs and took a shower.'"

Less experienced producers might find themselves ceding more ground to the contestants than they want to give up; but Puck always prepackages tempting offers like these, and almost no one wants to leave a good deal on the table.

"Fine," Jess concedes—and then with a dash of vanity that verges on homophobia, adds "Enjoy the show," as though Puck were so starved of intimacy that they needed to engineer girl-on-girl situations at work. If only Jess could see the string of women Puck has brought home from My Sister's Room the last few nights.

Jess exits the tent and strides across the lawn toward Erica's chaise while Puck returns to Ron's side. "Ready?"

Ron looks to be suppressing annoyance. "Have you ever thought about telling me what you're planning before you start doing it?"

"Where's the fun in that?"

Puck checks the monitors as the camera crews move into place before pulling on a pair of wireless headphones to make sure they can hear every word of what's about to happen. By the time they're tuned into the correct audio feed, Jess is standing over Erica, who flips over on her chaise lounge to find out what the other girl wants. Across the pool, Jason is maintaining his death-tight grip on Monica's hand, perfectly playing the part of dutiful boyfriend, but Puck knows how fragile that façade can be. The *Homewreckers* boys always crack; the only question is how spectacularly.

"I heard you could use a back rub," Jess says, and Erica, who's not quite as clever, struggles to piece it together.

"What? Who said that?" Erica asks—but it's fine; they can edit out this preamble in post.

Jess has to subtly tilt her head toward the video village before Erica understands what's happening. "Oh, um, yeah," she says, flipping back over on the chaise and reaching an arm backward to point at a random spot. "I guess I kind of have a knot right . . . *here*."

For all of Jess's protestations, the girl really leans into the performance now that she knows Micah is watching from on high. Puck even asked the PA to put a pair of binoculars on the bathroom windowsill in case he wants to get a closer look at the proceedings. After slowly removing her swim cover-up, Jess climbs onto the chaise and straddles Erica's butt. She presses her hands down firmly between Erica's shoulder blades, kneading her muscles like a cat making biscuits. It looks like the introduction to some bad lesbian porn, but that's exactly how Puck wants it to come across. The streamer *did* say they needed more boyfriends to watch this season, after reviewing the latest audience demographics. This is one way to do it.

"Here?" Jess asks, pitching her voice down to the exact right level of huskiness, while still making sure she's speaking loudly enough for Jason to hear.

"Ooh," Erica purrs. "Can you do it a little harder? I feel *really* tight."

Jess applies even more pressure, putting all her weight into her palms, shifting her body suggestively with every press and caress.

Ron shoots Puck a knowing look and whispers, "You're a genius," but Puck holds a single finger up to their lips.

"Shhh," they joke. "I'm trying to enjoy the movie."

But it's not a movie. Not really. It's more like a play with an ensemble cast—dozens of players whom Puck can choreograph blindfolded and with earplugs in, moving them up and downstage at will. If the PA managed to set everything up correctly, this could be the defining moment of the season—and it's only week three.

Jess leans over to dig her elbows into Erica's upper back, pointedly directing her cleavage in Jason's direction. Puck checks another monitor: Monica is stone-faced, watching in horror as the two sirens put on a sexy show across the pool. Jason can't help but peek, but only for a half second at a time. His internal battle is pointless. Puck knows he's not going to be able to keep it up—well, not in *that* sense anyway. Meanwhile, on the second story of the mansion, Micah is putting the binoculars to good use, as Puck confirms with a quick upward glance. The twin lenses might as well be window decals.

"You really know what you're doing," Erica says as Jess continues to work her back.

Puck grabs a walkie off a folding table and holds down the button. "We'll have to blur it in post," they whisper to the crew, "but I need a zoom on Jason's swim trunks."

Across the way, a cameraman obeys, redirecting his lens toward the man's crotch. An entire monitor in the video village is now taken up by Jason's growing bulge.

"Is that good for you, baby?" Jess asks Erica, loud enough for the entire backyard to hear, and even Puck thinks that's probably laying it on too thick. But based on the tent that pops up in Jason's swimsuit, it was perfectly calibrated for maximum impact. Would it be too much to add a *boing* sound effect in the final cut?

"Houston, we have liftoff," Puck gleefully announces.

It all happens fast after that, with the cameras springing into action to capture every development: Monica notices Jason's erection and drops his hand in disgust. She storms around the pool to confront Erica and Jess, who "know exactly what they're doing," as she repeatedly insists at ever-increasing volumes, but the girls play dumb.

"Can I not give another girl a massage?" Puck hears Jess say.

Jason, meanwhile, is chasing after Monica, hunched over, stammering out apologies even as he tries to hide his crotch with his hands.

Then Erica stands up and yells right back in Monica's face, the tension that's been building between them this season coming to a head. And finally, an unexpected cherry on top: Erica shoves Monica into the pool, a splash punctuating their shouting match, leaving everyone in stunned silence. The show's insurance won't be happy about that, but the audience will be.

Puck turns to find Ron shaking his head in a mixture of joy and disbelief. He got what he wanted, and then some.

"But wait," Puck whispers to their boss. "There's more . . ."

"More?"

"Yup."

Puck isn't sure this coup de grâce is going to happen, so they're going out on a limb with this infomercial-style tease. But then, right on cue, a scream from somewhere inside the house pierces the silence.

Ron looks alarmed. "What was *that*?"

"Oh, your new PA made sure that Micah was watching from the upstairs bathroom," Puck says, deigning to nod in the kid's direction. "And he may have also made sure Alexa caught him peeping. With binoculars, even."

Ron's grin goes from satisfied to devilish. "And I'm guessing a crew followed Alexa up there?" he asks.

"You're a bright bulb," Puck says. "They should make you an executive producer or something."

"Cute."

Puck smiles, reaching over to flick the bill of Ron's ballcap. "I'll put in a good word for you before my vacation."

Chapter 2

Hours later, as the rest of the day crew shuffles off to their cars, Puck returns to the front porch and their now borderline-inedible croissant, plucking off the pocket lint in a futile attempt to make it appetizing again. But the new PA seems determined to keep them from eating it. He reappears just as Puck starts into the pastry again, his greasy brown hair slicked back, beanie clutched in his hands like he's a Dickensian street urchin approaching an industrialist for a spare farthing.

"Hey, I, uh, just wanted to tell you that was incredible today," he says.

"What's your name?" Puck asks, after swallowing a bite.

The kid has earned that by now, even though he's still firmly on the bottom rung of the *Homewreckers* ladder. It takes more than a day's worth of good work to distinguish yourself here, but he worked miracles earlier, somehow securing that pair of binoculars with only a minute's notice.

"I'm Nick," he introduces himself.

"Well, today was all thanks to you, Nick," Puck says, not bothering to cover their mouth as they chew. There were six hours of follow-up interviews after the poolside fracas, and they need calories right now more than they need to look delicate. "I asked for a lot and you delivered."

There are ways in which Nick reminds Puck of themself when they got hired on *Homewreckers* as their first real job after college: young, eager to help, awed by how easily they could extract emotions from a bunch of twentysomething human guinea pigs. It's a heady feeling when you first exercise power over the contestants, and Nick has gotten a taste. But unlike Nick, Puck never carried themself with such meekness. They acted like a producer even when they were first hired as a glorified coffee-fetcher, and these days they act like the showrunner, which, for all intents and purposes, they are.

"How do you come up with that stuff?" Nick asks, shuffling his feet like he wants to sit down next to Puck but is too skittish to ask for an invite. "I mean, how did you know what everyone was going to do before they did it?"

Puck shoves the rest of the croissant in their mouth, crumpling up the wax paper. "Let me tell you something about people, Nick," they say between swallows. "They don't actually want what they *say* they want."

Puck grants the PA mercy, patting a spot next to them on the porch. Nick hurriedly sits, but he looks skeptical. "So they're liars?"

"Worse," Puck tells him. "They're fools, and they think we're fools, too."

Nick's face goes blank. He's not following.

"Take Jason," they continue. "During his entry interview, he tried to convince us he was a 'changed man.' He thought we'd buy it, too. He kept blathering on and on about wanting a family with Monica. He couldn't *wait* to have kids, a house, a dog, the whole kit and labradoodle. To quote the Bard, he doth protest too much."

"What does that even mean? 'Protest too much'?"

Nick may be helpful when it comes to arranging pawns on the board, but he's not destined to become a grandmaster, is he?

"It means Jason was selling it too hard, past the point of believability," Puck explains. "He doesn't want a mortgage with Monica—he wants to put his face in Erica's ass."

Nick, taken off guard by the crude remark, makes a sputtering noise somewhere between coughing and laughter.

"And Jess," Puck proceeds, unbothered, "she thinks she wants Micah, but she doesn't."

"How do you mean?" the PA asks, still not understanding.

"Jess uses male desire to shore up her ego. It almost doesn't matter *who* it comes from. If she actually *got* Micah, she'd be like a dog catching up with a car. She wouldn't know what to do. The fact that Micah wants her even though he's technically *with* another woman is what makes Jess feel real. Like she exists outside the borders of her own insecurity."

Nick mimes an explosion coming out of his ears. "Wow. Did you study psychology or something?"

Maybe it's because they're tired, but Puck decides to let some honesty slip out: "No, I'm just a queer person who's spent my entire adult life watching straight people live theirs."

Nick laughs. "And you think we're that predictable?"

"More often than not," Puck answers wearily. They really should head home if they're going to drive up to North Carolina tomorrow. "Look, to get places on this show, you have to remember that everyone is lying about themselves constantly," they continue through a stifled yawn. "And it's up to you to figure out what they *actually* want. Once you crack that, predicting how they'll act on those desires is the easy part."

If Nick were smarter, he'd ask Puck if they were lying about themself, too. He'd ask if what they thought they wanted in life was what they *really* wanted. If they were ignoring something inside themself by constantly pulling on other people's strings. And if Puck hadn't hit their limit on truth for the day, they'd say they don't know. That they can see through other people, but their own heart remains frustratingly opaque. Instead, Puck stands up and brushes the crumbs off their pants.

"Ron mentioned you were leaving for a few days," Nick says, suddenly sounding forlorn. "Something about a wedding?"

Is the kid trying to make small talk? He may be "Nick" now, but they're far from being friends. Puck is *this* close to demoting him back to anonymity.

"Yup. For a week, actually," Puck says, leaving it at that.

"Who's getting married?" Nick asks anyway, undeterred by the curtness.

Puck briefly considers answering Nick for the hell of it, detailing the whole saga of their college friend group. It might feel good to tell *someone* how much they've been dreading this week in the Blue Ridge Mountains. But with the beautiful havoc they just wrought together back at the pool, there's more than enough drama for Nick to handle already. Telling him about Mia, Zander, Damon, and Lena would be drama overload, and he should stay focused on *Homewreckers*.

Besides, Puck has already lingered on set too long. At this rate, they'll only have about half an hour back in their Decatur apartment to cram a suit, their formal Docs, and, somewhat optimistically, their strap-on into a backpack before sleep takes them. Then they have a five-hour drive to the resort in the morning.

"The question isn't who's getting married," Puck says, opting to remain elliptical, "but *should* they."

"And should they?" Nick prompts.

"Well, if you have to ask, they probably shouldn't," Puck tries to joke, but they can hear the anxiety in their voice.

They turn to leave, weighing whether they need to stop and buy any travel toiletries on the way home. With the filming of *Homewreckers* and all of its sundry spinoffs, it's been years since Puck has taken real time off work—not that this trip feels like a vacation. If anything, this wedding will be a watered-down version of the show, full of drunk straight people making bad decisions, but with all of Puck's authority checked at the door.

"At least it'll be nice getting away from all these lunatics, huh?" Nick says, gesturing at the house.

Most people would feel relieved to get some time away from a job this stressful. Puck can only pretend to be one of them.

"Yeah," they tell him. "Should be nice."

Sunday

Chapter 3

The dirt road that supposedly leads to the Athenian Hotel is so long that Puck pulls over after five minutes to make sure they didn't take a wrong turn off 276. They don't want to end up on the front lawn of some shotgun-toting moonshiner, which is a stereotype they're allowed to conjure up in their mind because they're actually *from* this part of the country. The endless rolling forests of Appalachia still feel like home, the spruces and firs waving in greeting under a morning mountain breeze, but the familiarity is only comforting so long as Google Maps has a signal, and right now Puck's phone is about as useful as a licked finger held aloft.

Eventually, though, the dense tree canopy opens up to a breathtaking view of the resort, perched on a manicured hill at the end of a paved driveway lined with stately elms. Those trees typically don't grow at this elevation, but the Athenian can afford the upkeep.

This place occupied an almost mythical status among Puck's grade-school friends in Johnson City. Was the Athenian in Tennessee or North Carolina? Both. The property was just *that big*. Had anyone actually ever *been* there? No, but someone's friend's rich parents once stayed there for their tenth wedding anniversary, *supposedly*. Legend was the hotel had everything: an entire fleet of shoeshiners, manicurists, barbers, chefs, sommeliers, and golf caddies who would tend to your every need the moment you set foot on the lobby's polished marble floor.

In other words, the Athenian is exactly the kind of place that only Damon McLeod's family can afford to rent out for a week, and exactly the kind of place Mia would have scoffed at once. *Mia and Damon*. Even thinking about those two names together makes Puck squirm in the driver's seat. It's a pairing as wrong as peanut butter and anchovies, which is why it's so frustrating that everyone seems to be letting this happen. If no one objects at the altar, Puck will be tempted to do it themself.

Few people know the burden of being right about everything quite like they do. As early as high school, Puck realized that gender was the world's biggest scam, invented to sell razors to girls at one and a half times the cost. Love was another conspiracy. At Emory, they could count the number of lesbian undergrads—as they saw themself at the time—on two hands. Everyone was already each other's exes by winter break. Puck mostly spent college watching over Mia's love life instead, which is how they know it has definitely taken a wrong turn for her to be marrying Damon.

After gently easing their beat-up Subaru over a completely unnecessary speed bump, Puck pulls up beneath a white-columned portico to the grand entrance of the Athenian. A valet in a crimson uniform jogs performatively toward the driver's-side door. Puck doesn't relish handing over the keys to an ancient Subaru Forester that has had its Check Engine light on for nearly a year, but they do it anyway, asking the valet to "take good care of her" as a joke.

Instead, the obsequious valet treats the request solemnly, promising "she won't get a scratch," which makes Puck regret saying anything.

A more welcome sight is Mia. She's standing at the top of the carpeted stairs in an A-line denim dress that would hang like a burlap sack on anyone else. Her wavy blond hair looks freshly blown out, and it probably is.

When Mia was assigned to be Puck's roommate during their first semester at Emory, they stereotyped her on sight as a homophobic Southern belle—the kind of woman who would go to a bachelorette party at Lips but say that gay marriage "just isn't right." But then she turned out to be one the most accepting straight girls at Emory, even holding Puck's hand when they came out as lesbian to their parents over the phone sophomore year. Never has an ally looked more like a Fox News anchor. Nothing about her support felt put-on; she didn't always know the right words, but it mattered more that her heart was in the right place, especially when all the other pretty blond girls on campus could be such menaces.

"Puck! You're here!"

Mia rushes down the stairs as Puck drops their backpack on the ground and opens their arms wide for a hug. Their increasingly intense shooting schedule has kept them from seeing their old roomie in the flesh since . . . when? Three years ago at her and Zander's apartment in New York? So much has changed: Her relationship with Zander went south as his substance use got worse, but two years later, she had her chance encounter with

Damon, followed by her baffling decision to move to Raleigh to be with him. Everyone has been trying to make sense of the relationship since, especially Zander, who considered Damon one of his closest friends.

Puck's connection to Mia has suffered, too. How do you acknowledge when a best friendship has become merely a good one? Their old stream of voice memos, astrology memes, and Instagram messages slowed down to a trickle after she got together with Damon. Puck knew that Mia *knew* that they disapproved, and that tension was laced through every message without needing to be openly stated.

They try not to let any of that show as they squeeze Mia back. "I didn't think this place was actually real," Puck says.

Mia looks around at the landscape surrounding the resort, layer upon layer of gentle green domes, stretching forever in every direction. "Isn't it dreamy?" she asks, her sweet perfume only adding to the effect. It's not enough for her to be gorgeous; she has to smell like rosemary and fresh flowers, too.

"Your perfume is incredible," Puck says as the hug ends.

"Oh, it's called Pansy. Do you want some? It's from Lush. I have more!"

"No, I prefer more abstract aromas like Grandpa's Sweater or Monopoly Money."

Mia's laughter could power a major metropolis, and the McLeods are probably looking into that possibility. Damon's family made their fortune in "food processing," which always struck Puck as a dystopian juxtaposition of words. As far as they understood it, somebody further up in his family tree had figured out a new way to debone a chicken and, as a result, Damon had never had to work a day in his life. Not that he'd acted rich back at Emory; he often bummed meal swipes off Puck before retreating to his frat house with bowls full of pasta to fuel all-night *Super Smash Bros.* sessions.

The Damon that Puck knew in college barely noticed women, and Mia had never paid much attention to him either, not even after graduation when his big brother made him trade his Wiimotes for barbells. But now Mia's wearing a diamond the size of a hubcap on her finger. Puck spots the glimmer of it as Mia gestures down at their backpack.

"Is that all you packed?" she asks, before answering her own question. "Of course that's all you packed."

Puck let Mia use half their closet space back in college to store her voluminous collection of thrifted shoes because they didn't need much room of their own.

"Who's here so far?" they ask as they walk with Mia up the stairs to the entryway.

They don't want Mia to give them the full guest list; they only want to know about the five members of the old Emory crew. Mia and Damon made two. Zander, whom Mia still invited despite everything, will have to third-wheel his ex's wedding. And Lena, poor lovesick Lena who always had a hopeless crush on Damon that no one took seriously, rounded out the group.

"Lena got in last night," Mia says, stopping to wave both hands in front of a finicky automatic door that has been awkwardly retrofitted into the Vanderbilt-era architecture. "You just missed Damon," she continues. "He left to go pick up his grandparents from Asheville, but he'll be back late tonight."

There's a telling pause, and Puck feels the need to prompt her.

"And Zander?" they ask.

Mia answers quickly, and as matter-of-factly as possible.

"Early tomorrow morning. Redeye." Just as hastily, she adds, "Come on, let me take you up to the suites."

Puck had hoped the subject would be less sore on the verge of Mia marrying someone else, but apparently not. For a few seconds of silence, Mia leads Puck through the opulent lobby of the Athenian, past a bubbling fountain and a veritable army of bellhops. Perhaps Puck shouldn't have broached the topic immediately, but they're all going to have to confront it soon enough.

Mia dated Zander for two years in college and six afterward; she's only been with Damon for one. Little about Mia's tortured relationship with Zander suggested it was going to last forever, especially with him drinking as much as he did. They had zero trouble in the bedroom—quite the opposite, as Puck sometimes saw too closely in the dorm—but make-up sex was never going to be a foundation for an actual adult life.

Still, rebounding with Damon and committing this hard to the bit is concerning. Puck can't believe Mia is marrying the guy who only ever had eyes for Princess Peach right in front of the ex-boyfriend who used to give her screaming orgasms that could be heard all the way from Savannah.

The engagement has made everything awkward in overlapping and overwhelming ways: Damon and Zander's friendship is in a tense period of détente that Puck can't parse. Lena seems gutted that Damon is leaving bachelorhood behind for the only other girl in their old friend group. And Mia has been worryingly uncommunicative about all of it, leaving Puck caught in the middle, navigating multiple smaller text chains while the main group chat stays quiet.

It was Mia's right to break up with Zander. Puck never expected them to be in rocking chairs together in their eighties. But there were so many other rich men in the world she could've landed besides a McLeod—and that's all that Damon, once a harmless nerd, seems to have become these days. No, for some reason she made the only choice that could tear the entire crew apart.

As they step into a waiting elevator, Puck decides the only way out of the conspicuous silence is to run straight through it. "Mia, are you sure you're OK with Zander being a groomsman?"

The questioning can pass for genuine concern for now. Back in school, Puck was always the one most sensitive to Mia's feelings, especially because Zander could be so reckless with them. They lost track of the number of late-night arguments the couple had that were quickly forgotten the moment Zander texted an apology or an "ily" the next morning. Meanwhile, Zander came to rely on Puck as a conduit for communication whenever Mia wouldn't talk to him—a gay mediator in a never-ending battle of the sexes.

"Of course I'm OK with it," Mia says, pressing the button for the fourth floor. "I know things got a little awkward last year, but we're all on good terms now. Right?"

She sounds like she's trying to reassure herself more than anyone else. "Good" is a laughable descriptor for how things feel right now. As recently as last week, Puck had to call Zander to convince him he should still come to the wedding.

"Right," Puck lies, as the old-fashioned floor counter in the elevator dings away.

"That reminds me, though," Mia says, sounding eager for

a change of subject. "Do you really not mind being one of the bridesmaids?"

When Puck first came out as nonbinary, shortly after college, they might have bristled at being slotted into such a gendered category, and they certainly wouldn't blame others for feeling like that. But lately, when forced to choose, they prefer dancing on top of labels to avoiding them altogether. And if there have to be groomsmen and bridesmaids at this incredibly upscale affair, they'd rather spend more time with Mia than with this new version of Damon they barely recognize.

"I'm fine rolling with the bridesmaids, so long as you don't mind half of them being in love with me by the end of the week," they quip.

Out-and-proud lesbians may not have been abundant in college, but that didn't stop Puck from seeing action. Mia and Zander liked to play a game with them at the few parties they managed to coax Puck into attending: The couple would point out the soberest, straightest girl in a crowd and Puck would secure permission to kiss her by the end of the night. They were "a makeout wizard," as an awed Mia once dubbed them. But honestly, it didn't take supernatural skill: A few minutes of eye contact, a little conversation, maybe a quick brush of the knee, and *boom*. Women were a lot more bisexual than Mia thought they were.

"No seducing my bridesmaids!" Mia insists, only half joking, as the elevator door slides open on the fourth floor. "Be good, Puck."

"'Good'? I'm not sure that word is in my vocabulary." Puck has been making up for lost time since graduation, and Mia is vaguely aware that they have slept with virtually half of the queer women in Decatur by now.

"None of my bridesmaids are gay anyway," Mia says. "At least as far as I know."

"And we all know how good your gaydar is," Puck deadpans. "Remember when you thought I was just 'artsy'?"

"No! I thought you were 'alt.'"

"Yeah, I was just *really* into Vampire Weekend," Puck jokes.

Mia laughs again. For a moment, as she leads the way down a long hall, it feels like the pair might be able to find their old groove again, even if in a very different environment than a dorm with concrete walls.

The carpet of the Athenian, like all the staff uniforms, is a deep shade of crimson. Polished brass wall sconces, originally built for candlelight, now house faux-flickering bulbs, the late nineteenth century returning by way of the twenty-first. The whole estate, with its Gilded Age finishes, has a reassuring permanence compared to the flimsy McMansion where they film *Homewreckers*, which threatens to fall down around Puck, Buster Keaton–style, at any moment. But despite the age of the hotel, there's not a speck of dust on the baseboards. It's foreign seeing Mia in a place this well-maintained.

Puck's old roommate has always taken great care of herself, less so her surroundings. Back in college, she slept on hideous electric purple sheets from Target that were almost never washed. Puck shuddered to think about how much of Zander's DNA was in them by the time they moved off campus together senior year. And their Brooklyn apartment was a wreck too. Mia and Zander always offered their couch on Puck's handful of visits to the city, and Puck always—respectfully—declined, choosing to stay in a hotel instead, though nothing as bougie as the Athenian.

Was Mia's taste always this expensive, just waiting for the right checkbook to come along before it could be activated? That can't be the case—Puck couldn't have misjudged her so badly—but it's difficult for them to not wonder if her values have shifted, and for the worse. Why else would she get with Damon, a guy who seems to have sacrificed his entire personality on the altar of his trust fund?

This past year, Puck watched in horror as Mia posted endless Instagram photos of her international vacations with the McLeod heir, seemingly oblivious to the risk that luxury could have rapidly diminishing returns. Sure, Damon can take her to the Maldives, but at least Zander had the spark of life in him.

Puck barely recognizes this version of Mia, who can say a phrase like "wedding itinerary" without even hearing how staid it makes her sound. As she leads Puck deeper down the hallway, the bride-to-be runs through the schedule: Tomorrow afternoon, there will be croquet for the bridesmaids and groomsmen, while the other early arrivals play lawn games: "Darts, bocce, the usual," she rattles off. Tuesday is a spa day for the bridesmaids while "Damon goes skeet shooting with the boys."

On Wednesday, the divide between the sexes will collapse briefly for the duration of a chartered bus ride to Asheville, but once they get there, they'll split up again for eleventh-hour bachelorette and bachelor parties: "Yoga, shopping, and tapas for the girls—and you, if you really don't mind being lumped in," Mia says. Puck assures Mia that they'll happily join the women that day, but that they draw the line at penis straws.

"Don't worry," Mia replies with a smile. "I can still return the crate I ordered."

The celebration proper kicks off on Thursday with a catered picnic on the front lawn "for all one hundred guests," Mia continues, and then Friday is the main event: an outdoor ceremony in the botanical garden, followed by a cocktail hour in "The Court," a restaurant on the top floor of the Athenian, before ending with a glitzy reception in the grand ballroom. It sounds expensive. It sounds exhausting. And honestly, it doesn't sound like Mia.

"Remember when our idea of a fancy night out was getting milkshakes from the Cook Out on Ponce?" Puck asks, hoping their old roommate is still in there somewhere. "Banana pudding?"

"You know, I actually wanted milkshakes as our late-night snack," Mia replies.

That's encouraging. But Puck notes the past tense: "Want*ed*?"

"Oh, we decided against it," Mia says, which only raises more questions for Puck. *She* wanted them, but *we* decided against it? What's the real story here?

"Damon shot it down?" Puck asks, trying to ascertain the truth.

"No, Damon would never—"

"So who?" Puck doesn't let her finish, but after their years of living together, Mia should be used to having information wrung out of her.

She gives Puck a little side-eye but relents. "Damon's family thought milkshakes would be tacky. His mom said late-night wedding treats were a 'middle-class affectation.'"

Puck resists the urge to punch a wall. The ancient studs in this place would give them tetanus anyway. "The McLeods aren't gods, Mia. You don't have to do what they say. You know that, right?"

Maybe Mia has changed even more than Puck feared. This girl used to be an untamable stallion. That's what made her relationship with Zander so powerful—and so tempestuous. They both did exactly what they wanted, which worked wonderfully when they wanted the same thing, and horribly when they didn't. Mia may have grown up and mellowed somewhat, but it's hard to picture her taking orders from anyone, let alone the baby boomer duchess of a boneless chicken fortune.

"I mean, Puck, they're paying for all of this," Mia says, lowering her voice. "I had to make *some* compromises."

"Compromises?" Puck asks, matching the hushed tone. "Is this a wedding or a hostage negotiation?" It's blunt, but they used to be able to call her out like this. Puck hopes Mia can stand up to an iota of friendly scrutiny.

"It's an *expensive* wedding," Mia whispers. "Maybe if I were paying for some of it, I'd stand my ground more, but you know that my parents are in no position to help. And I'm not exactly working right now."

What? Puck assumed that Mia had found work after following Damon down to North Carolina—at least a substitute teaching job. Even SAT tutoring would be a gesture toward financial independence, albeit a token one. Mia loved her kids up in New York. They kept her grounded even when her life with Zander was in tatters. And yet she's trading thirty adoring faces for *this*? To become Damon's housewife?

"But you're looking, yes?" Puck asks, stopping just short of a bend in the hallway, failing to hide their judgment. "For work?"

"I've been pretty busy with the wedding."

Christ. Mia was the last person Puck would have expected to get Stepford Wifed but now she is bending to convention, just like everyone else.

"I know, but afterward?" they press.

"I don't know."

"You don't *know*?"

The look on Mia's face is equal parts angry and chastised. This was too much out of the gate, Puck realizes, but they can't contain their disappointment. Mia opens her mouth to respond but before she can speak, Damon rounds the corner and almost runs headlong into both of them.

Mia goes pale.

"Oh, hey, Puck!" Damon says, a bit startled himself. "When did you get in?"

Before Puck can answer, though, a visibly anxious Mia stammers, "Damon, I—I thought you'd left already?"

"I was just heading out," he says. "But I can't find the fob for the Tesla. Do you know where it is?"

Damon was always handsome, but sometime after college he grew into his looks. He abandoned all that pasta and started guzzling protein shakes instead. He threw out his stained *My Hero Academia* T-shirts and adopted the uniform of most monied Southern men: boat shoes, polos, and shorts that frankly should leave more to the imagination. Puck doesn't need to know that much about the shape of Damon's junk. No one does. Not even Mia, ideally.

But still, it looks like drag on Damon. Somewhere beneath all that salmon clothing, Puck hopes he's still the same guy who used to shout, "No items, Fox only, Final Destination!" at two a.m. with the exuberance of a child on Christmas morning. Sometimes he'd even play *Smash Bros.* one-handed, just to level the playing field with Puck, but of course he'd win anyway.

That endearing enthusiasm is gone from his voice now. "Hey, how's the TV thing going?" he asks Puck with disinterest, turning toward Mia immediately afterward. It's clear he was only looking for his fiancée and doesn't actually want to catch up.

"It's going great," Puck reports, but they can't resist adding a little barb: "I'm ending relationships every day!"

The sentence hangs in the air for a moment as the bride and groom both grapple with its implications. Mia laughs uncomfortably, but Damon is the one who tries to bat it down. "Well, hey, remember you're on vacation, OK?"

Puck holds up their hands in mock innocence. "Don't worry, lovebirds, I'm off the clock!"

"I was just walking Puck to their room," Mia says. "Come with us, and then I'll help you look for the key."

A look of annoyance flashes across Damon's face, but he agrees. As they continue toward the room, Puck mentally reviews the conversation they just had with Mia before Damon appeared in the hallway like a *Shining* ghost. They notice she hasn't yet said a single loving word about her betrothed: Nothing about how happy she is, or how excited she is to start a life with him. Women are under no obligation to gush about their partners, but brides-to-be aren't supposed to pass the Bechdel test. She's giving up her career for Damon *and* she's not even obsessed with him?

"Room 444" Mia announces, stopping in front of the last room. "*Finally*. God, this place is huge."

"Ooh, it's a corner suite," Damon adds. "Nice."

But the mood between them feels off. Puck suspects Mia's still thinking about the job conversation. No one likes to be accused of abandoning who they are, especially by the person who knows them best. Or used to, anyway. It always seemed to matter to Mia that Puck didn't see her as being like the other girls. Their questioning must have gotten to her. Well, good. It should have.

"A corner suite, you say?" Puck jokes, taking a battering ram to the awkwardness with an obnoxious British accent. "Well, this calls for merriment indeed."

Neither Mia nor Damon can muster the enthusiasm for a polite chuckle. Instead, Mia hands Puck the key card, also crimson, embossed with the Athenian's logo: a white lowercase alpha symbol.

"Enjoy the room," she says, holding on to the card a second too long before letting Puck take it.

It's a pointed gesture: The McLeods are indeed paying for all this, including Puck's accommodations. Is it really their place to be questioning this wedding? That seems to be the message. But years of working on *Homewreckers* have trained Puck to bring up the very subjects that contestants want to avoid. It may feel cruel in the moment, but it's beneficial in the long term; without some pushing, most people surrender to society's expectations. At least that's how Puck justifies what they do. And maybe this is all Mia needs: a little push.

"Oh, Damon!" Puck says, as the couple turn to walk back down the hall. "Mia was telling me about your late-night snack predicament. And I was thinking, I can always drive to the nearest Cook Out and sneak you both some milkshakes."

Damon looks unsure of how or if to respond, trying to gauge the situation. Mia goes dagger-eyed.

"That could be cute," she says, through a painful grimace. "Except not a milkshake. Damon's keto now."

Oh, God. It's worse than Puck imagined.

Monday

Chapter 4

"You are aware that the best restaurant in the state is upstairs, right?" Puck asks Zander.

He's bent over the stovetop in his room, vigorously whisking eggs in a stainless-steel bowl, a gorgeous mess of dark curls bouncing atop his head. Puck wasn't even aware any of the suites in the Athenian had their own kitchens, but apparently this one was custom-built for the live-in staff of the wealthy family who once occupied the adjacent penthouse, and Zander was able to convince Mia to reserve it for him as a condition of his attendance.

"Do you trust them to make you an omelet more than you trust *me*?" Zander fires back, and it's a point well-taken.

No matter how highly rated the Court is, the swanky hotel restaurant would find a way to over-chef this dish. They'd use Gruyère instead of the cheddar Zander procured on his drive here last night and herbs de Provence instead of the parsley and chives he is currently chopping up, his knife moving so rapidly that it becomes a silver blur against the cutting board. What Puck needs is something simple and filling; they slept fitfully last night, conking out on the couch in their street clothes, still agitated by their conversation with Mia. A fistful of overpriced M&M's from the minibar was the only thing in their stomach at the time, so they're counting on this breakfast to restore them to life.

"Hey, I'm not complaining! I just don't want you to have to work during your week off," Puck clarifies.

"If I'm going to come all the way down here and watch Mia get married to a guy I thought was my friend, I at least need to eat my own fucking food," Zander says. He adds three pinches of salt and a few grinds of pepper to the mixture in the bowl, then gives it a couple of firm whisks. "I can't live off wedding catering for a week."

Puck could think of worse fates: seven years of crafty, for one. "Are you going to make your own reception dinner too?" they ask.

"I don't know, man," Zander says, pouring the eggs into the hot buttered pan on the stove. "I haven't thought that far ahead."

When Puck came out as nonbinary, Zander was the only straight guy who seemed to understand that it didn't mean Puck was just a woman with an asterisk. He had always been weirdly attuned to Puck's masculine energy in college, and that pronouncement just gave him permission to bro out with his friend even harder.

Mia used to say the two of them together were "dangerous," which really just meant they enjoyed each other's company with an ease she coveted. She would try to get Zander's attention at a group hang, but he'd be too busy ranking Christopher Nolan movies with Puck in the corner. He was an *Interstellar* guy; Puck was partial to *Memento*, and both of them pretended to understand *Tenet* when it came out, only to later admit over text that they had each watched hours of YouTube explainers afterward.

"Well, I'm glad you're here, Zan. I've missed you."

Puck means it. They haven't seen him face-to-face in three years, ever since the last time they visited New York. Of the Emory crew, he's the only one who has never made a remotely judgmental comment about Puck's choice of profession. It's probably because he has survived working in New York kitchens—loud, chaotic, and definitely unethical spaces that have to be constructed the way that they are to serve meals at price points diners can tolerate.

For years living with Mia in the city post-graduation, he worked his way through roughly a dozen restaurants, hopping between kitchens and participating far too enthusiastically in the post-closing nightlife. It was only after Mia left him that he got serious—and then sober. After that, he quickly climbed his way to where he is now: the executive chef of some buzzy French-Italian place in the Meatpacking District. But like Puck, he knows that entertaining people isn't something you can do while keeping your hands clean.

"I missed you, too," Zander says, checking to see if one side of the omelet can lift off the pan without folding it just yet. "But I can't believe I'm here. She's really doing this, huh?"

Puck exchanged texts with Zander after the breakup, feeling not exactly guilty but more . . . *odd* about back-channeling without Mia's knowledge. Their fraternal dynamic usually came with feminine supervision, which was suddenly absent. Zander has been in denial for the last year. But even so, Puck was expecting him to have some fight left. Mia "doing this" was far from inevitable. Weddings are not weather events. And Zander's a hot chef making six figures who has more than a year of sobriety under his belt. Plus, he has the weight of history behind him; Damon's just got a Black Card.

"I guess she is," Puck says, toeing the line between commiseration and uncertainty.

Zander sprinkles the cheese and herbs into the omelet with a precision that even Puck finds sexy. He watches it cook for a moment longer before sensing exactly when to make his move. "I definitely can't compete with this place," he says, setting his spatula down on the countertop. "My family couldn't afford to stay here for a *night*."

Puck understands Zander's frustration. But Mia isn't some cartoon character who would get dollar signs in her eyes and run off with the rich guy, tempted as Puck was to apply that theory to her yesterday. No, there has to be a deeper emotional truth underlying her decision to pick someone like Damon. Mia enjoys going to Mykonos, sure—what hot girl who looks good in a floppy hat wouldn't?—but there's something else that gives him an edge over Zander. Or at least, over the version of Zander who Mia dated. It must be security, plain and simple. Puck puzzled over it for hours last night, and in the end decided that a refreshing boringness is probably the best thing Damon has to offer Mia—but next to the old Zander, that's enough.

Zander's right to have a chip on his shoulder about the money angle; he was the only one in the group going to Emory on financial aid. But he could afford to realize that *he's* actually the elusive full package now: hot, talented, and reliable. He can't take her to Mykonos, but he *can* take her to Miami, and can anyone tell the difference if you crop the photos right? Sand is sand. Water can be made turquoise with the right filter.

"I don't think it's just about the money, Zan," Puck gently suggests. "Besides, Damon's part of this, too. Why not blame him?"

Zander is laser-focused on plating the omelet, garnishing it with the remaining chopped herbs, but he pauses at the question. It's something Puck has been trying to ask about in circumspect ways for the last year.

"I can't really blame anyone except myself," Zander says, returning to his work, fastidiously wiping the edges of the plate with a clean white cloth. "I know how badly I messed up. I hate what I put her through. Someone else was always going to give her a better life. But Damon? Fuck."

Puck's having a hard time squaring this with what Zander just said. He's at once trying to take responsibility for his actions—an AA lesson, no doubt—while sounding bitter about how everything went down. The truth is probably somewhere in between: He's repentant, but he also wants Mia back. His anger with himself is real, but it can't completely paper over his disappointment with his friend.

"Well, I wasn't expecting it to be Damon either," Puck says.

Zander ignores the comment. He rotates the plate slightly, beholds his creation, then looks up with that winning smile of his. "Voilà," he declares. "One classic omelet, made to order."

Puck already has their fork clutched in their hand, tines pointing up, like a barbarian eager to skewer a hunk of meat. Zander slides the plate over the counter and Puck takes their first bite. It's exactly what they needed.

"All I know is that Damon can't compete with *this*," they continue, barely managing to stop eating long enough to get the words out. "This is incredible. Do you know how many plates of sad overdone scrambled eggs girls have eaten in boys' apartments the morning after? It's one of the world's great injustices."

Zander smiles. It doesn't matter how many times someone compliments his cooking; the praise wriggles its way into the core of him each time. Puck can relate. Even after seven seasons, whenever they hear someone say they're "hooked" on *Homewreckers,* Puck grins like a child whose finger painting just got stuck to the fridge. Nothing compares.

"Well, if omelets alone were good enough, maybe I could have gotten her back," Zander says. "And then we wouldn't be here."

Puck sighs. Do they really have to spell this out again? "We've always been straight with each other, yeah, Zan?" they ask between mouthfuls.

"Yeah, sure. Why?"

He moves around the kitchen island to stand opposite Puck, as though he needs a slab of granite between them to guard against whatever hard truth is about to get hurled his way.

"What time is it?" Puck asks, and Zander looks back at them, confused.

"What?"

"Check the clock. What time is it?"

"Eight thirty . . . five?" Zander squints to read the grandfather clock over in the sitting area. "Why? Got somewhere to be? Croquet isn't until noon, I thought." He emphasizes the point by sliding over an itinerary that lists the day's activities in an absurd amount of detail, including notes about dress code and an hourly weather forecast. Puck found the same paper slipped under their door this morning.

"No, but when you were with Mia, how often were you awake at eight thirty-five *a.m.*?" they ask him.

Zander smirks. "I mean, sometimes I was up this early because I had been out with the line cooks all night, but yeah, I get your point. I know I can't expect her to forgive me. Besides the restaurant, the regret is all I think about."

Puck had fielded the frustrated phone calls from Mia through those early years in New York. She was up every morning at six to get ready for her teaching job, and by the time she got home in the late afternoon, Zander had already left for dinner service. At best, the couple got a few hours together on Zander's off days, and sometimes they made the most of them. Puck saw occasional photos from the Rockaways.

But the low moments were really low, like when Zander stumbled back into their Crown Heights apartment with an obvious case of the cocaine sniffles and threw up in the kitchen sink while Mia was trying to make her morning coffee. Women don't forget stuff like that. But Puck doesn't need to scold Zander for his past behavior; staying in the bro zone is the best way to keep him in a good headspace.

"Girls aren't complicated," they tell him. "Maybe sometimes they want you to *think* that they're delicate, emotionally complicated little puzzle boxes. But that's just PR. At the end of the day, they want someone who's around. And I hope you know that's all Damon is now that he's gone corporate: around."

Zander grabs a spare fork, leans over the island, and steals a bite of his own handiwork, even though he already ate before Puck arrived. "You're right."

It's Puck's turn for a proud smile. "About women? Of course I am."

"No. About the omelet. It *is* incredible."

"C'mon, Zan. I'm trying to impart some sagely wisdom here."

"I mean, I hear you, dude. But there's nothing I can do about that now."

Nothing? Puck can feel an idea solidifying in their mind. It took root, however subconsciously, when Mia essentially admitted to giving up teaching for Damon. It emerged for the first time as an uncomfortable joke about "ending relationships every day."

But seeing their best guy friend this downtrodden has solidified it: If Zander's not going to stop Mia from making the worst mistake of her life, then Puck will have to. They produce people for a living. How hard can it be to produce their friends? This wedding can just be *Homewreckers: Emory Edition*.

Mia may enjoy the calm of being with Damon now, but she'll regret it one day. If she doesn't come to her senses soon enough, she'll probably have a kid with him, maybe even multiple. The inevitable divorce will be difficult, especially if the McLeods made her sign a prenup, which they almost certainly have. At worst, she'll have to stay in North Carolina for years because his lawyers will secure joint custody, trapping her in a state she only moved to for a man. From there, it'll be a long road back to the Mia she used to be, if she can ever claw her way back to herself. Zander will have long moved on by then too, leaving only Puck to help her get back on her feet.

They can see that future so clearly—but they're also best equipped to stop it. This week doesn't have to feel like a time bomb anymore, or at least if it does, it can be one that Puck is actively trying to defuse. For starters, it'll help if Zander drops the defeatist attitude, ideally before he sees Mia for the first time at croquet.

Puck picks their next words carefully. "Well, you're here, aren't you?" they ask, and before Zander can respond, they stand up to wash their plate, making a deliberate amount of noise while doing the chore. They don't want the comment to land like some profound suggestion; better for it to sink in over the course of the day.

"Hey, can you make me breakfast again tomorrow?" Puck calls over their shoulder. "I'd like French toast, please, ideally with a raspberry compote."

They place the dish on a drying towel and turn around to find Zander smiling. *Good.*

"I'll see what I can do," he promises.

Chapter 5

Puck all but power-walks back to Room 444, overtaken by the notion.

This wedding can be stopped. It *should* be stopped. Sure, their friends might be less pliable than *Homewreckers* contestants, and they're probably unwilling to make big scenes on demand, but modified versions of the same tricks will surely work on them, too. They're only human. And while they might not be aware they're on a makeshift episode of reality TV that isn't even being filmed, this scheme will be for their own good, Mia's most of all. It might even be kind of fun, and Puck was *not* expecting to have a good time here, given the circumstances. But circumstances can be controlled.

Puck unlocks the door with their key card and bursts into their room, which barely looks occupied. Between the vintage armoire, the dresser, and the walk-in closet where Puck hung their tailored suit, only a small fraction of the suite's storage space is being put to use. But it's not a room anymore—it's a video village, minus the monitors. A base of operations for what comes next. Puck sits down at the enormous oak desk by the east window, energized by their newfound clarity.

Outside, they see the garden where Mia and Damon plan to get married on Friday—squares of white and purple wildflowers tamed into a checkered grid, with stepping stones leading up to a low platform. Mia and Zander might be two especially wild species, but they'll still grow wherever Puck plants them. It won't be Puck's first time putting them in their proper positions. Hell, Mia and Zander are probably the reason why they were so successful on *Homewreckers* in the first place.

Back at Emory, Mia was Puck's point of entry into a broader social universe. She wholeheartedly supported them in their queerness, so they would have taken a bullet for her in return. The mild friend-crush Puck developed for her only deepened their affection. Doing de facto Secret Service duty for their roommate introduced Puck to everyone else: Zander, the boyfriend, became unavoidable—and in the rare event he wasn't in their dorm room, he was off playing *Dark Souls* with Damon, passing the controller back and forth between every boss attempt.

Then there was Lena, a lanky campus activist whom Mia vaguely knew from high school, and who wriggled her way into the crew based on that tenuous connection alone. Really, she just wanted to get closer to Damon—and not for his family's money, given her allegiance to Bernie Sanders. What she saw in him was always a mystery, but it didn't matter; Damon ignored all her awkward flirtations.

The dynamics of the group had always been like a TV show to Puck. Mia and Zander's Libra–Scorpio romance was better entertainment than any episode of *Game of Thrones*. There was even a certain beauty in witnessing Lena's unrequited yearning, like waves crashing against an unforgiving rocky shore. But the more they hung out with the heterosexuals, the more involved Puck became in their lives.

Soon, they were a messenger, an arbiter, and a confidant. Lena saw Puck as a sympathetic ear and a sign of her own virtue: She was one of the only straight people to come to the LGBTQ+ affinity group every week, which Puck only attended to try to hook up with girls anyway. Even Damon used Puck as a sounding board, mostly to complain that "*Brawl* had made *Smash* more casual," or that "the Moonlight Greatsword in *Dark Souls 2* had been nerfed," whatever that meant.

It was overwhelming at first. A loner in high school, Puck had simply never spoken to so many people simultaneously. But then they learned how to maneuver, from brokering the peace between Mia and Zander to giving Lena the tough love she needed on Damon. They had to triangulate, deflect, and soothe, often in the same night—and they *loved* the thrill of doing it right. It's no wonder that they ascended the *Homewreckers* ranks within a couple of seasons.

They spent years keeping this group together, which means they can easily pull a couple of them apart if it's what's best for the whole herd. Should Mia actually get back together with Zander? Maybe. He's changed a lot. Most of their fights, probably 90 percent, were about his drinking, and the other 10 percent were about the consequences of his drinking. But also, maybe not. All they know is that Damon is the wrong choice for Mia's wild spirit, and if Puck doesn't stop her from marrying him, they're all in for a lot of heartbreak: Lena will be even more jealous and lovesick than she already is, Damon and Zander's friendship will be unsalvageable, and Mia could lose everyone.

This is just the slightly more mature version of dragging Mia home from a party before she does something stupid. You never get too old to need rescuing from yourself.

Puck fishes their AirPods out of their backpack pocket and puts on some music, ready to brainstorm. Anyone else might be so afraid of committing a few minor sins that they'd sit back and watch the wrong couple exchange vows. But it would be the greater wrong to do nothing. Of this Puck is certain. That quote about good men allowing evil to happen applies to reality show producers too. Puck slides over the hotel stationery, uncaps the complimentary fountain pen, and writes, "To-Do List."

The key to Mia is Zander, Puck knows, and it's a miracle that he's here at all. In the immediate aftermath of the Damon–Mia relationship reveal, he predicted over a FaceTime call with Puck that Mia's "fling" would be over in a few weeks and then she'd come "back home." Three months later, she posted the rock on Instagram. Even after Zander got his "save the date" in the mail, his confidence was unshaken, but the invitation itself sent him on a spiral that apparently still hasn't ended.

The first step in Puck's plan is to simply get the old couple next to each other. Puck jots down "M + Z" in the notepad.

The sexual chemistry between the pair has always been palpable, even during the periods when they claimed they couldn't stand each other. Puck hasn't looked at straight porn since the day they discovered the existence of the alternative, but even *they* get a little excited by the thought of Mia and Zander fucking each other in secret at this wedding. Mia's blond tresses would get all mussed up, Zander would pin her arms over her head, and, well, Puck needs to stop daydreaming like this if they're going to get through the rest of their bullet points. They can't listen to Paramore, write down a semi-Machiavellian hidden agenda, and have weirdly erotic thoughts about their best friends all at the same time.

"M + Z" isn't enough, though, as Puck knows from their day job. People can keep cheating a secret for years—and while Mia's more conscientious than your average *Homewreckers* girlie, Puck can't rely on her to pull the plug. No, the most reliable way for infidelity to actually break up a relationship, as obvious as it is, is for the offending party to get caught.

Which is why the second step in Puck's plan isn't rocket science. In fact, it's similar to the strategy they used on set right before coming here: Damon has to *see* the sparks fly between Mia and Zander. By now, he must realize that he doesn't thrill Mia the same way Zander did. Puck would be willing to bet that the only way he can get Mia wet is to take her to a beach. So, if Damon sees Zander and Mia in flagrante, or even just looking at each other with lust in their eyes, he'll crack.

"D 8 Z and M," they write down, with the "8" representing eyeballs.

But creating these kinds of openings will be difficult without access to their usual tools. On *Homewreckers*, if they want to move somebody somewhere, all they have to do is bark a few commands into a walkie. Here, the marionettes are much harder to manipulate.

That's where Lena could come in handy. The shock of Damon getting together with Mia after years of unrequited longing certainly seems to have driven her to the brink, judging from her recent Instagram behavior. This past year, Puck has watched her vacillate between making her profile private and public, posting all sorts of vaguely inspirational quotes and infographics about "dating yourself." *Grim*. She waited years for Damon to notice her, only for him to betray Zander and catch Mia on the rebound. The fact that a tree-hugging borderline ecofascist like Lena would even want to be with a McLeod remains confounding as ever, but her crush makes her tragically useful.

"L," Puck jots down, but then they hold the pen in place, ink seeping into the paper as they think about what they can do with her.

Puck is not entirely unsympathetic to Lena's plight. After all, she's the one whose future most closely mirrors their own likely fate. If there were some type of person between a nun and a monk, that's the life Puck will probably be living once they run out of single women to take home for a night.

They look up from the page and take in their vast suite. It's silly that a little extra space can be enough to make a person feel so alone. Last night, before falling asleep on the couch, Puck had a pang of homesickness for their condo back in Decatur. *Homewreckers* pays enough money for them to afford the down payment on a house by now—they even looked at a place in East Atlanta a couple years ago—but what would Puck do with all that square footage? Buy more plants that die within a month? There's no chance of anyone else moving into their imaginary house anytime soon. The strap Puck packed for this wedding is in high demand back home, but partnership doesn't seem to be in the cards.

Queer women tend to be so principled that after they find out how Puck earns their living, they decide sleeping with a "hot masc," as they are often labeled, is no longer worth the moral compromise. The last girl Puck dated worked for a nonprofit that was fighting a "Don't Say Gay" bill in the Georgia state legislature.

One night, over drinks at Leon's, the two compared how they had spent their days: Samantha had gone all around Fulton County collecting testimony from queer youth to present at the Gold Dome; Puck had spent theirs convincing a *Homewreckers* hunk to oil his abs before a volleyball game. Samantha called it quits over text the next day. "Different priorities" was the way she phrased it, which was fair, because Puck saw the notification right after planting a gay porn magazine under a contestant's pillow so that his girlfriend would find it later.

As for the handful of gay women with more questionable politics? Well, they weren't into all of Puck's "gender stuff," as a particularly terrible date once put it. Back when they still used both "she" and "they" pronouns, Puck made the mistake of giving one hot girl a pass, only for her to *never* alternate between them. Now that "she" is completely off the table, it's much easier to pick out the rotten apples.

But Puck feels certain they'll end up alone, just like Lena. The only difference is Puck is resigned to a life of perpetual singledom whereas Lena still shares nuggets from Brené Brown about "cultivating love" or whatever. Even after a decade with nothing to show for it, she still only has eyes for a guy Puck once saw pour used cereal milk back into the jug because he "liked the flavor."

Lena's single-mindedness is exactly why she'll make a good substitute PA this week. Puck looks down at the notepad, thinking about how she can help with each component of the plan. Lena is definitely an expert at cornering Damon. And if she can pull Damon away from Mia, that creates space for Mia and Zander to cozy up next to each other. This way, Puck can have plausible deniability for the entire plot.

Besides, this could even be productive for the poor girl: Maybe Lena needs to spend some more time with Damon as a full-on adult to realize that her crush on him ought to be put to bed once and for all.

They wish they could level with Lena and enlist her to help with this scheme directly. It'd be so much easier to do this with at least one ally. No, she has to remain an unwitting accomplice, and she has too many moral scruples to get involved anyway. If this is going to work in a way that leaves the Emory crew with any hope of remaining friends afterward, they all need to feel like they've arrived at their own conclusions. If anyone were to find out about Puck's involvement, they'd be able to use their outrage as an excuse to return to their comfortable delusions. But it won't come to that.

"Use," Puck writes in front of the blotchy "L" at the bottom of the note as a reminder, and even *they* feel the slightest twinge of guilt at that. But they nearly leap out of their chair when they feel a tap on their shoulder, whip around, and find the actual flesh-and-blood Lena towering over them.

"Lena, Jesus!" Puck shouts, ripping the AirPods out of their ears with one hand and flipping the notepad over on the desk with the other. They're trying to figure out how she got into their room when they notice that in their haste to enter, the door fell against the security latch.

Lena gestures at her own ears. "So sorry, Puck, I tried to get your attention but . . ."

"No, no, it's great to see you," Puck interrupts, remembering to breathe.

It's only after looking her up and down that Puck notices how different their friend is. This is Lena, but it's also *not* Lena.

It's not that Puck hasn't always considered her beautiful. Back in college, they liked to tell her, somewhat problematically, that she'd "clean up if she were gay." The lesbians at that campus affinity group were always devastated to learn Lena didn't play for their team. She wore weird stretchy dresses with ironed-on prints of horseshoes and lassos, and graphic T-shirts with wolves howling into phosphorescent sunsets. Her wavy hair spilled out everywhere, fraying into a thousand split ends well past her shoulders. Her glasses were thicker than car windows. If she had gone to Sarah Lawrence, she would have been among the most coveted women on campus, but she was at Emory, where beauty norms were decidedly more confining.

And now? The Lena standing in front of Puck is jaw-dropping, by conventional standards. She hasn't had any plastic surgery done that they can tell. What she has done though, is gotten Lasik, apparently, because the glasses are gone. An artfully shaggy chin-length bob now frames her cherubic face. She's finally dressing for her height, with a long collared dress cinched with a tie around her waist, but she hasn't entirely given up on the whimsy, either, judging from the pin of a hippopotamus eating an ice cream cone on her left lapel. It's a lot of little changes that add up to an almost cinematic, *Princess Diaries*–style transformation.

Puck stands up to take it all in.

"You, um, got a haircut?" They don't mean to make it a question, but the inflection happens of its own accord. They can't believe what they're seeing.

"Yup," Lena says, confirming the obvious as she hugs Puck, her chin clearing the top of their buzzed head. "I finally did the big chop for Locks of Love."

Lena's heart was always so inconveniently large. Puck secretly hated walking to class with her at Emory because she was physically incapable of ignoring all the petitioners collecting signatures for various causes. Somehow, Lena had infinite patience to listen to organizers proselytize about the climate crisis, gun violence, and reproductive rights, even though she knew their statistics and talking points better than they did. Meanwhile, Puck just wanted to get to Comp 101 so they could flirt with the hot goth girl in the back row.

"Did you donate your corneas to charity, too?" Puck asks.

Lena looks puzzled for a moment before the joke clicks: "Oh! The glasses. I mean, I know you're being silly, but I did give all my old pairs to a nonprofit."

"Of course you did," Puck says, holding an arm out toward the center of the room. "Come, sit. My suite is your suite."

Lena can act as altruistic as she wants, but Puck is certain that the wedding is the primary motivator for her makeover. No way is she going to watch Damon get married without one last major bid for his attention. Taking a laser to your eyeballs isn't all that extreme in the grand scheme of desperate romantic behaviors.

"How was your drive?" Lena asks, pausing to choose between a restored velvet couch and the hulking leather armchair in the corner of the sitting area.

"It was quick," Puck says, making Lena's choice for her by taking the armchair. "How about yours?"

Lena sits off to one side of the couch, too humble, it seems, to take up space in the center. Puck has never found the same easy banter with Lena that they did with their other Emory friends. Small talk with someone so aggressively agreeable can feel like waiting for a progress bar to fill up.

"The drive was good!" Lena chirps. "Mia's maid of honor gave me a ride from Raleigh. Robyn. She's so sweet."

Somehow, everyone besides Puck and Zander has ended up in the Research Triangle. The McLeod family has an office there, where Damon accepted some nepotistic C-suite position after college. His first-ever job on LinkedIn was being the vice president of some made-up-sounding department. Lena followed him like a lost puppy, landing an internship at a local conservation network that eventually became a full-time job with a focus on preserving bird habitats. She doesn't believe in driving anymore, hence her glorified hitchhiking to the Athenian. And now, of course, Mia's there too.

But wait, *maid of honor*? Puck knows it's tradition to have one, and yet Mia hasn't ever mentioned this "Robyn" person. Who is she and where did she come from? As much as they would have been uncomfortable with the designation, Puck wonders why *they* weren't asked to be the "*person* of honor." Mia's been with Damon for a year and she's already replacing her oldest friends? Another warning sign—and more proof that Puck's plan is essential.

"So," Puck asks, "who from Emory have you seen so far?" What they really want to know is whether Damon has seen Lena yet.

"Mia, obviously. And I ran into Zander on the way here, but I didn't catch Damon yesterday. I think he was in Asheville."

Interesting. Puck keeps the small talk going for a minute. Lena shares updates about a forest she's trying to save from development because it's a critical habitat for the "red-cockaded woodpecker," and Puck recounts a few recent *Homewreckers* feats to barely disguised looks of disapproval. Lena would fit right in with Puck's judgmental ex. But even as they chat, Puck keeps thinking about the last line on the upside-down notepad: "Use L."

When they wrote it, they meant to use Lena *as a distraction,* a persistent gadfly who could drive Damon away from Mia long enough for Puck to pull off their machinations. But now, seeing Lena, and knowing just how superficial men can be, the field of possibilities has expanded considerably: They can also use Lena *as a weapon.* Damon may not have noticed her back at college, but he certainly will now.

Chapter 6

Puck feels like a disgraced detective who had to hand in their gun and badge. On *Homewreckers,* they can ask for any information they need and some harried lowling will procure it. Here, they have to do their own investigating. After their chat with Lena, they took some time to mull over the plan a bit more before heading downstairs for a chat with the Athenian concierge.

The resort, it turns out, has a nine-wicket croquet course. What's more, Puck's learned that the hotel only has six balls to share across a total of twelve people in the wedding party, which likely means they will need to split into six teams of two. As the concierge explained the rules of the game, Puck was already plotting: If there was anyone in the group who could take charge of assigning teams without it seeming out of character, it'd be a producer—and now it's time to put that theory to the test.

On the expansive back lawn of the Athenian, the bridesmaids and groomsmen are fiddling with their mallets as they mill around a placard detailing the rules of backyard croquet. They're reading certain lines aloud, debating their meaning over the distant din of the other wedding guests throwing cornhole bags and playing Jenga with enormous blocks.

"What does it mean to 'take a mallet-head'?"

"I think it means you can move the ball one mallet away if you hit somebody?"

"Like, the length of the whole thing?"

"No, just the bottom part, I think."

"Are we playing the 'poison' variant? Or are we doing 'cut-throat'?"

They're almost making it too easy for Puck, who has so far been observing everyone's interactions from the sidelines with interest. After he arrived a minute ago, Zander gave Mia a hug hello, but with Damon watching, it had to be cursory and completely drained of affection. He then extended his hand out to Damon for a handshake, only for Damon to pull him in for one of those bro embraces that ends with a lot of vigorous back patting. It reads as overkill, like Damon's trying to make up for the easily apparent awkwardness between them. Lena, meanwhile, has been busy lacing up her shoes, which look as new as her eyeballs. Damon hasn't seen her yet—at least not that Puck has noticed. The rest of the wedding party seems confused by the croquet equipment. Some are examining the colored balls as though they're looking for billiard numbers. No one is taking charge.

Perfect.

"OK, everybody, listen up!" Puck announces, loudly clapping their hands once, using their set voice to cut through the chatter. "Let's make this easy: We'll split up into six teams of two. Everybody will take turns hitting their team's ball through the little gates—"

"Wickets," a brunette in a blue workout set corrects them as she joins the group.

"Yup, the wickets. And the first team to get their ball through the last *wicket* and then hit this little pole—"

"The starting stake," says the newcomer, again, infuriatingly.

"Thank you," Puck says, trying to disguise their annoyance. "Yes, the starting stake. If you hit the stake after getting your ball through the last wicket, your team wins. Don't worry about all the other rules on the sign. They're too complicated for us to bother with them."

"Do you play a lot of croquet or something?" the interrupter asks them when they're finished, a hint of mockery in her voice.

Who is this girl? And where did she acquire all of her nine-wicket know-how? Puck wasn't expecting to be hung out to dry in front of the group like this. "I played all the time as a kid," they lie to the late arrival, hoping she doesn't try to chat with them about the finer points of getting "roqueted" and all the other nonsense they tuned out during the concierge's spiel.

"OK, so what now, Captain?" the athleisure-wearing woman asks, still needling them. This relentless public teasing is not a great start for Puck's first official act of sabotage.

"Let's pick teams," they announce, pushing past the sarcasm to procure their phone from the pocket of their khaki jumpsuit. "I'm going to write down everyone's name in this randomizer app, and it'll split us into pairs. That way we don't all end up with someone we already know."

There is, of course, no randomizer app; this is a ruse for Puck to get to choose who gets paired with whom. And the entire wedding party is going to go along with it, even if a few people are looking at Mia and Damon for permission to enlist. The lesson Puck took away from the Stanford prison experiment is that everyone is already living inside of it every day, doing whatever the person with the most charisma or the biggest office tells them to do. Puck doesn't bother waiting for a consensus to emerge; instead, they open the Notes app on their phone and approach the first groomsman.

"What's your name?" they ask, loud, clear, authoritative.

"Peter," he says. Puck now recognizes him as Damon's brother. The best man. A gym bro in the family business whom Puck blames, at least in part, for Damon becoming the kind of guy who's obsessed with airport lounge access.

Puck moves down the loose line the wedding party is beginning to obediently form; Philip Zimbardo would be proud or ashamed, they're not sure which.

"Francis" is next. Preppy. Pink shirt. Puck didn't know popped collars had come back in style, and they wish they hadn't.

"Phil." Dead-eyed. Wearing a button-down and a puffy vest even though it's seventy-eight degrees outside. Probably a friend Damon made at work.

"Anya." Mia's childhood friend. Came to visit her at Emory once.

Puck skips over Lena and Zander but makes a show of jotting down their names anyway. Next up is the girl in the two-piece set. Her hair is pulled back into a slick ponytail of almost impossible tightness. Her green eyes narrow as Puck approaches. They already don't like this woman. She looks like she would have called Puck a "dyke" in high school—to their face, even.

Before Puck can ask her name, the woman says, "You must be Dr. Croquet, given all your expertise."

Puck tries to joke their way through the dig. "I prefer Croquet, PhD. And your name is?"

"Robyn. R-O-B-Y-N."

So *this* is Robyn. Puck is disappointed to discover that Mia's maid of honor is apparently a pedantic bitch. This isn't the DMV; Puck doesn't need to know the spelling of her name.

"Robyn. Like the annoying little bird, got it," Puck says, then immediately moves to the next person: a groomsman named Tom whom Puck vaguely remembers as an old college buddy of Damon's from his peak gaming days—someone who didn't otherwise travel in their friend circle.

As Puck writes down Tom's name, they shoot a glance back at Robyn to find her scowling, presumably over the bird remark. Puck hopes she stews over it for the entire game. Or match. Whatever the fuck they call a unit of croquet, though she probably knows that, too.

Puck keeps moving past Mia and Damon to collect the name of the final bridesmaid, Willa, who looks way too fashionable to be standing in the middle of a clearing in southwestern North Carolina. Wearing a strange asymmetrical dress with multiple cutouts and a pair of platform sandals, she's dressed for the runway, not croquet. At least Puck can now say they're not Mia's oddest-looking friend.

"OK!" they call out to the group after giving all the names a quick once-over. "Let's find out our fate."

They tap a random place on their phone screen and nothing happens, obviously, but the song-and-dance buys them time to start mapping out teams in their head.

"Francis and Willa," Puck pretends to read off their screen. The collision of their outfits should be fun to watch, if nothing else. The groomsman and bridesmaid step toward each other, Francis regarding Willa leerily.

"Phil and Tom," Puck says next. They're not going to do *all* opposite-sex pairings. The men high-five as they link up, so they must already know each other.

And now that Puck is partway through the team assignments, they can lay their first trap: "Damon and Lena."

Puck watches everyone's reactions carefully. Lena, of course, lights up despite herself but then tries to tamp down her excitement. Damon, a few feet to her right, frowns involuntarily; he's spent a decade knowing that Lena is in love with him, and to his credit, he has been nice about it. But as far as anyone knows, it's the "randomizer app" that chose the teams, so he'll have to endure another hour of being pursued.

Damon scans the group, looking for Lena, even though she's standing a couple feet away from him. "Is she here yet?"

Does he really not see her? She says hi from surprisingly nearby and Damon's eyes widen. "Oh, Lena. Hey! I didn't recognize you without all the . . . you know . . ."

"Yeah, I did Locks of Love," Lena says, completing his thought.

"I, uh, love it a lot too," Damon says, not following.

Does Puck detect a smile on his face? This is promising. Mia doesn't clock the expression, nor does it seem like she heard Damon's flustered comment, despite standing right next to him. At some point, she must have noticed that Lena started dressing differently—they live in the same city, after all—but she's been conditioned to not consider her as a threat, which is perfect. Now Damon is free to spend the entire afternoon with what is an undeniably attractive straight woman in a short white dress. Croquet might not be the sexiest sport, but it still involves a lot of bending over and talking about balls, so maybe it'll do something for him.

What Puck can't do, though, is pair Mia with Zander. That'd be suspicious, not to mention needlessly risky. Part of producing is knowing when to go for broke and when to let a plot line build. It's tempting, given the condensed time frame here, to just jam the former lovers together right away and hope for fireworks. But Puck has to do this carefully. There will be more opportunities to get them alone between now and Friday. For now, it's a good enough start to put Lena on the board.

"Mia and Peter!" Puck declares instead. The bride and the best man. An inoffensive pick to everyone but Zander, who Puck spots stifling a grimace. Was he hoping the "app" would pair him with Mia? Maybe he's got some fire left in his belly after all.

As they look over the rest of the list, Puck realizes they're quickly running out of names, and it's getting harder to keep track of who they've paired off. So, without thinking, they call out the first two people they notice who haven't been matched yet—"Zander and Anya!"—not realizing who that leaves remaining.

"I'm with you, then, Dr. Croquet," Robyn says, and it's obvious to Puck she's not happy with the outcome, even though she's keeping her look of disdain just on the right side of undetectable to the group at large. What is this girl's deal?

"Yup, Robyn with a 'y' and Puck," they confirm, looking down at their phone for full effect, worrying that they might be overselling the whole app schtick. But they seem to have gotten away with it.

The wedding party assembles by the "starting stake," as Robyn called it, and because Puck assigned the teams, they all naturally turn to them for guidance on the order of play, too.

They rattle off the colors of the balls at random, accidentally assigning their own team first. Already they feel like they're making too many unforced errors, but that's mostly because of Robyn's rude interruptions. Regardless, Puck can get this back on track. The hard part of this particular subplot is over. So why are they still feeling rattled as they line up their first shot?

Puck whacks the ball embarrassingly far afield of the first wicket, eliciting amused chuckles from the wedding party. "Easy, there!" Zander teases. The unsurprising truth is they've never touched a croquet mallet before in their life.

"I'm a little rusty," they try to explain to Robyn, who ignores the excuse.

"What kind of a name is Puck anyway?" she asks, while they wait for the rest of the teams to take their first hits. "Were your parents hockey fans?"

"Were yours Batman fans?" Puck fires back a bit childishly, but they don't care. They're too busy watching Damon as Lena takes her first hit. It's not just her hair and wardrobe that have changed; the way she carries herself is more poised, too. Lena delicately tucks her hair back behind her ears as she prepares to hit the ball. Her dress clings to a body that was there all along but never shown off, stretching against her curves as she swings and connects with the ball. Is Damon noticing this? Puck tries to track his gaze, but Robyn pipes up again, dividing their attention.

"Puck is such an uncommon name, though," she says.

"Well, my parents didn't name me that," Puck brusquely replies, not even bothering to look over at this nuisance next to them. Instead, they're trying to read Damon's expression as Lena returns to his side.

"How'd I do?" Puck overhears Lena asking him.

"A lot better than Puck," Damon says, and Lena laughs.

Puck doesn't mind if some flirtation comes at their expense, so long as it will help them later on.

"So it's a nickname then," Robyn presses, testing Puck's already thinning patience.

"No, Puck is my name; I just chose it myself."

Mia is lining up her shot, and from where Puck is standing, it looks like Zander is all but ignoring Anya to keep his eyes locked on his ex. Their suggestion over breakfast must have worked fast. Maybe *too* fast? Should Puck rein him back in today? The pacing matters here; he shouldn't come in too hot, and historically, that has been difficult for Zander to resist doing.

"And why'd you pick Puck?"

Robyn. *Again*. Puck is done with this. "Because it rhymes with my favorite word," they say, whipping out the answer they only fall back on when they're extremely annoyed.

Francis interrupts the awkward conversation. "Team Robyn: You guys are up again."

"Excuse me," Robyn says, turning to Puck. "I have to go fix your mistake."

Puck watches as Robyn strolls across the lawn to their team's blue ball. It matches her workout wear perfectly, and Puck hates Robyn all over again just thinking about her outfit—and her exposed midriff. Croquet isn't SoulCycle; this is a sport old British people play on cruise ships. Puck's stray hit left their team's ball at an almost impossibly acute angle several yards from the wicket, but Robyn is unfazed. She lines up the shot, practice-swings the mallet like a pendulum between her legs a few times, and then strikes with confidence, sending the ball gliding across the grass and bouncing off one side of the wicket before passing through it. The group is so stunned that some of them start applauding. Even Puck is rendered momentarily speechless.

"You didn't tell me you were an expert," they say when Robyn returns to their side. "I should give you my PhD."

Robyn is not amused.

"You know, I've been planning this wedding with Mia for months," the maid of honor says, finally unloading on Puck while the other teams take their second turns. "I went to *three* croquet lessons just so I could be sure this day went well. And then you waltzed in and dumbed down all the rules before I got here."

"I didn't realize," Puck says.

"You didn't ask" is the maid of honor's stern reply.

Puck may be the de facto leader of *Homewreckers*, but Robyn clearly takes her title here seriously. In all their scheming on the hotel stationery, Puck never stopped to consider—though it probably should have occurred to them—that every wedding already has its own producer. This one is a type-A nightmare in Lululemon.

"So *that's* how you know what a wicket is," Puck says in an attempt to deflect Robyn's annoyance. Can't they just laugh about this and move on?

Robyn frowns. "It's almost your turn again. Try to do better this time."

Puck tries to mimic Robyn's technique, and their next hit gets commendably close to the second wicket, but their head is spinning the entire time: Is Robyn going to get in the way of the plan? Can something be done to . . . neutralize her? She seems *scarily* committed to ensuring this wedding goes well, far beyond what her role requires, and this will certainly make stopping it more challenging. But Puck has dealt with stubborn contestants before. So many people come onto *Homewreckers* thinking they'll get to call the shots, and they have to be humbled. Robyn can be put in check too.

But as Puck walks back to Robyn, taking in the look of her all the way from her trendy white Sambas up to her perfectly shaped eyebrows, they're even more alarmed by another, even more urgent sensation rising within them: They do, unfortunately, need to fuck this hot mean girl as soon as possible.

Puck should be celebrating that, only a few feet away, an increasingly competitive Damon is now *this* close to teaching Lena how to use the mallet by straddling her from behind. He starts to scoot his hips close to hers, then thinks the better of it.

"Watch me," he says instead, stepping around in front of her and modeling the ideal form.

"You're a pro!" Lena responds, without a hint of irony, and it's exactly the kind of flattering comment Damon would have found annoying coming from her in college, but now it looks like he's flexing beneath his polo to try to impress her. He's treating her completely differently now that her face is no longer hidden behind a pile of hair like Cousin Itt. Puck's plan is already working, and it's only been in effect for an hour.

Maybe they *shouldn't* rein Zander in; maybe it's time to step on the gas, especially if this Robyn girl is going to be a problem. Could they wrap this whole thing up tomorrow? What are they meant to be doing again? A spa day? Or was it the picnic? Robyn is probably the one who slipped those itineraries under everyone's doors, Puck realizes. Is she going to wake up at four a.m. every day this week to consult the weather forecast?

More importantly, what is she doing *before* that? Does she have any availability in the middle of the night, perchance?

Puck is admittedly having trouble concentrating because they're consumed by the thought of pulling this girl's ponytail as they ride her from behind, her face buried in bedsheets, moans of pleasure only barely muffled by the mattress. Then, after she came, she'd flip over and look up at Puck, her skin dewy with sweat, and ask, "Is that all?" And no, it wouldn't be all.

Puck shouldn't want to hook up with the most spiteful, normative-looking woman at this wedding, but that may be exactly why they want it. They crave Robyn in a way they're almost too ashamed to admit to themself. Puck *should* want to sleep with some alternative-looking cater-waiter with a nipple ring, not a woman ripped straight out of a Macy's catalog. But even though they can commandeer this croquet game with ease, trying to force their body to want anything other than what it wants would be pointless.

Later, though. Puck doesn't want to lose focus, for Mia's sake. Protecting their friend's future happiness is a lot more important than bedding a bridesmaid. But if Lena doubles Puck's chances of success, maybe Puck has time for two missions.

Chapter 7

The bartender wants to know what kind of vodka Puck would like in their sea breeze, but Puck refuses to dignify a question that unnecessary with an answer.

"The clear kind," they say dismissively.

Puck rarely feels the need to resort to the bottle, but it turns out trying to influence their friends is more anxiety-inducing than corralling a bunch of hot strangers who signed up to generate drama on television. They made some headway today, but the stakes of all this hit Puck immediately after croquet: If they don't successfully break up the couples on the show, they can always try again next season with a new set of faces. But if they don't wrestle Mia free from Damon, they could lose her for years, maybe even forever. Yes, their visits are infrequent, but Mia's still their best friend—or at least Puck thought she was. The fierceness she once had is already fading.

Puck can't have that, and their head also hurts from doing this all without a fleet of employees. They spent the end of the croquet game talking to Mia as much as possible so she didn't pull Damon away from Lena, and also trying to smooth things over with Robyn, all while fending off fantasies about what the maid of honor looks like underneath her Lycra. It was confusing. And it was a lot to juggle. Horniness and deviousness don't blend well when there's too much stress in the cauldron too.

When the wedding party disbanded twenty minutes ago, Phil asked for the name of "that randomizer app" because "it might be useful for team-building exercises at the next company retreat," and that proved to be Puck's limit. They lied, rattling off some fake name like "Teamstr, without an 'e,'" and hurried off to the bar to decompress.

The space itself is welcoming enough. Between the checkered marble tile and the gold columns separating the bar from the rest of the lobby, the impersonal luxury of the Grove, as it's called, reminds Puck of the Cheesecake Factory at the Lenox Square mall, but made from more expensive stuff than drywall. The topiaries filling the space between columns are actually real, and they're apparently thriving under their watering schedule, unlike Puck's wilting pothos. If only the bartender were less of a pretentious twit. Puck would take a five-dollar margarita at the Factory over this interaction any day.

"If you're really fine with any vodka, I'll just give you the house brand," the bartender says, and then turns around to select some glorified paint thinner from a shelf near the floor.

Puck is debating whether they should take the drink back to their room to avoid any further conversation when a familiar alto voice sounds behind them. "Hi."

They turn to find Mia standing there, alone. "Mind if I join you?" she asks.

Puck pulls the adjacent high-top closer to them and lowers their voice. "Sure, but fair warning: I think the bartender hates me."

"What did you do?" Mia whispers back a little excitedly as she accepts the seat.

"I don't know how to act rich," Puck answers, still in a hushed tone. Then, without thinking, they add, "Can you teach me?"

Mia looks wounded for a moment, but then the bartender clears his throat and they both swivel forward to face him.

He plunks a glass of orangey-pink liquid down on a coaster and announces, "Sea breeze." Then, voice dripping with disdain, he adds, "With Smirnoff." His frown disappears as he turns to take Mia's order. "And what can I get you, miss?"

Puck didn't get a gendered salutation, which they were grateful for, because they're not sure which one this man would have picked. Anyone who thinks there are essential differences between vodka brands isn't likely to have a very fluid conception of gender.

"A French 75, please." Mia recites her order, and Puck has no idea what that means. Is she ordering an extremely expensive wine? A 1975 vintage?

"Great choice," the bartender says, with the same condescending tone one might use to compliment a dog who can shake hands. "What gin would you like?"

OK, so it's a cocktail. Surely Mia doesn't have an opinion on this question, right? She's not *that* far gone. The ritziest thing Puck ever saw her drink back at Emory was a Blue Moon. But she responds right away.

"Aviation."

Did she go to finishing school before she joined the McLeod family? Or is this Robyn's doing? Puck wants to comment on it, but the bartender hasn't left yet. Instead, he's standing there stroking his chin, as though this drink Mia ordered is some great philosophical paradox that needs unraveling.

"Aviation's a solid choice," he says, "but can I actually recommend Empress? The herbaceousness of the spirit would cut through the sweetness of the lemon and champagne beautifully—and it's a really unique purple color."

Putting legal poison in your body shouldn't be this complicated. Whoever coined the term "mixology" deserves to be drowned in Everclear. But instead of dismissing the bartender and sticking by her original choice, Mia smiles.

"That'd be great. Thanks for the recommendation."

Who is this docile young woman, and what has she done with Puck's tiny but feisty roommate? Did it really only take Mia a year of living among the McLeods to learn how to stomach this kind of treatment? Being told what to drink, what to wear, and how to behave? Puck takes a sip of their sea breeze in an attempt to wash down the bitterness rising within them, and maybe they *should* have asked for top-shelf vodka, because it tastes terrible, like cranberry-flavored nail polish remover.

"So, Robyn's an *interesting* girl," Puck says after their throat recovers, putting just enough spin on the adjective to suggest they find her infuriating.

"Oh, Puck, you know I would have asked you to do her job," Mia says. "But with you being nonbinary, I figured you wouldn't want to go *that* far—and besides you've been so busy with your show, and things haven't been the same since, well, you know . . ."

It's the closest Mia has come to acknowledging that getting together with Damon has put distance in their friendship, but she walks back from the edge of saying it aloud, and Puck is glad for it. They don't need to go there quite yet. Not until they've had more to drink.

". . . and I just really needed someone nearby to help me plan, is all," Mia finishes, opting for a less hurtful conclusion to her sentence.

Puck had watched the meticulous blueprints for this wedding come together online. Mia's Pinterest activity has been off the charts. Over the last year, she made *nine* different moodboards for the flowers alone: three apiece for the cocktail hour, the ceremony, and the reception. Puck wonders now how much of that was actually Robyn's doing.

"Robyn lives in Raleigh too?" Puck asks, and at this point they're also just trying to gauge how easy it would be to visit her for a weekend. This astringent sea breeze is doing nothing to abate the contradictory blend of annoyance and almost cartoonish lust they've felt ever since they paired themself with Robyn by mistake. A long-distance hate-fuck buddy could go a long way toward alleviating their Atlanta loneliness; it'd introduce some variety into Puck's routine at least.

"Yes, we met at a barre class after I moved in with Damon," Mia says. "I forgot to bring grippy socks, so Robyn loaned me a pair. After class, we exchanged numbers and she sent me a calendar invite for brunch the next day with a photo of the menu attached and her recommendations circled. That's just how she is."

Puck is trying to decide which detail from that story they find the most obnoxious when the bartender returns with Mia's deep purple French 75. He carefully sets it down on a coaster, wraps a spiralized lemon peel around one side of the rim, and then looks up at Mia, expecting praise. Where was Puck's garnish? Do nonbinary people not deserve citrus?

"Wow," Mia says, trying to appease him. "It looks *gorgeous*."

But instead of leaving to tend to another customer, he just stands there, waiting for Mia to take a sip, and Puck can tell even *she* is starting to lose her patience with this whole song and dance now. That's refreshing, at least. Mia isn't a lost cause yet. But she still needs some help dealing with this bartender, so Puck does what they have always done best: intervene.

"Hey, uh, barkeep?" they pipe up, sounding as boorish as possible. "I think you forgot the, uh, lime wedge for my sea breeze here."

The bartender looks annoyed but walks to the other end of the bar where Puck spotted the garnish tray earlier. Only then can Mia enjoy a sip without having to please an audience.

"Thanks for that," she says. "He's a little much, isn't he?"

"A *little*? I want to turn his face a 'unique purple color.'"

Mia nearly spits out her drink but manages to swallow her sip before returning to the subject at hand. "Anyway, Puck, I know Robyn's a lot, but she's been a lifeline for me. I hope you like her. Please be nice."

"I will," Puck says, and Mia has no clue just how nice they hope to be.

The bartender returns to deliver a small white bowl with a lime wedge sitting in it, and Puck pointedly refuses eye contact to discourage him from staying.

"So you do barre now?" they ask Mia. "Is that part of a wedding workout plan or something?"

They know they're being a little shady, but Puck genuinely wants to know the extent of Mia's acculturation to aspirational Carolina womanhood. In college, Mia's idea of a workout was walking up the stairs to the computer lab on the third floor of the student center.

"I started working out in New York," Mia says. "We're not twenty-one anymore, you know."

Mia's talking about metabolism, Puck realizes. But her response hits them in a softer place, too. Back at Emory, it was easy for Puck to believe their life was just like Mia's, just with a twist. A queer garnish on a classic cocktail. In the hermetic bubble of a college campus, separated from broader civilization, a straight girl and a lesbian going through some gender trouble could feel more proximate to each other than they otherwise might. However different they might have been on the inside, most of their day-to-day lives took place in the same two-hundred-square-foot room, a world away from the world.

But after graduation, when Puck stayed in Atlanta and Mia moved to New York with Zander, phone calls weren't enough to preserve that feeling. Their friendship didn't weaken right away. But there was a gradual undertow Puck could sense as the structures of their lives started to diverge. All the friends Mia and Zander made in New York were other straight couples; they didn't adopt some new queer weirdo to occupy the hole Puck left in their heart. It sometimes made Puck wonder whether Mia's support back in school was accidental. If Residence Life had paired her with a College Republican, would she have been just as nice to *her*? Did she even *want* a gay friend?

Not that the same principle didn't apply to Puck in reverse. They dove headlong into Atlanta's lesbian scene after graduation.

And they didn't try to find some normie but surprisingly funny hot blond woman to serve as a substitute for Mia. In fact, outside of *Homewreckers,* they almost never have occasion to interact with straight people anymore. Being queer, Puck has come to realize, is like living abroad in your own country; you mostly hang out with the other expats.

By age twenty-seven, shortly before Mia broke up with Zander, Puck could tell they were starting to speak different languages. On those rare visits in person over long weekends, the old magic was still there. But otherwise, Mia was unironically using phrases like "biological clock," while Puck was dealing with a new wave of younger lesbians complaining about a "top shortage." Mia was deep into a years-long relationship, dealing with trust issues and shared utility bills; meanwhile, Puck was entertaining a revolving door of fleeting partners Mia could barely track.

Sometimes they laughed about the differences between their life paths. But in Puck's worst moments, the disparity fed their deep, almost unutterable insecurity that queerness was a sort of perpetually delayed adolescence. It felt sometimes like heterosexual life at least had the dignity of evolving seasons, while being queer was a sort of eternal summer, pleasurable but ephemeral, and ultimately meaningless.

So, it's hard not to feel like this Robyn girl has replaced them. Like she represents Mia's commitment not just to this wedding, but to an entire universe that doesn't include them. Indeed, as attracted as Puck is to Robyn, they have to admit she looks like the mascot for straight girls, and Mia is signing up for varsity.

"Well, maybe I'll take up croquet as a workout when I get back home," Puck jokes to Mia, returning to the conversation.

"How much do you think a mallet weighs? Five pounds? Think I can get bulging triceps like Peter?"

But it seems Mia's not in the mood for humor, either. She looks down at her drink, picks off the lemon rind from the rim of her glass, and plunks it down in the bowl next to Puck's unused lime wedge. A grand piano starts playing in the background. Mendelssohn, maybe, if Puck's memories of playing flute in orchestra are still intact.

"Listen, Puck," Mia says, her tone more sober than Puck wants to be right now. "I've been thinking about our conversation in the hallway yesterday."

"And?" Puck doesn't like where this is headed.

"And I want you to know that I'm happy," Mia continues, her voice hitting a pleading note that catches Puck off guard. "*Really* happy."

"I didn't say you weren't—"

"You didn't have to," she interrupts. "I know what you're thinking. And I know how it looks: me moving here with him, me not working. But it's not forever. Damon just came into my life at a time when I needed a break anyway."

A "break" is how it starts. Treating a trip to HomeGoods like the main event in a day? That's how it ends. It's jarring to hear her talk like this, as though her life is a lazy river and she can just float along until she feels like rejoining the rapids. Puck doesn't have and never will have the luxury of kicking back while a husband provides everything. And Mia—the old Mia—wouldn't have wanted that either.

She sounds uncannily like the hundreds of women who have come on *Homewreckers* over the years and tried to persuade the producers that they're head over heels in love with the world's most mediocre men. But this could be a situation in which she is looking, at least subconsciously, to be questioned. If you're really sure of something, you shouldn't need to persuade anyone else to believe it too.

They can level with Mia now. They don't want to be too reckless, but there's space for some real talk, and they decide to take it. The plan can get thrown in the bin if this works. No one ever needs to know what Puck was prepared to do.

"So, you really want to get married? To Damon McLeod? At the Athenian?" they ask, hopefully keeping their exasperation within acceptable limits. "Do you know how crazy that would have sounded to us back at Emory?"

Mia looks hurt, like she wasn't expecting Puck to double down on their doubts. "But we're not back at Emory," she insists. "We graduated nine years ago. And Damon's really sweet, actually. I *want* to marry him, and yes, he just so happens to come from money, and yes, his family just so happens to be able to afford this big, beautiful resort. But you know I couldn't care less about all this stuff, right? I'm not some snobby bitch. I'm still me."

Puck could say that no one should ever describe the man they want to marry as "really sweet, actually." They could say that "coming from money" is a hell of a way to acknowledge that Damon belongs to one of the wealthiest families in the United States. And if they were feeling extremely uncharitable, they could say that Mia might not be a snobby bitch, but she's certainly figuring out how to blend in. Befriending Robyn is a pretty good start.

But if they're going to keep their cover, and it looks like they'll have to, Puck decides it's best to play it cool right now.

There was a window for honesty—the old kind they once shared during late nights back at the dorm—but it has passed. Mia's so deep in this thing that there's no reaching her with conventional methods. Just like those *Homewreckers* girls, she needs to come face-to-face with what she actually wants before she can admit she's been telling herself a lie. It's only Monday. There's still plenty of time left.

"And I'm still me, I guess," Puck says with a shrug. "Kind of an asshole."

The peace offering hangs in the air.

"Not an asshole," Mia offers. "But a little blunt. Always have been."

It's true. By virtue of being the only queer person in their friend group, Puck always had something of a permission slip to utter uncomfortable truths. It was the one area where their outsider status was an advantage. But it may not work as well outside of Emory, they're realizing. At least, not with Mia.

"Look, I'm sorry about yesterday," Puck says, gesturing around at the columns and the varnished wood cabinetry behind the bar. "This is just a lot. You can acknowledge *that,* I hope. We used to do six-dollar Mondays at Moe's, and now look where we are."

"I know," Mia says. "But we're roomies . . . right?"

There's a shakiness to the question—a quaver in Mia's voice that she maybe doesn't intend, but doesn't go unnoticed. Twice during this conversation, she has made a point of reminding Puck that they're not in college anymore, but now that she wants to brush everything under the rug, they're "roomies" again? That's how Puck can tell Mia is at war with herself. But the time for diplomacy is over. The kindest thing Puck can do for Mia is form an allegiance with the deeply buried part of her who knows this is a bad idea—who like Puck is probably already seeing and bracing for disaster.

Puck scoops their terrible drink off the bar and holds it aloft. "Cheers to you and Damon."

Mia regards them warily, then decides to accept the olive branch. She grabs her cocktail and clinks it against Puck's glass. "Cheers."

There's probably a curse for toasting a union you plan to disrupt. For now, this drink is punishment enough.

Tuesday

Chapter 8

Puck is trying to relax in the sauna, but they made the mistake of offhandedly asking Lena if climate change is going to make the whole world feel like this room one day, and now she's monologuing about the apocalypse.

". . . and here in the Southeast especially, the problem isn't the heat itself so much as the combination of heat and humidity," Lena is saying as Puck keeps their eyes glued shut, trying to think cheerier thoughts. "That's called the 'wet-bulb temperature' and when it climbs too high, your body can't cool itself off with sweat anymore like it does when you're in dry heat."

"Are you saying it'll feel more like a steam room?" Anya asks Lena.

"That's a great comparison," she says, sounding a bit too enthusiastic to showcase her knowledge. "Picture the entire region as one big steam room. Basically, your body will never be able to get back down to a normal temperature, so you just, well, die."

"Speaking of steam rooms . . ." Anya starts to say, and Puck briefly opens their eyes to see the bridesmaid standing up and cinching her towel tighter. "Anyone care to join me?"

Puck hopes Lena doesn't follow, not because they want to hear more about suffocating on doomsday, but because they need to talk to her privately. Tonight, when the guys get back from skeet shooting, Puck wants to get Mia and Zander together for the first time, which means distracting Damon. It's time to "use L," which means talking to "L" *alone.*

"I'll come find you in a little bit," Lena tells Anya, to Puck's relief.

The other bridesmaid shuts the door as quickly as possible to keep the heat trapped inside, leaving Lena and Puck by themselves, sitting on opposite wooden risers. Puck takes a second to consider their next move. They want to know about everything that's happened in North Carolina over the last year. And they know what they need Lena to do later today. But this girl can be so sincere that there's never an easy way to break the ice with her.

"So, Lena, do your conservationist friends know you're away partying with the McLeods?" they say, taking a wild and somewhat impulsive stab at an opening line.

"The McLeods are one of our biggest donors now, actually," Lena says. "It's a bit of an offset situation given their overall impact, but they gave us three million dollars last December."

That's unexpected news for Puck, though it doesn't make them feel any warmer toward the family. That donation, however sizable, is probably a rounding error for them. Still, this could be a way to gather some useful information.

"Did Damon arrange that?"

Lena tilts her head and considers the question for a moment. "I'm not sure he even knows about it. In fact, I haven't seen Damon and Mia since the engagement party. I met Mrs. McLeod at a women's conference a while back and she asked me to connect her to our fundraising lead. Then one day I heard my boss scream from her office. I thought somebody had died."

So Damon's *mom* made the donation. That makes more sense: It's exactly the sort of thing wealthy white women do to make themselves feel better about belonging to business empires. How far does three million go, Puck wonders, toward saving the birds that drink from the same waterways the McLeods pollute? But they need to stay focused on the wedding. Lena's been in North Carolina this whole time; she must have some actionable intel.

Shared disbelief could be the right tone to strike if they want to shake something useful out of her. They can invite Lena into a circle of confidence—without being *fully* honest, of course. "This is kind of surreal, right?" Puck asks, leaning forward on the sauna riser.

"What, the Athenian?" Lena says. "Yeah, it's pretty wild. I won't complain about a free spa day, though."

"No, I mean . . . Mia and Damon," Puck says, taking a more hushed, conspiratorial tone. "I still can't get it through my head that they're actually getting married."

For a second, Lena looks like she might cry, and Puck regrets addressing the subject so forthrightly. But then she clears her throat and collects herself without so much as a sniffle. This is a woman who has practiced bottling her emotions. Puck isn't close enough to Lena anymore to ask directly about her feelings for Damon, but her face just gave away how fresh they are.

"That makes two of us, I guess," Lena says, breaking the silence.

"Why *are* they together?" Puck asks. "Do you have any . . . local insight?"

Puck has heard Mia's recounting of the start of the relationship over the phone a few times: After she broke up with Zander for what she swore was the last time, she left their Brooklyn apartment and went to live with a friend in the East Village. She was grabbing a Coke from the bodega one Saturday afternoon a couple years later, bare-faced and still in her pajamas, when she ran into Damon, who was traveling in New York on business. It seemed like an unignorable coincidence. He took her out to dinner that night so they could catch up, and there was "just a different energy to him," Mia liked to say. But there were never more specifics offered.

"I mean, it makes perfect sense," Lena says. "Damon's very nurturing."

Puck chokes down a laugh. Damon barely took good care of his Pokémon in college, and yet Lena is now talking about him like he's an emperor penguin incubating an egg. Puck feels like they're living in another reality. Is the grown-up Damon McLeod some kind of Rorschach blot that straight women see as only exactly what they want to see? He was completely inoffensive in college, but "sweet" and "nurturing" is pushing it. Lena keeps talking before Puck's bewilderment becomes noticeable.

"I understand why Mia likes him," she continues, casting a nervous glance at the small glass window in the sauna door. "I just can't believe she's doing this to *Zander*. And so soon."

Puck has to read between the lines here. A self-styled empath like Lena would never admit to feeling personally betrayed; instead, she has to couch her concern as being for someone else. In Lena-speak, what she's really saying is "I can't believe Mia and Damon are doing this to *me*." It's the closest she'll come to confessing how hurt she is, and the fact that she has to do it so obliquely is genuinely heartbreaking.

Strategically, however, her emotional investment is helpful. The thought makes Puck feel like a cat-stroking Bond villain, but they have to remind themself this plan will ultimately benefit Lena, too. She'll never land Damon despite how well she's dressing now, no longer looking like she covered her body in superglue and rolled through an entire Buffalo Exchange every morning before walking out the door. Lena shouldn't have to spend the next decade watching someone she's known since childhood buy a house and have babies with the man she loves. Let him marry a stranger instead. Doesn't the Tyson Foods family have a single daughter? Surely the chicken world is due for some royal intermarriage.

"Did Damon say anything about Zander yesterday?" Puck asks Lena. "During croquet?"

"No," Lena says, then smiles. "He mostly just really wanted to win. I guess Mia made him stop playing video games a few months ago and I think his competitiveness needs an outlet. You remember how he was with that one game in college."

"*Smash*," Puck confirms.

"Right," Lena says. "I was so bad at it."

Damon complaining about Mia to Lena is music to Puck's ears, as is the fact that Mia is placing behavioral restrictions on Damon. Puck may be gay but even they know you should never get between a man and his PS5 controller. All is not well in the state of North Carolina. There are plenty of preexisting fractures they can press on here. With Lena's assistance, of course.

Like all the best ideas, this one comes suddenly. "Hey, that reminds me, can you do me a favor when the boys get back?" Puck asks.

Lena nods. "Sure."

"I'd already heard about that video game ban, so I bought Damon a Switch 2 as a secret wedding present. It should be small enough for him to hide somewhere. I want to sneak it into his room. Can you pull him away somewhere for a little while tonight? Ask him for help with something?"

Puck knows Lena won't be able to resist the prospect of some alone time with Damon, especially if it's framed as being for his benefit. But before Lena can agree, Puck feels a burst of cold air come from the entrance to the sauna. They turn to find Robyn, her toned body barely hidden by a short white towel wrapped around her torso, standing in the doorway.

"You," she says, and it's obvious from her stern tone that she doesn't mean Lena. "I need to talk to you. *Now*."

Eyebrows raised, Lena looks back and forth between Puck and Robyn, then decides it's the perfect moment to follow Anya to the steam room. "I can help you with that thing later, Puck," she says, almost tripping in her hurry to clear the room.

"Lena, hang on . . ." Puck tries to say, but it's too late.

The door has barely swung shut behind Lena when Robyn starts laying into Puck, her voice quaking. "What's this I hear about you asking Mia if she *really* wants to marry Damon? Are you insane?!"

In their panic, Puck tries to remember if they spotted Robyn anywhere near the Grove after croquet. Was she eavesdropping? Hiding in the topiary? No, Mia must have told her. Did she really go running to her new best friend as soon as they made up? That makes Puck feel even more alienated from Mia than they did yesterday. She won't share her deepest feelings with Puck anymore, but she will with *Robyn*?

As the maid of honor waits for an answer to her angry question, Puck glances longingly at the door, wishing they could just get up and leave. Right now would be a great time to visit the cold plunge. But Robyn is standing squarely in front of the exit, immovable and pissed the fuck off. Her bare feet might as well be combat boots.

"That's not what I said," Puck claims, not even sure if they're lying or not.

"So why did Mia tell me just now at the nail spa that she's been in her head about the wedding ever since you said it?"

She just *had* to mention that she was getting a mani-pedi with Mia, didn't she? The start of the spa day had made it clear where Puck fell in the pecking order: There were six in the group but only three chairs in the nail salon, so after a few seconds of looking awkwardly at each other, Lena, Anya, and Puck realized they should shuffle off to the sauna while Mia, Robyn, and Willa chose their colors.

"I was just trying to understand her choices," Puck says, but if they want to keep off the back foot, they've got to go on offense, fast. "If you had known Mia for longer than a few months, you'd know this is a big shock for us."

"For *you*?!" Robyn takes a step closer, and as Puck turns their head downward to avoid the fury in her eyes, they notice her pale-pink pedicure. She picked a good color, at least. "This is *Mia's* wedding, not yours. Who gives a fuck about *you*?"

Puck makes a living off straight culture, but this is the kind of heteronormative hogwash they can't stand. A wedding doesn't give a woman carte blanche to ignore the rest of her social circle. No one else should have to subscribe to that shared psychosis. "We're still people, Robyn with a 'y,'" they say, standing but still only coming up to her chin. "Our feelings matter, even at this little party that you planned ever so perfectly."

Puck knows they shouldn't lose their cool. And they know they're sinking their chances of ever getting Robyn in bed. But there's just something about this girl that makes Puck feel instantly on edge. She's like a toothpaste stain on a mirror that won't go away no matter how hard you try to rub it out.

"Mia was a wreck before she moved here, you know," Robyn says, lowering her volume but not her intensity. The fact that she's deliberately ignoring all of Puck's personal digs only makes her more maddening. "That curly-haired boy you all love so much messed her up *bad*. But she's finally happy."

"And I'm not allowed to check in with my best friend?" Puck asks, taking a step forward to show Robyn they're not going to tuck their tail between their legs and run away. "Are you her maid of honor, Robyn, or her fucking babysitter?"

Even when she's sneering, Robyn still somehow looks like she belongs on a billboard. The woman is incapable of making an ugly face. Her eyes are narrowed in anger, but even as Puck bears the brunt of her outrage, they wonder how wide Robyn would open them as she came. Not that Puck would *ever* touch this absolute brat. They want to spank her a lot more than they want to fuck her. Damn it, maybe they want to do both.

"She needed some caretaking after the way she was treated!" Robyn yells, the wooden walls of the sauna absorbing the echoes. Finally Puck's attack lines seem to be getting on her nerves. "Do you know how sick I am of hearing about the *Emory crew*? Zander broke that girl, you all apparently fucked off, and *I* had to pick up the pieces."

"Wait," Puck fires back, dialing up the sarcasm to a dangerous degree. "I thought this wedding was about Mia, remember? Not your martyr complex."

"Just shut the fuck up from here on out," Robyn commands. Puck's disappointed that she's given up on creative insults, but they can at least admire her directness.

"Trust me, not speaking to you will be easy," they quip.

"No, shut the fuck up around *Mia*," Robyn says, her voice now eerily calm, each syllable carved out of ice. "Read my lips: She's getting married. To Damon. She's trying to enjoy herself. And the last thing she needs is for some lonely little"—Robyn pauses while searching for the word, looking Puck up and down—"*loser* to ruin that for her."

Puck smiles. What they already suspected has been confirmed. Robyn looks like a bully, and now she's taken her mask off.

"Oh, I get it," Puck says with a snicker, taking another step closer, almost exhilarated that they don't have to pretend they didn't sense this familiar brand of hostility anymore. "You're just homophobic, aren't you? You think I'm a freak?"

Without hesitation, Robyn brushes the accusation away. "I didn't say that."

"Oh yeah? You didn't have to!" Puck yells, unable to maintain any sort of boundary anymore between the anger they feel and the alarming level of arousal that seems to have switched their brain off altogether. Something inside of them must be wired wrong, because for some reason they want Robyn now more than ever. They want to slap this girl right on her stupid, plump, perfect cheeks. They want to hear a whimper escape from her lips. They want Robyn to hit them back. They want to get out of this sauna before they start dripping more than just sweat onto the floor.

"You're a loser because you came to a wedding and asked the bride if she wants to go through with it!" Robyn shouts back, some spit landing on Puck's face. "Who does that?"

They stare back at her, pointedly refusing to brush the saliva away.

"Are you sure this isn't all because I've got less hair on my head than you have under that towel?" Puck asks, feeling the words slip out before they can second-guess the boundary they're crossing. "How often do you and the rest of the Pumpkin Spice Brigade go for waxes back home? Weekly?"

Robyn smirks. "I truly don't give a shit if you're gay or whatever."

Puck laughs. "Real convincing."

"I mean it," Robyn says. "You'd be hot if you weren't so selfish."

Puck loses any scrap of self-control they had left. "And I'd take you right here if you weren't such a bitch," they say.

Robyn thrusts a hand out toward Puck and they flinch, then quickly realize she isn't trying to hit them. She's grabbing the knot on the front of their towel. She pulls them closer to her, their faces now centimeters away. "Fucking try me," she says.

And then Puck closes the distance. They're kissing Robyn, swallowing her spit instead of just letting it sit on their face. They're feeling Robyn's hungry grip on the nape of their neck. They're pushing her up against the sauna door, reaching a hand down to feel for the bottom edge of her towel. For a moment, they consider fucking her where they stand. Puck can hold the door shut; they will only need one hand to make Robyn come anyway. But they have just enough self-control left to stop, pressing their fingers against her upper thigh instead.

"At least when I'm kissing you," Puck pants out, "you can't talk."

Robyn's towel has been jarred loose. Her once-tight ponytail is getting mussed up from all the motion. She still looks mad, but also amused, and most importantly, like she wants more than anything for Puck to keep going. She gives Puck a sly look.

"Why do you think I kissed you back?"

Chapter 9

Two hours later, Puck still hasn't forgiven Anya for coming back into the sauna in search of a missing hair tie at exactly the wrong moment. Just when the makeout session was getting somewhere, the sound of the other bridesmaid's footsteps forced Puck to pull away from Robyn and act like nothing at all had happened.

They've been antsy ever since then—a contrast to Willa, Lena, and Mia, who remain blissed out from the day's treatments, their skin as poreless and shiny as the low marble table they're all gathered around in the Athenian lobby.

"The boys are almost back," Mia says, checking her phone.

"Boo," Willa jokes. "And just when we're the most relaxed we've ever been."

Puck has been bristling more than they expected at how casually everyone uses gendered language here: *The boys* this, *the girls* that. But it's hard to get hung up on that right now because Mia's words barely break through their reverie anyway. They're wishing they could rewind time, put an extra hair tie on Anya's wrist, and see what they could have done to Robyn without any interruptions.

Maybe they just need to fuck her once, good and thoroughly, to get it out of their system. That's usually what happens with the straight girls Puck "turns" for a night: After the thrill of the chase is gone, the bubble of attraction simply pops. Being someone's experiment is fun, but only once. And yet, despite outward appearances, there was something about the way Robyn pulled Puck toward her that felt . . . experienced? Like she wasn't at all intimidated. Straight girls often cross boundaries out of entitlement, acting like their touch should be inherently flattering for Puck, but Robyn's approach felt different. More self-assured. So why does she dress like a Barry's class might break out at any minute?

Puck is still trying to solve the Schrödinger's box of Robyn's sexuality when the groomsmen strut into the lobby wearing matching orange hunting vests that were probably purchased for this occasion alone. Even worse, they're loudly boasting about massacring clay pigeons.

"Phil, you were a killer out there," Tom is saying loudly, his volume not calibrated to the sanctitude of the lobby, where the bubbling fountain has so far been the only background noise.

"Yeah." Peter mimes Phil's movement, bursting through the sliding door as he cocks and fires an imaginary shotgun. "Buh-duh, boom!"

Lena, no fan of killing make-believe birds that aren't even shaped like birds, audibly sighs. It's days like these that Puck experiences gender most clearly as a masquerade that would be funny if it weren't so annoying to sidestep. What if Zander wanted a pedicure or Willa wanted to fire a shotgun? These are all young—and if they're close enough to Mia to be invited,

Puck would hope somewhat progressive—people in their late twenties and early thirties and they still readily divide themselves along gendered lines, based on . . . what? The way people have "always" done it? If Puck didn't want to spend most of this week with Mia, they would have been more vocal about how distinctly 1950s the entire wedding itinerary felt. They might have even chosen shooting over the spa—and it seems like some of the groomsmen would have gladly given up their spot. Francis, in particular, looks crestfallen, like he didn't perform as well as he wanted to. And Zander looks downright bored.

Puck stands up to intercept him as the groomsmen approach. "Are the big strong men back from hunting so soon?" they joke as the rest of the guys move out of earshot behind them. "Why, we haven't even had the chance to bake all the berries we gathered into a pie!"

Zander laughs. "Yeah, this caveman shit is not for me. The only shotgun I care about is the one in *L.A. Confidential*."

"The sawed-off one? From the shootout scene?"

"Mm-hmm."

"So good," Puck agrees. "Why can't we all have a movie night this week, instead of you guys going off to war while we beautify ourselves?"

"Yeah, well, take it up with that Robyn girl," Zander says. "She seems to be in charge around here."

Puck casts a nervous glance around the lobby. Apparently, one never knows when Robyn is about to stampede into a room. For now, the maid of honor is safely out of sight, probably printing off a dozen photocopies of tomorrow's itinerary or hand-sewing the picnic blankets for Thursday. What is she getting out of this wedding, exactly? Puck knows what it feels like to be in friend-love with Mia, and the kind of devotion that can inspire. But is that all this is? Is Robyn's neuroticism over the wedding purely protective? Robyn may just want the same thing Puck wants—for Mia to be happy—but Robyn would be wrong about what that means in practice. And there's nothing more frustrating than someone with completely misplaced confidence.

"She's a handful," Puck agrees, and even that phrasing evokes images that are difficult to shake off.

Zander shifts his weight on his feet as though he's about to head elsewhere, which Puck can't have. There are other, more painstaking plans in the works, but even this interstitial moment is an opportunity, they remind themself. There's a notepad upstairs that says "M + Z" on it, and "M" and "Z" are indeed both here, not to mention the "L" who's supposed to help.

"I think I'm gonna go upstairs and make a sandwich or something," Zander says. "Do you want one?"

As perfect as that sounds, food can wait. There's work to be done.

"Hang on a second, Zan," Puck says, before whipping around to locate where Lena went, hoping that she remembers their conversation in the sauna. She's still sitting at the marble table, so Puck backtracks a few steps, listening to make sure Zander doesn't wander off somewhere. Fortunately, they soon hear him strike up a conversation with Francis.

Meanwhile, Puck leans down to whisper in Lena's ear. "Hey, remember that thing?"

Lena turns toward Puck, looking momentarily confused, but Puck nods almost imperceptibly toward Damon, who's chatting with Peter nearby.

"Oh, right," Lena says, a little too loudly for Puck's liking, but then she launches out of her seat. Puck keeps one ear trained on Lena as they return to Zander, just as Francis heads over to the bar with Phil and Tom. So far, this is working out perfectly.

"Sorry about that, Zan," Puck says. "I'll come up for a sandwich, but Mia, Willa, and I were about to have another cucumber water. We got hooked on the stuff back in the spa. Want one before we go up?"

Zander considers the invitation. Behind him, Puck can see Lena pulling Damon aside. They can't hear all of the conversation, but based on the few words they *do* catch and Lena's odd hand gestures, it seems like she is talking about needing something heavy moved, and that'll have to do. Damon takes the bait a lot more eagerly than he would have back in college, and the pair disappear together, with Damon offering a hurried explanation to Mia as he walks by: "Sorry, babe. I'll be right back; I just need to help Lena for a second."

Zander clocks Damon leaving, which is great, because the groom's departure seems to be enough to tip the scales. "Yeah, sure, I'll have one," he says. "Even though I pity the poor guy who has to slice cucumbers all day."

"OK, have a seat, I'll bring over a tray," Puck says.

"You don't need any help?"

They try to say "Don't worry, I've got it" with as relaxed an air as they can manage, but internally, Puck is sweating. Even small moments are a lot to orchestrate alone.

They watch Zander long enough to make sure he sits down at the table with the girls before darting off to the Grove. The same smug bartender from yesterday afternoon is, of course, the one Puck has to ask for four cucumber waters. "Please," they add, even though he doesn't deserve the politeness. A minute later, when he brings a tray over to Puck, he orders, "Just bring this back when you're done"—no "please"—and Puck promises to comply, even as they fantasize about decapitating him with it.

Puck doesn't command remotely the same respect here that they do on *Homewreckers*—and these "contestants" could just get up and leave at a moment's notice. There's no guarantee Mia has stayed put or that Zander didn't get distracted. But when they return to the lobby, everyone is still in place, chatting away. In fact, Zander has thoroughly enraptured Willa—a predictable and not entirely unwelcome development. Men with his looks who can cook tend to have that effect on people—life's two great needs, sex and food, wrapped up in one pretty package.

"So, what's your favorite thing to make?" Willa is asking Zander, and Puck can see her fantasizing about dating him already.

"At the restaurant or at home?"

"Either."

Willa fawning over Zander could help Mia realize what she's missing out on, which is why Puck doesn't mind the third wheel right now. As *Homewreckers* has proven many times over, the triangle isn't just the strongest shape, it's also the sharpest wedge.

They set the tray down, and Zander picks up one of the glasses with a brief "thanks" to Puck as he considers Willa's question.

"The dishes at the restaurant don't really feel like mine. I like making them, but it feels like doing paint-by-numbers for somebody else's vision."

"At home, then," Willa prompts, not even hiding her interest.

Puck scans Mia's face for a reaction but her eyes betray nothing. Upon closer inspection, though, she does seem to be keeping an especially tight grip on her cucumber water. Intellectually, of course, Mia must know that Zander is available to be pursued, but it's another thing to watch your bridesmaid make a bid for your ex.

"Probably a breakfast sandwich," Zander finally answers, flashing a smile that could make an entire sorority pass out.

"What kind of breakfast sandwich?"

Oh, she's down *bad.* Puck can see that Willa's thinking about all the scenarios in which Zander might make her breakfast. Meanwhile, Zander is clearly ramping up to some borderline pornographic description.

"Well, I'm from Jersey," he says, scooting forward in his seat, "so it's gotta be Taylor ham. Sear it on the cooktop, fry the eggs in the fat while you toast a kaiser roll. Add a couple slices of American cheese on top at the last minute, just long enough for it to melt, and boom. That's heaven between buns right there."

Puck takes note of Zander's word choice, and while they appreciate how good he is at commanding a woman's attention, they do need him to appeal to one *particular* woman. Fortunately, though, Willa notices that Mia is also here.

"Did he ever make that for you, Mia?" she asks, then immediately apologizes. "I mean, sorry if that's an awkward question. I just know you two used to date."

The statement catches Mia mid-sip and she looks startled for a moment before collecting herself. "No, no, it's fine," she says, after swallowing. "When we first moved to New York, he'd make one of those for me when he got home from the restaurant in the mornings. I'd be waking up for school. He did that for a while."

"What happened?" Willa asks. "Too much of a good thing?"

Willa is doing the Lord's work right now, asking questions that a surreptitious Puck no longer can. Maybe they should add her first initial to the notepad stashed in their nightstand.

Mia and Zander eye each other, silently debating whether to answer, and if so, who should. Sensing the tension, Willa tries to defuse the situation, saying, "Sorry, sorry, I'm prying. I've been told it's a problem."

But Zander jumps on the conversational grenade with a quickness that surprises even Puck. "What happened is I started drinking even more than I was already drinking, which was a lot, and then I started mixing pills in there too, and that started making me really drowsy, so I tried to counteract it with cocaine before I got home, but then I'd be on the comedown just as I walked in the door. So yeah, the breakfast sandwich was the first of many casualties." Zander takes a breath, then gulps down the rest of his cucumber water.

"Oh I didn't know—" Willa stammers, "I mean, Mia didn't mention . . ."

"Zan, I—" Mia starts to say, taken aback by her ex's outpouring of honesty.

But Zander stops her. "It's OK. If I were Mia, I'd want to forget all about it too. I wasn't very much fun to live with. But for what it's worth, this cucumber water is the hardest thing I've had since Christmas, so there's that."

Puck suspected some sort of mention of his sobriety was coming, and they've been hoping to find out how much Mia knows about it. First, her eyebrows lift in genuine excitement. "Really, Zan?" she asks. And then there's a glimpse of another emotion—a sadness behind Mia's own flashbulb of a smile. Part of her must be imagining an alternate present where Zander had gotten sober while she was still with him. *Perfect.* But Mia contains the tinge of regret before anyone spots it.

"Yeah, I mean, I'm not out of the woods yet," Zander responds.

"In this case, literally," Puck chimes in, gesturing toward the forested hills outside the lobby windows, sweeping their free arm around them in an exaggerated circle. "Eh?"

There's a painful silence.

"Puck, that was bad," Mia says. "Even for you."

"We like bad jokes in AA," Zander adds. "There's an awful one about nonalcoholic beer and incest. But even we have our limits."

"Wait, what's the joke?" Mia asks.

"It's too dirty for your virgin ears," Zander fires back.

"Well, tell it to me, then," Puck insists. "I can take it."

"Yeah, but you're banned from this conversation now," Mia says.

There's a rightness to this: Mia and Zander ganging up on Puck to tease them for being a showy try-hard; Puck watching the two of them flirt, even though Zander could probably make the case that his sly retort about Mia's "virgin ears" was barely acceptable for two people with a long romantic history. Puck doesn't feel like they're in the Athenian anymore: No, they're back in the old dorm room, the natural order restored. This is how it *should* be.

Willa shifts in her chair, perhaps realizing that Mia can still command Zander's full attention if she wants to, but that's fine; the bridesmaid has served her purpose. If this were *Homewreckers*, Puck could basically order Willa to be dragged away with a vaudeville hook so that Mia and Zander could have the chance to start going at it already. But this is, sadly, a real wedding in the middle of the mountains with no contracts, cameras, or cash incentives at their disposal.

Instead, Puck counts it as a small victory that the exes are even talking to each other. If Ron were here, he'd want something explosive; for now, Puck will have to settle for quietly monumental. Real life can't move on reality TV's timetable, much as Puck wishes it could.

Chapter 10

When Puck returns to Room 444 at the end of the night, they find Robyn waiting outside their door. She's wearing black leggings and a crimson zip-up that perfectly matches the carpet of the Athenian hallways, which probably isn't a coincidence given the amount of advance research she seems to have done.

Puck can't decide whether this girl is a welcome sight. Is she here to say that what happened back at the sauna shouldn't happen again? This wouldn't be the first time that an ostensibly straight girl has gotten buyer's remorse. Usually, Puck doesn't mind when it happens; in fact, it seems like those women typically expect Puck to be more broken up about it than they are.

But this time, Puck is surprised to find themself bracing for a disappointment they shouldn't feel. They'd hate to admit to Robyn how badly they want to pick up where they left off. For all they know, though, the maid of honor is just here to yell at them some more.

"Is this another ambush?" Puck jokes, procuring their key card from a pocket. "Should I call security?"

Robyn gives a mock laugh in reply: "Ha ha."

Puck brushes past her to open the door and Robyn follows them into their room without a word. "Well, I guess we know you're not a vampire!" Puck calls over their shoulder, emptying the contents of their pockets onto an end table with a clatter.

"What?"

Robyn is apparently unfamiliar with Victorian literature, but on the other hand, that probably means she ended up with some kind of legitimate job after college. What did Mia say she did again? Medical sales? Business-to-business marketing?

"Vampires have to be invited in," Puck explains, turning to face their sexy trespasser and deciding they're too tired to try guessing her true intentions.

Robyn says nothing, looking unamused as always, leaving Puck to fill the silence. "So are you, like, queer or what?" they ask with a yawn. Their evening sandwich with Zander became an impromptu movie night after they realized *Heat* was on cable, so Puck could easily turn in right now.

Unless, of course, Robyn has other ideas. Bluntness seems like the right approach with her—the only way to actually pin her down. Her intensity can only be met with intensity, an equal and opposite reaction.

"I made out with you, if that counts," Robyn answers, as she walks past Puck and sits down in the leather armchair, clearly expecting to stay awhile.

Puck's curiosity is piqued by the vagueness of her response. Robyn looks about as straight as they come, with flat-ironed hair and no visible piercings beyond her ears. Then there are those eyebrows, which are the most vexing of all. Usually, Puck can tell a girl's sexuality by her brows alone, and the shape of Robyn's is giving Kinsey zero. She looks like a woman who would unironically say she wants to marry a man who "reminds me of my dad." If Mia and Zander had dared Puck to try to make out with her back at Emory, even *they* would have demurred.

"No, but I mean, have you done anything like that before?" Puck asks, realizing how invasive the question might be midway through posing it.

"And would you like to volunteer your entire sexual history?" Robyn responds. "Or do you think having a shaved head means no one gets to doubt how gay you are?"

Puck is taken aback. "It's just that you don't look like anyone I've ever . . . you know . . ."

"What's the matter?" Robyn interrupts their stammering. "I thought it was your favorite word."

"Made out with!" Puck locates the words they want to land on. It's annoying how this girl keeps getting the better of them. "Jesus! You know what I mean."

"Some of us dress for the weather, you know," Robyn says, crossing her legs. "I'm living in North Carolina in the Trump era. I kind of like flying under the radar right now. But I could show you my AO3 account if it would assure you that I'm into some freaky stuff."

Puck sits down on the velvet couch, reassessing what Robyn wanted out of this secret meeting. They had assumed she either wanted to fight or fuck, but now she's bringing up assimilationist politics and fan fiction? This conversation is inscrutable so far.

"And that's how you think of me?" Puck asks. "*Freaky*?"

Robyn rolls her eyes and leans forward in the chair. "You really need to get over how radical you *think* you are," she says. "Do you think you're the first person in history to use they/

them pronouns or have sleeve tats? Like, *half* my friends back in Raleigh are nonbinary. You walked into this hotel like no one's ever seen one of you before."

"One of me?" Puck asks, but even as they balk at the phrase, their eyes are inadvertently drawn toward Robyn's cleavage, plainly exposed by the way she's positioned in the chair now. Is she not wearing a bra underneath the zip-up?

Robyn laughs. "I know you act hot and tough and in charge, but all you seem to want to do is catch me in some kind of verbal trap where you can prove I'm victimizing you. It's not going to fly with me." She puts her hands on her knees. "I promise."

Puck isn't used to people outmaneuvering them in conversation. And they're feeling equally discombobulated by the way Robyn's zipper is hanging on for dear life. If she just leans forward a little more . . .

And yet beneath all the horniness, something about Robyn's statement pricks them. Back at Emory, Puck stood out, which had its drawbacks, but the ego boost of being a big fish in a small pond outweighed most of them. Being all but sequestered on *Homewreckers* hasn't helped. The world must have changed more than they know for people like Robyn to be completely unbothered by their existence. But if they can't impress her with their "radical" vibe, as Robyn puts it, how is Puck supposed to get her in bed, they wonder, their mind settling into a single shameful track. They don't want therapy; they just want to finish what they started in the sauna.

Puck stands back up to try to find a task they can busy themself with, mostly as a distraction. "I'm thirsty," they announce, turning around and walking over to the minibar in the corner of the room. "Do you want anything? Reading me like that probably has you parched."

Robyn ignores Puck's pity parade. "Did you drink the Red Bull in there yet?" she asks. Puck squats down to peer through the glass door of the mini-fridge and sees the energy drink, a galling ten-dollar price tag attached.

Mystified by the decision to have caffeine this late, Puck reaches for the can anyway. "You want a Red Bull at *midnight*?"

"Yeah, I figure we're going to be up for a while," Robyn says.

Puck sorts through the contents of the fridge for another moment, remembering that the McLeods are footing the bill for the entire wedding, which changes their calculus. They settle on a spiked seltzer.

"For a while? Doing what?" Puck calls back to Robyn, peeling the sticker off the can. "Trying to prove to each other that we're queer?"

"Sure. I can think of one way to do that," Robyn says.

Puck stands up with the drinks in hand and turns around to find Robyn already topless, her crimson zip-up neatly folded on the glass inlay of the coffee table, a mischievous smile on her lips. Puck nearly drops the cans on the floor, but they disguise their shock long enough to play it cool.

Robyn's intentions are nakedly clear now. At least behind closed doors, her libido overrides her objections to Puck. But they're not going to perform for her on demand. They already lost control once around her, and they're determined to keep their composure from here on in. Let her squirm for a second. Let her sit with the arrogance of her own presumptions.

"I've seen boobs before, you know," they say, as nonchalantly as possible.

They resist the urge to pounce on Robyn and instead sit down on the couch, refusing to look at her breasts, and making direct eye contact instead. Robyn doesn't flinch.

"So you've seen them all, is that it?" she asks, leaning back again in the chair, as if to prove how comfortable she is with the overture she's making. When she folds her arms over her chest, Puck can't help but steal a glance—and Robyn catches them in the act.

"I mean, yours are nice . . ." Puck admits, unable to pretend like they didn't look.

Robyn is trying to torture them—and goddamn it, it's working. Again.

"But you can do without them," she finishes the thought.

Desire itself is hyperbolic, but still, Puck has never needed anything more than to put their hands all over Robyn's body. Not that they can confess that. With enormous effort, they eke out a response—"Definitely"—knowing that they're already losing. They've probably already lost.

"Oh, maybe I'll take my drink to go, then," Robyn says, and starts to rise from her chair.

Puck knows they should let her leave—or at least let her pretend to start making an exit. That's the only way to get the upper hand back. But after getting cut off in the spa, Puck can't let another opportunity slip out of their grasp. It almost kills them to admit it to themself, but it would kill them more to not have her tonight.

"Don't," they say, their desperation too painful to spread across more than a single word.

There's no use pretending anymore. They need this. Puck slides off the couch and drops to their knees in front of Robyn's armchair. They haven't let themself be in a position this submissive in at least five years, and the last time it happened, Puck had to block the girl from their phone to stop thinking about the shame of having been so vulnerable with her, of showing the cracks in their stone. But they also haven't been so thoroughly bested by someone this femme ever. There's topping from the bottom, and then there's absolutely dominating from the bottom, and Robyn is essentially leading Puck around on a leash right now. She has been since she walked in, as much as they hate to admit it. And there'll be no avoiding her this week. Puck will have to think about how pathetic they felt in this moment every time they see her for the next four days, all while dealing with the stress of trying to undermine her carefully laid plans. But for now, Puck needs this more than they need to feel in control. They need to suck on her.

"Oh, *now* you think I should stay?" Robyn coos.

Puck looks up, past the curve of Robyn's breasts, directly into those piercing green eyes, and nods.

"Are you still thirsty?"

Puck nods again. They can't believe they're doing this, but they can't stop now.

Robyn cups her right breast and leans forward, lowering her nipple toward Puck's mouth. They accept it, quelling the urge to start licking her voraciously, which would betray how horny they really are, and instead settling for gentle caresses with their tongue. Maddeningly, Robyn doesn't immediately throw her head back in ecstasy as Puck might want her to, but instead chuckles softly to herself, like she's pleased with how pliable this person became at the mere sight of a tit. Unfortunately, this only makes Puck want Robyn even more. They close their eyes and lose themself in the act, tracing a slow circle around Robyn's areola, then reversing direction. Robyn lets out a soft moan at that—and it feels like a tiny gift, offered almost as encouragement rather than reward.

"Remember earlier . . . when you called me a bitch?" Robyn says, pulling her breast back, leaving Puck wanting more.

Even at the absolute peak of their arousal, there's a limit to how degraded Puck is willing to feel. "Well, you were being kind of a bitch," they manage, mounting a makeshift defense.

"Oh?" Robyn moves her left breast closer to Puck's mouth, but stops short of offering it.

"Yeah," Puck responds, not taking the bait, trying hard to keep their resistance from collapsing.

"Well, I think I'd like you to apologize," Robyn says, a demand in the guise of an observation. She won't settle for anything less than absolute control, will she? If Puck keeps ceding ground, she'll only take more. They have to draw a line somewhere.

Puck smirks. "Not gonna happen."

With alarming swiftness, Robyn stands up. "Mind passing me my shirt then?" she asks, looking down dismissively at a still-kneeling Puck on the floor.

God, she is fucking relentless. Puck considers for a moment whether playing "Robyn Says" is really worth their dignity. How much of this is sexual play and how much of this is a humiliation ritual meant to punish them for what happened yesterday? Is there any difference between the two for her? And does Puck even care? The feeling between their legs is the same either way. They've come too far to go back now. Puck looks up at Robyn, who hasn't budged an inch. There's only one way to get her to sit back down.

"I'm sorry," they mumble.

Robyn stays standing.

"*For*?"

Puck shouldn't entertain this for a second longer. They can get up and walk out of the room at any moment—no, wait, this is *their* room, damn it. They're so drunk with need, they're not even sure *where* they are anymore. Which is probably another sign there's no point fighting this urge.

"I'm sorry for calling you a bitch," they dutifully respond.

"Now with my name," Robyn orders, a smug smile painted across her face.

"I'm sorry for calling you a bitch, Robyn," Puck responds, feeling a twitch as they utter the final two syllables.

"Good."

And only then does Robyn sit down and allow Puck to return to their work. Puck moans into Robyn's breast, overcome by the unexpected pleasure of having their authority so thoroughly and completely subverted.

"You really want to please me?" Robyn asks, and this time Puck can tell from the throatiness in her voice that she's feeling it now too. Puck nods, staying focused on what they're doing with their tongue.

"I want you to touch yourself while you do this," Robyn demands, and Puck stops licking for a moment to grapple with the suggestion.

There are women Puck has dated for months who never once saw them have an orgasm. They much prefer giving over receiving, and might even do it exclusively if their partners didn't sometimes want to participate in their pleasure. But Robyn is nothing like those women, and the way she cuts straight through

Puck's self-image is as erotic as it is terrifying. As if they had any choice, Puck undoes the top button of their pants, reaches a hand down the front of their Hanes, and feels themself. And then they're lost in it all, their mouth back on Robyn's breast, their hand working themself toward climax, Robyn reaching down past Puck's head to also touch herself. Puck wants to stop and ask if they can just eat Robyn out instead, but she seems very particular about how this happens, just like she's particular about everything. Puck feels Robyn's back arching, shoving her breast even deeper into their mouth. They feel themself getting closer. Almost—

And then Robyn's phone dings. Feverish and focused, Puck tries to say "Ignore it," but their mouth is full, and besides, Robyn's already checking her phone. "Hang on, it's Mia. She says the dress isn't fitting right."

"Can't she wait?" Puck asks, pleading, their hand now motionless in their pants.

But Robyn is already standing up again, gently pushing Puck's head off her. "I'm still the maid of honor at a wedding, you know," she says. "I can be your milkmaid later."

She quickly pulls on her zip-up before walking away, leaving Puck all but whimpering for her to stay. After they hear the door latch behind Robyn, Puck doesn't even move somewhere more comfortable. They keep touching themself until they're a shuddering mess on the floor.

Wednesday

Chapter 11

People like Puck find out who they are in the backs of school buses—liminal, lawless spaces where freedom only engenders cruelty. It's where Puck first heard the whispered rumors about them, then the slurs, and eventually the silence of simple isolation. They couldn't wait to leave for college. Next to Tennessee, going to Emory felt like fleeing to Northampton. So it's with some reticence that Puck steps onto the yellow party bus that the McLeods have hired to take the wedding party to Asheville this afternoon. When Mia first mentioned they were renting a bus, Puck was picturing a sleek black motorcoach, not a time machine back to ninth grade.

"Remember, there's a three-hundred-dollar fee if someone throws up," Peter reminds the groomsmen as they pile into the converted cabin ahead of Puck, prompting some of the group to cast an accusatory look back at Phil.

"C'mon, that was *one* time," Phil protests.

"Yeah, and we're *still* banned from the Hatteras ferry," Tom says, conjuring an image Puck wishes they could blot from their mind.

In a bit of accidental symbolism, Puck climbs into the bus behind the men but in front of the women, who seem a little more cautious about the vehicle, and for good reason. The interior looks like Vegas on wheels, with blue and purple LED strip lighting around the entire perimeter, and faux-leather bench seating on either side of the central aisle. Mercifully, there is no stripper pole in the back, but it wouldn't look entirely out of place with the prevailing aesthetic. Instead, there's a built-in chest in the rear of the bus that must be a drinks cooler, complete with a wet bar that probably pulls water from a tank Puck wouldn't trust. They sit down so that the girls can finish piling in behind them and see Lena trailing right behind Damon, just like old times.

"Are there seat belts?" Lena asks, surveying the situation.

"Lena, it's a *party* bus," Damon tells her, but there's a fondness to his tone.

"You can still die on a party bus."

"Well, then you just go to party heaven, baby!" Damon jokes, and even though it passes for jocularity, hearing anything even approaching a pet name coming out of his mouth is telling. Puck hasn't had time to check with Lena about how last night went, but this is one of the lightest exchanges they've heard these two have, maybe ever.

Anya makes a beeline for the alcohol while Willa runs her fingers around the edge of one of the window frames. "Wow, it looks like they used upcycled vinyl from an actual school bus for the trim," she observes, and only Robyn is able to mirror her interest.

"Yeah, I wanted to find something with just a hint of charm," she says, slipping past Puck without any acknowledgment, like she wasn't half naked in front of them a short time ago, ordering them to touch themself for her pleasure.

Puck debated trying to track Robyn down this morning, but decided it would read as too desperate, even though they were basically performing dog tricks at her command earlier. The impulse to connect with her was concerning in and of itself: Are they really so lonely that they want to "talk about last night" with someone who drives them up a wall in every other context but that one, and yes, even that one? Why are they offended that this girl hasn't even said hi to them? Are their feelings actually—*ugh*—hurt?

"You did a good job." Puck hears the compliment—really a bid for attention—slip out of their mouth before they can stop it.

Robyn turns to look at them, a mixture of amusement and confusion on her face. "What?"

"With the bus, I mean," Puck says, wishing they could simply run off the vehicle, but there are too many people clogging the aisle now.

Before Robyn can respond, Mia squeezes between them on her way to the bar. Meanwhile, Zander is lagging behind the entire group, making conversation with the bus driver in the way that fellow service industry workers always seem to zero in on each other. Puck wishes he would join the party. They are saving the centerpiece in their plan for tomorrow, but it requires as much table-setting as possible.

If they could just pull everyone for interviews, ask them how they feel, and plant ideas in their heads, this would all be so much easier. But this is going to be a tough environment: Trapped inside a moving vehicle, with limited room to maneuver, both figuratively and literally. Back at *Homewreckers*, Puck likes to divide and conquer the contestants when they clump too close together; group scenes have never been their strong suit, and those tend to make for worse TV anyway, with all the cross talk.

Helping their cause, though, is how everyone looks absolutely delicious today. The wedding party decided to show out for this excursion. Mia is in a short navy dress that is perfectly cinched in all the right places. Zander's V-neck cuts low enough that some of his chest hair is peeking out, and for the same reason that many lesbians find Hozier kind of hot, Puck can admit it's working for him. Even Damon looks good in a pair of brown loafers, some fitted pants, and a patterned button-down. But it's Lena who's the real showstopper in a gingham dress with an almost scientifically calibrated amount of leg showing.

Once they arrive in Asheville, according to the itinerary Robyn slipped under their door mere hours after Puck's mouth was on her nipple, the bridesmaids are doing a hot yoga class, which means all this work getting dolled up will shortly be undone. But with the exception of Willa, perhaps, these seem like the kind of girls who wouldn't dare let a man lay eyes on them without makeup, so they'll probably just reassemble themselves afterward. Robyn included. Does she really have nonbinary friends—or was that just a bluff?

"Are you going to teach everybody how to ride a bus, too?" Robyn asks, reappearing by Puck's side with two mimosas and offering them one. The gesture lands in an indiscernible space somewhere between threatening and welcoming. Yesterday, Puck would have been sure Robyn wholly hated them, but now it feels like there is some affection underneath the teasing. How are they supposed to tell the difference between meanness as a form of flirtation and simple cruelty? Puck warily accepts the flute, careful not to spill it as the bus pulls away from the Athenian and into the woods.

If Robyn wants to keep the tête-à-tête going, Puck can play along.

"No lessons today, I'm afraid," they say. "My expertise is restricted to lawn sports." What they really want to do is acknowledge whatever the fuck happened last night. But saying, *Hey, remember when you shoved your tits in my face and I licked them and then you left and I kept masturbating on the floor?* might not go over well in mixed company.

"A shame," Robyn says. "I was looking forward to some pointers about how to sit on my ass."

Before Puck can respond to that barb—or was it meant to be suggestive?—Peter dings his champagne glass for a toast, then grabs on to a siderail as the bus turns onto 276. The few members of the wedding party still standing scramble for a seat.

"Hey!" Peter shouts as the murmurs die down. "Hey, everyone! I won't talk long because I've got to save my *real* speech for the reception, but I just wanted to say it means a lot to me to see how many of y'all came out to support my baby brother."

"Pete, c'mon," Damon protests.

"No, no, no, look, these people need to know what a fucking dork you were, and how proud I am that you're all grown up now," he continues, to a light groan from Damon. "With some help from me, of course."

Puck steals a glance at Robyn, who is gritting her teeth through this cliché-ridden excuse for a toast. It's reassuring to know her contempt has multiple targets—and in this case, Puck shares her enmity. Next, Peter is probably going to say something about how Mia is out of his kid brother's league.

"I mean, look at Mia," Peter says on cue, and Puck detects the slightest narrowing of Robyn's eyes at the instruction. "*Damon* and her? People are going to think he's a Make-A-Wish kid who won a meet and greet with a supermodel."

It sounds like a line he stole from a Vince Vaughn comedy but bastardized in the delivery. Whatever its origin, it's embarrassing. "Stop," Mia protests, but her nervous laughter betrays her, as good-natured as she tries to make it seem. She must know how asymmetrical this arrangement looks from the outside.

"Am I wrong?" Peter asks the group, refusing to let it go.

Although they wouldn't use the same words, Puck doesn't disagree with Peter's hackneyed observation. Mia is indeed too good for Damon. But it's not just because of her beauty, which is of course the attribute Peter is choosing to focus on. It's because she has long experienced emotions more complicated than the momentary joy of defeating a *Dark Souls* boss. Mia's a fully matured human; Damon only grew up a second ago, relatively speaking, with a big push from Mommy, Daddy, and Big Brother. If you can call abandoning your only real hobby "growing up."

"OK, OK," Damon groans. "Move it along, Pete."

Peter shoots him a playful warning glance, like he's considering doubling down *again* just because Damon told him to stop, but ultimately he concedes: "Cheers to Mia and Damon," he says, hoisting his glass, but then with a smirk, he adds, "I guess dreams really *can* come true."

At that Puck swears they hear Robyn mutter "Jesus Christ" under her breath before reluctantly raising her glass. Puck drains half their mimosa in one sip, then immediately looks toward the front of the bus at Zander, gauging his reaction to all this.

He's stone-faced, nursing a Liquid Death, rightfully unamused. It must be hard to watch your ex go through with this; it must be unbearable to watch it happen on a party bus.

Yesterday, when they first hatched their plan, Puck felt more neutral on the question of Zander and Mia *actually* getting back together so long as the wedding itself was stopped. Their relationship was combustible all the way to the end, so it seems unlikely that Zander's sobriety alone could repair it. But then again, that was the root of their problems, wasn't it? Still, it's hard to overcome the compounded resentment that comes from years of cleaning up after someone else's mess. Even if Mia could forgive him, could she really forget all the emotional energy she spent along the way? All those nights she worried he might not come home at all? And yet, if they *could* get through that reckoning, Puck thinks, how beautiful would it be that they grew up together, moved past a challenge that could have destroyed them, and then grew old? They could have all the familiarity borne of time with all the cohesion of surviving a shared trauma—or Mia could have a loveless marriage full of lie-flat airplane seats. Great dick or Delta One, take your pick. Puck doesn't want to think too many steps ahead, especially when they still need to get "M" and "Z" alone together for the first time, but maybe there's a world where they *do* actually work.

Puck shouldn't waste any more time nudging things along. And thanks to the gender-divided itinerary, this ride may be their only chance today to talk to everyone. They need to get a temperature check on Zander, investigate why Damon and Lena are so buddy-buddy now, and find out how Mia's feeling about her ex-boyfriend getting clean. But before Puck can move next to Zander, Robyn takes advantage of the post-toast silence to issue an announcement of her own.

"Hi, friends!" she calls out. "I want us all to have fun today, but you should have seen on your itineraries that we're going to do a little icebreaker first."

Puck really needs to start reading these papers more closely; they've been glazing over the subheadings and ignoring the concerning number of bullet points below them. An icebreaker is going to eat up the time they badly need. This week is already going by faster than Puck thought it would, especially with the bridesmaids and groomsmen splitting up so often.

"What were you thinking, Robyn?" Mia asks over the light chatter that's broken out on the bus, directing the group to respect her maid of honor's plan.

"Two Truths and a Lie," Robyn says, and Puck has to stop themself from groaning.

This game won't reveal anything—just quirky, outlandish-sounding factoids that don't have anything to do with who people actually are. Puck doesn't need to know whose cousin played for the Lakers, or who saw Timothée Chalamet on vacation in Paris. No, if they're going to have to spend the first stretch of this ride participating in a conversation starter, Puck at least needs to be able to extract some valuable information.

"What about Truth or Drink?" Puck chimes in, knowing that Robyn will hate the suggestion, but not caring. They pissed her off yesterday, and she still came over, so fuck it. "We've got drinks on the bus, and besides, it cuts right to the chase . . ."

Puck lets the suggestion trail off into awkward silence, but they can bear it—and they *do* want to make this seem like more of a suggestion than a command, even if the outcome is the same. Puck knows they'll all go along with it eventually, just like everyone followed orders at croquet. What they can't do, though, is look at Robyn, for fear her gaze might literally light them on fire. If last night was any indication, they're going to be sexually tormented into apologizing for this later, probably with a bar of soap stuck in their mouth or something. Even so, they can't let today's best opportunity go to waste.

"Can I just do the Truth part?" Zander asks from the front of the bus, holding up his garish green-and-yellow seltzer can.

Fuck. Puck admittedly hadn't taken Zander into consideration when they proposed the change, but he seems open to the idea. Does he want to hear some unadulterated truth from Mia too?

"Except for Zander, we've all got to use something harder for this than mimosas," Phil says, already fumbling around in the shelves above the bar for liquor—and Puck now sees how that ferry disaster might have happened.

The idea already has momentum behind it, but there's one hurdle left to clear. Puck finally braves a look at Robyn: She isn't thrilled. Her mouth is tightly shut. But Puck also sees a flicker of curiosity in her eyes, like she's trying to figure out what they could possibly be up to. What's wrong, after all, with telling the truth?

"Robyn? Would that be OK with you?" Mia checks in.

Robyn casts one last suspicious glance at Puck, and appears to weigh the suggestion in her mind, but accedes. "Sure," she says, curtly, making her displeasure known.

Red Solo cups are quickly filled with an unidentified clear liquor and passed down the aisle, with everybody but Zander taking one.

"How should we do this, Puck?" Mia asks, setting her empty mimosa flute in one of the cupholders built into the bench seats.

Puck doesn't want to overcomplicate things, but they do need people—a few *specific* people—to be more honest than they otherwise might be in this setting. The longer this game goes on, the better. "Well, I think everyone should get the chance to ask one question that everyone has to answer," they say. "And we can go around clockwise."

Robyn, of course, raises an objection. "Won't that take forever? The drive is only an hour long."

"Yeah, and won't we get wasted?" Peter asks.

But Puck is ready with their rejoinders. "Not if the questions are quick," they say, "and not if everyone tells the truth." And then they issue the death blow: "Why don't you start, Robyn?"

"Fine," Robyn says, swirling her red cup discontentedly, "what if everyone just says where they first met Mia and Damon?"

Does she not know how to play this game? Who would be uncomfortable sharing that?

"Do you want to go first?" Puck prompts, more to needle her than anything else.

"Sure," Robyn says, speeding through it. "I met Mia at barre, and I met Damon a couple of weeks later at brunch."

Peter, sitting to Robyn's right, chuckles a bit at the question. "I met Damon at home, obviously. Mom says I called him 'an ugly potato' when she brought him back from the hospital, so Damon hasn't changed much, I guess. And I think I first met Mia when Mom, Dad, and I came down for his graduation."

Damon picks up the figurative baton. "Hard to say when I met myself," he says, smiling at the stupidity of it in a way that even Puck finds endearing, a flash of his more boyish demeanor slipping through. "But I met Mia through Zander. We were all at Emory and she came over while we were gaming." He leaves unmentioned the fact that Zander and Mia dated for most of their adult lives.

Puck largely tunes out the rest of the group's answers while they try to calculate a question of their own—something a little risqué and potentially revealing that could still pass for being socially acceptable. They're glad there are a few members of the wedding party sitting between Robyn and themself, because this exercise needs some time to pick up steam before Puck injects their question.

When Willa asks everyone to share "the most embarrassing fact" about themselves, Puck wants to kiss her on the mouth, because that's exactly how this game needs to unfold, even if the answers—like Anya's "I still sleep with a teddy bear," or Tom's "I peed myself in eighth grade"—are fairly lackluster. Both Willa and Francis opt for the Solo cup on that one, and Puck probably should too, if they were strictly following the rules.

The most embarrassing thing they could admit to is that they Photoshopped a picture of their head onto James Dean's body in seventh grade to see how it would feel, but instead they opt for a less vulnerable—but still queer—admission: "My mom wanted to know why Rachel Weisz was my phone wallpaper when I was a teenager, and I told her it was because she was my 'style icon' and not that I was a huge lesbian," which elicits a few nervous laughs from the group.

"What was the reason for your last breakup?" Anya asks when her turn arrives, but she immediately second-guesses her choice. "Oh God, I shouldn't have asked that, because even I don't want to answer it," she adds, tilting back her Solo cup in shame.

Tom blames his last breakup on a move, and then it's Zander's turn. He had no trouble being honest in a small group yesterday, but Puck wonders how he'll respond to this prompt in front of everyone.

"For anyone who doesn't already know, my last breakup was with Mia," Zander says, shooting her an apologetic glance. "And the reason we broke up has a lot to do with why I'm drinking a 'severed lime' sparkling water," he adds, looking down at his Liquid Death and reading the macabre flavor name off the can.

"Oh, Zan, you don't have to—" Mia hits a note of tenderness that's all the more surprising because of how public it is. Damon's *right there*.

But Zander interrupts her. "Sorry, Mia, I don't want to make it awkward. I would have picked 'drink,' except, well, I kind of can't."

The mood in the bus gets heavy for a moment, which Puck can't have. There are still three-quarters of the circle left to go. It's Zander himself who rescues the vibe. "I *can* chug the rest of this, though," he announces, then cranes his neck back and starts draining the seltzer.

Puck starts a semi-ironic chant of "chug, chug, chug," and the rest of the bus joins in after the first round, clapping until Zander hoists up the empty can. The group laughs and cheers before settling back down.

By the time it's their turn to answer, though, Puck's mood is decidedly less ebullient. Their last breakup is not a topic they want to discuss, especially in front of Robyn, who does seem very interested in their answer indeed, judging from her intent gaze and the mischievous curl of her lips.

They could just lie. Or Puck could say that Samantha broke up with them because she thought being a reality TV producer was "a slippery slope to fascism," garnering some extra sympathy by saying that she did it over text. The Emory crew know all about Puck's work—and have side-eyed it for years—and they'll probably never see the rest of these people after this week, so they shouldn't give a damn what anyone thinks. But then there's Robyn, sitting across from them with that dumb Cheshire grin. Pissing her off is fun but, oh God, it seems they actually care how she perceives them. They must, or something would have come out of their mouth by now.

But *why*? She's been nothing but mean to them—publicly, at least, and privately, too. And it's not like there's any world in which Robyn wants to *date* them, right? Puck hates themself for even entertaining the thought—for even wanting to hope—but there's something about her that compels a fascination that can't be satisfied in a week alone. They shouldn't feel this. They don't want to feel this. And yet.

"Well?" Robyn nudges them.

Puck locks eyes with her, lifts up their cup, and burns their throat with a sip of vodka.

"That bad, huh?" Robyn asks, and the group laughs, but she just smiles, her expression bemused and knowing at the same time.

Puck is still reeling during the next couple of answers, only focusing again when Mia's turn arrives. Everyone is now painfully aware, if there ever were any ignorant stragglers, that

Zander was Mia's last breakup, so she should have no trouble answering. He broke the door down and all she needs to do is step through it. She could easily defer to Zander's explanation and let the game continue. So why does she look like she's struggling to decide what to do, pouting ever so slightly?

"I think we've probably heard enough about my last breakup," she says, and takes a sip of her drink, a brief hush falling over the group at even the slightest possibility of the bride being sad.

Francis, though, fails to respect the mood. "If I talk about my ex, I'll want to drink anyway," he announces, "so I might as well cut out the middleman." The rest of the line drinks, too—even Robyn, seemingly out of a desire to be done with the subject more than anything else.

But Puck's not going to ease up now that it's time to ask their question. If anything, the pump is primed for even more forced vulnerability.

"How many people on this bus have you kissed?" they ask.

Across the aisle, Robyn's eyes widen and her nostrils flare. She clearly wants to keep their recent tryst a secret. And she can't be happy that another question will resurface the subject of Mia and Zander's relationship. But as far as Puck's concerned, Mia should be thinking about all the times she's kissed Zander, and how much better that must have been than anything she's ever done with Damon.

"Puck!" Lena shouts, scandalized by the question.

"It'll help paint a picture," they explain, grabbing on to Anya's knee for stability while the bus takes a turn. "I mean, we all know about Mia and Zander, but surely some of *you* have dated each other, right? I'm still getting to know everyone."

"Well then, you go first," Robyn prompts, but the venom in her voice makes it clear she *definitely* doesn't want to be included in Puck's total count.

"I'm only at one," Puck says. Robyn looks briefly panicked, but it's not her they're counting.

"That time when I was drunk?" Mia asks, and half a dozen pairs of eyebrows raise in unison, some out of surprise; others, Puck is sure, out of titillation.

"You'll have to be more specific!" Puck jokes back.

"It happened more than *once*?" Damon asks, as his brother elbows him in the ribs.

"We never *made out*," Puck clarifies. "It was just the occasional drunken 'I love you so much, bestie' smooch, you know? No one else has ever done that?"

"No, I can't say I have," Phil says with a derisive laugh—an unsurprising interjection coming from him. It's just shy of homophobic, but still awkward enough to bring the conversation grinding to a brief halt until beautiful, perfect Zander resuscitates it.

"I don't know, you should try kissing the homies goodnight sometime," he says, and coming from someone with his inherent charisma, it'd be enough to turn any straight man bisexual.

To Puck's left, Tom answers, "I guess I'm at zero."

"Francis and I dated for six months in high school," Willa adds. "So I've got one. Two if you count Phil, which I don't."

"Well, fuck you, too," Phil says, toeing the line between vindictive and playful. Clearly there's history there, but Puck can unearth that another time.

"Never again," Willa emphasizes.

Only then does Puck notice that Lena, sitting across from Willa at the back of the bus, looks especially flushed. She's only taken one sip in the entire game, for the breakup question, so alcohol alone can't be responsible for the tomato-red hue of her skin. "We have to actually say?" she asks. Is she *trembling*, too?

"Well, yeah, that's the whole point," Puck confirms, their curiosity growing. "Unless you want to drink again."

"Yeah, but we kind of know you've kissed at least one person now," Anya says, drawing even more attention to Lena's nervousness.

Whose name could Lena possibly be nervous to utter? Is she gay now? Did Lena have a lesbian fling with one of the bridesmaids that no one knows about? Puck admittedly didn't even consider Miss Goody Two-Shoes when posing this question to the group. Lena probably requires notarized consent before kissing someone.

"Yeah, I mean, I'm at one . . ." Lena says, and everyone—especially the Emory crew—looks at each other.

"Who, Lena?" Puck asks, unable to contain their curiosity, and not wanting to.

"I only had to say the number, right?" Lena stalls.

But then Damon of all people speaks up: "OK, fine. Lena and I dated for three months during senior year."

"You *what*?!" Puck can't stop themself.

"Yeah, um, what?!" Mia echoes. She's not quite as exasperated as Puck, but close enough.

The non-Emory contingent shifts their gaze around the bus nervously, recognizing that this history precedes their entry into Mia and Damon's lives. The bride looks dumbfounded, but also increasingly betrayed the longer the silence lasts. College was nine years ago now, but still, Mia's husband-to-be probably should have told her about this . . . relationship? Fling? A dare gone wrong? Sensing Mia's confusion, Lena tries to defuse the situation, even though it's Damon who owes her an explanation.

"It was nothing," she says. "I think he was mostly just bored."

Damon doesn't endorse Lena's theory, but he does deign to offer some context for his near decade of silence: "I had ignored her crush on me for so long that I thought you guys would make fun of me if you found out we were *actually* dating." But judging from the regret that flashes across his face, he has barely enough social adroitness to realize how that could come across. "Not that it would be embarrassing to date Lena. Now, I mean. Well, not then, either. But it was just that I never . . . fuck, you know what I mean."

Damon is going red now, the anxious nerd reemerging from beneath the preppy veneer. Across the aisle, Lena can't stand to see him feeling so self-conscious.

"It's fine," she assures him, but then she leans forward to look down the bus bench at Mia. "*Is it* fine? I'm sorry, I guess I always assumed he'd told you. Sometimes *I* even forget it happened."

Puck doubts that very much. Lena has probably written her own fan fiction about the failed relationship. The last two days, she's been looking at Damon with that same hopeless, forlorn expression she had back in college, even if she's trying to convince herself she doesn't need him. But she did have him once, briefly, which must make it that much harder to let go for good. Mia stays silent, weighing how to respond as Lena's expression grows more pleading by the second.

Instead, Zander interrupts. "I guess there *were* a couple months where you kind of fell off the face of the earth, Damon.

Did you two hook up over spring break or something? I remember knocking on your door the week after we got back and I swore I could *hear* you inside, but you didn't come."

Except he probably *did* come, Puck thinks. All over Lena. How could they have missed this? Puck prides themself on their perceptiveness but an entire three months of Lena and Damon having sex somehow eluded them. They should be forced to resign from *Homewreckers* for not having noticed.

"Yeah, it was right before graduation," Damon confirms.

"Jeez, Damon, leave some for the rest of us," Peter says, somehow finding the most vile way possible to try to lighten the mood. Meanwhile, Mia has finally figured out what she wants to say.

"So who broke up with who?" she asks, her face contorted into a chipper smile, but Puck can see she's processing the painful surprise.

"Mia, we don't need to talk about this now," Robyn says, trying to intervene.

"No, it's fine," Mia insists, regaining mastery over her expression, any shred of embarrassment or pain wiped away. "It was a long time ago now. I do just want to know. For the record. Before I marry this . . . well, this Lothario, apparently. Jeez."

"I broke up with him after I moved to Raleigh," Lena says, no longer able to meet Mia's gaze directly, dropping her head apologetically. *She* broke up with *him*? Puck is shocked for the second time in as many minutes. "I could tell he wasn't as into me as I was into him, and he was too scared to hurt my feelings and break up with me, so I did it for him. But I liked North Carolina, so I stayed, and I guess I never looked back."

The group is pin-drop quiet as Lena waxes introspective in front of all of them. The party bus is not living up to its name. But this reveal is, as a *Homewreckers* sizzle reel might promise, a "total game-changer." Puck can see Mia across the bus reassessing Lena, mentally refiling her friend as an antagonist, far from the former wallflower who didn't know how to use a makeup brush. Some healthy competition could be good for Puck's plan—but they also don't want Lena to be *too* visible on Mia's radar. The "Stay away from my man" part of Mia's lizard brain should remain deactivated for now. Better for her to keep reminiscing about the good old days with Zander instead.

On the other hand, Damon might be even more susceptible to Lena than Puck originally thought. Could Lena be more than just a distraction? Is there a contingency plan that involves her and Damon getting caught by *Mia* instead? The mood in the bus is still heavy, but Puck's mind is skittering through an array of hypothetical scenarios, trying to assess whether they should take a different tack. No, better to stay the course. Mia and Zander have the chemistry and the history to make this plan work. That's what matters.

Lena finally tilts her head back up, becoming even more keenly aware that the entire wedding party has been hanging on her words. "Well, look at me doing therapy," she says, and then attempts her version of a joke: "Whose idea was this anyway?"

"Puck's," Robyn answers, her narrowed eyes landing back on them. "It was Puck's."

Chapter 12

The most gender-affirming athletic wear Puck could find in their backpack ahead of this excursion to Asheville was a pair of basketball shorts and a Boygenius tee, which makes them stick out even more than they already do during this "bridal yoga" class. But being the group's queer duckling today comes with a consolation prize: They were assigned the yoga mat directly behind Robyn, which means they have spent much of the last forty minutes looking directly at her ass.

The group has gone through the same Vinyasa flow at least four times now, and Puck is finding the transition from downward dog to cobra to be especially suggestive when Robyn does it.

"Now lower your belly button all the way to the ground," the instructor says in the sort of soothing whisper that must have destined her to either work in a yoga studio or host a public radio show. "Lift your chest up. Breathe in. Now exhale."

Robyn breathes out like she's trying to prove something, forcing a loud "ahh" out of her lungs. Puck should have known she'd be a teacher's pet, even as an adult.

"Good, Robyn," the instructor compliments her—then, with a slight frown, she tiptoes between the rows of mats to correct Puck's form.

Puck feels the woman pressing down on their lower back. It doesn't feel like their spine should be able to make this shape. Right now, they're regretting not raising their hand at the start of class to signal they don't want personal touch. They've got more important things to worry about than doing cobra right—namely, looking at the way Robyn's red leggings hug her ass.

"Just like that," the instructor says, squatting in front of them now and gently pushing their shoulders backward. "Perfect, Puck." Of the many things Puck finds annoying about this woman—who definitely smells like she only uses natural deodorant—the worst is that she will not stop showing off her recall of everyone's names.

After the instructor moves on, leaving a trail of body odor in her wake, Puck looks around to see how the others are faring with the final minutes of this class.

Anya's eyes are closed as she loses herself in the flow. Lena is constantly looking back and forth at the instructor, then at the other bridesmaids, making sure she's doing everything precisely correct. Willa, meanwhile, has taken up the instructor's not entirely serious offer to spend as much time in child's pose as they'd like; she's wearing a black set with skulls all over, her face pressed to the mat, her body unmoving, just like she's been for the last ten minutes. Mia looks the most pristine despite the temperature, and weirdly comfortable in this environment, but she's still wearing the tacky plastic "Bride-to-Be" tiara from the party bus as a joke, which gives Puck hope. The irreverence hasn't been exorcised from her body just yet.

Puck wishes they had found time to connect with Mia during the remainder of the bus ride, but she was always flanked by a bridesmaid or a groomsman. A debrief of Lena's revelation will have to wait until later.

Mia shifts into downward dog, which reminds Puck to turn their head back toward Robyn so they don't miss a second of what comes next. This part—the part during cobra when this girl's butt forms a perfect dome on the mat—makes Puck wish their eyes were video cameras so they could rewind and rewatch this again and again.

They swear this girl looks more naked in her yoga clothes than when she's actually naked. The whole flow restarts for the final time, and Puck savors every last one of Robyn's movements, lagging a few seconds behind the transition to tabletop so they can sneak the best views.

If no one else were here, and Puck were the yoga instructor, they'd tell Robyn to stay in tabletop and the rest would follow naturally. But instead, the class ends in three minutes of child's pose, and Puck reluctantly whispers "Namaste" back with the bridesmaids before being dismissed to the relative cool of the changing area.

"Whoa, that class ran a little long," Willa observes as they regroup and retrieve their phones from their lockers. "We still have time to shower, right?"

"How *are* the showers?" Anya asks. "I forgot to bring my sandals."

Lena joins in on the anxiety-fest too. "Yeah, we still have time, right?"

It's bad enough that Puck is usually bundled in with women by default. But it's infuriating to have to endure situations like these, when girls just endlessly ask each other questions about what they *should* do instead of ever making a decision. Even trap shooting with Peter would be more appealing than this.

"We have time," Robyn announces on Mia's behalf. "I built a half-hour of wiggle room into the itinerary. And Anya, they're floor-to-ceiling waterfall showers that are cleaned before every class. You're fine. You won't get athlete's foot."

Robyn's hyper-preparedness is finally serving a good purpose. If she weren't here, the girls probably would have agonized about it until they had to leave anyway.

"When the maid of honor speaks, we listen," Mia says, giving Robyn's command the imprimatur of bridal authority, and the women begin collecting towels and washcloths from the baskets near the sinks. Puck follows behind them before retreating into one of the shower booths at the far end of the changing room. Already they're thinking about how to pass the time when they're done; ever since cutting off their hair, their bathing time has been dramatically reduced. A quick lather and rinse is all they need.

The shower is as pristine as Robyn promised it would be. The expensive soaps and shampoos have scent names that are all three words too long. What, exactly, is bergamot? Shouldn't lavender and honeysuckle be enough for one shampoo? But just as Puck squirts some gel on their hands, the shower door opens to reveal Robyn standing there in nothing but her towel. Before they can utter a word of protest, she steps inside and pulls the door shut behind her.

Startled, Puck manages to stop themself from speaking louder than the sound of the running water. "Excuse me?" they hiss, immediately turned on, but terrified of being found out. "I'm naked."

"I'd hope so," Robyn whispers back, undeterred. "You're in the shower."

Among all the bossy bottoms Puck has encountered in their life, this girl might be the most demanding. They have not known a moment's peace since meeting her, and they suspect they won't as long as they're within spitting distance of her. Has she already forgotten her annoyance over the bus icebreaker—or is she just really good at compartmentalizing her sex drive?

"Can we do this later?" Puck asks through clenched teeth. "Back at the hotel?"

Robyn stays put. "But you look hot *right now*," she insists, and Puck feels every movement of her greedy eyes from their fuzzy head to their tattooed arms to their hairy legs, with more than a few pit stops along the way. She is insatiable, even more so than Puck, which unfortunately only makes them want to rise to the occasion. But they'll have to be quiet in these showers, and they'd rather do things to Robyn that make a lot of noise.

"We're going to get caught," they whisper, and Robyn, who seems to always be scowling at them in public, has the audacity to break into an actual fucking pout.

She takes a step toward the water stream, loosening the knot in her towel. "I saw you looking at me during class," she coos, lips still turned down. "You always stayed in downward dog a bit too long after I moved to cobra. But I get it. You want to wait until *later*."

If she thinks she's going to mope and tease her way into making Puck fuck her in a shower ten feet away from their best friend, then, well, unfortunately she's right. But they can't let her know that yet.

“Can’t you be a good girl and wait?” Puck pointedly turns away from Robyn after asking the question and continues soaping up. They’re not going to make the same mistake they did yesterday and let themself lose the upper hand so soon. This brat can’t get *everything* she wants the moment she wants it.

“Who said I wanted to be good?” Robyn says, and then Puck hears the towel come off, and feels the woman’s body press into their back, followed by her searching hands reaching around Puck’s midsection. “Don’t you want to turn around?”

“If I do that, I’m going to have to fuck you,” Puck says, a little too loudly, in their most serious voice.

“Finally.” All the coyness is drained from her voice. She turned on her charms to get what she wanted and now that Puck has given in, they can get down to business.

“I’m not sure there’s enough time in your itinerary for me to do that as thoroughly as I’d like,” Puck says, as Robyn keeps exploring their body with her fingers.

“Oh, I’ll make room,” she whispers in Puck’s ear, and they nearly have to reach out to the wet tile wall for stability because of how weak their knees go at that. They turn around to find Robyn, lithe body loaded like a spring, her now-damp hair slicked back against her head. Puck looks down to confirm that their little barb about Robyn’s bikini area was indeed true before pulling her closer into the stream. For a moment, they savor the feeling of warm water flowing off the shelf of Robyn’s breasts onto their own body, and then they reach a hand down between her legs. They’re not going to have long.

“You need to stay quiet,” Puck warns, and Robyn only nods in response, taking the instruction in an infuriatingly literal fashion. Even when she's getting what she asked for, she still manages to be a fucking pain.

Puck works deliberately and expertly at first, pulling Robyn deep enough into the shower so that she can keep warm, but not so close that the water will get in the way of their handiwork. A lot of queer people act as though there's some kind of rocket science involved in fingering someone, like fucking a girl with your hands requires knowledge of hidden arcana that has been passed down from lesbian foremother to lesbian foremother for generations. But all it really requires is attention and focus while you kiss the right places. Puck starts with Robyn's neck while they keep rubbing her, then work their way up to her lips, remembering with some bemusement that this is technically only the second time they've kissed.

Robyn lets out an involuntary whimper as Puck feels her legs tighten around their hand, and they both stop for a moment, waiting to see if anyone overheard the noise. For an eternal second, they look straight at each other, Robyn's body urging them to keep going while her eyes insist they wait. But the only sound is five different streams of running water slapping against the bathroom floor at the same time. As a precaution, Puck grabs their unused washcloth, folds it in half, and after an assenting smile from Robyn, slides it into her mouth. *That's better*. They wish they could gag her in the outside world, too.

The groaning of plumbing in the background signals that one of the showers is already being switched off. They better finish this before too many bridesmaids congregate and it becomes impossible to pretend like they didn't emerge from the same stall. But whatever happens now, there's no way they're letting Robyn walk out of here without an orgasm. Not after two interruptions in a row.

With the washcloth in place, Puck can't kiss Robyn on the mouth so instead they look right into her eyes—and the same intensity that can make this woman's anger so severe is exactly what makes her arousal so powerful. She doesn't even blink, only nods, encouraging Puck to keep going. To keep touching her. Faster. To keep holding her gaze. To keep going until . . .

Robyn moans through the washcloth so loudly there's no way her orgasm went unheard, sounding almost in pain from the pleasure. She leans into Puck afterward, and they hold her upright so she can get her sea legs back as she savors her complete exhaustion—the highest compliment she could pay. But they've both got bigger problems than Robyn being wobbly on her feet.

"Um, is everything OK in there?" someone calls out. It sounds like Lena.

Puck exchanges a panicked look with Robyn, silently debating which of them should respond—or if they should just stay quiet and ride it out. But no, that won't work. Especially if it *is* Lena, who'd be too worried someone slipped and fell to wait much longer than a few seconds before rushing in to help. Puck is just about to open their mouth when Robyn spits out the washcloth and shouts back: "Yeah, sorry! I dropped the shampoo bottle on my foot!"

"Ouch!" the voice—definitely Lena—calls back.

"How'd you manage that, Robyn?" Mia asks. "My shampoo was bolted to the wall."

Puck starts to panic even more after hearing another voice come from the common area. How are they supposed to get out of the shower if *everyone* has stopped early to investigate the commotion? Robyn looks at Puck and shrugs. She's going to have to keep improvising.

"Oh, weird," she calls back to the group. "Mine was, um, loose."

Another shower stops and now the changing room is almost completely silent.

For all Puck's producorial skills, they have no idea how to squirrel their way out of this jam. Should they say that they ran into Robyn's shower to make sure she was OK after that yelp? No, no one would believe that, least of all Mia, who has watched them "turn" many a straight girl in the past—which is what Robyn apparently still is in her eyes. But again, it's Robyn who proves quickest on her feet.

Silently, she points first at herself, then walks her fingers through the air like legs toward the shower door. *I'll go first*, she's saying. Then she points at Puck, and holds her palm flat. *You, stay*. Then she taps her wrist, points again at Puck, and repeats the finger-walking gesture. *Wait a minute, then leave*.

Puck nods in agreement and then Robyn mouths, "Thank you," before turning the water off and slipping out the door, careful not to open it too wide. Puck stands there, starting to shiver, as they wait for the women to get dressed and reapply their makeup. They grab their towel from the hook on the door to try to keep warm.

"Did Puck finish already?" Anya asks after a few minutes of shuffling, stepping, and inessential conversation.

"Yeah, we're just waiting on them, right?" Lena says.

"They probably left already," Mia suggests. "They don't have much hair to wash."

She knows them so well.

"Yeah, I heard them walk out earlier," Robyn says with absolute conviction, and it frightens Puck that she might be an even better liar than they are.

Puck is freezing by the time the last footsteps finish echoing in the changing room, and then they race out of the shower, quickly throwing on their street clothes: another band T-shirt, a denim jacket, some rumpled black pants. Instead of taking the door that leads toward the reception area, they slip back into the fortunately empty studio, still warm from the class, and then dash toward the emergency exit, banking on its not being alarmed. Even if it is, they trust themself to think up some excuse. They hold their breath while they press the bar, but the only sound Puck hears when the door opens are running cars in the parking lot. Finally free, they jog around to the front of the studio where the women have presumably assembled, slowing down just before turning the corner so they won't be gasping for air when they run into the girls.

And there they are, standing in front of the Sprinter van waiting to take them shopping. Mia's pulling her phone out of her bag, looking around in confusion.

"Hi!" Puck pants, still a few yards away.

"Puck!" Mia calls out. "I was just about to call you. We've gotta get downtown."

"Sorry," Puck says, coughing to cover up their breathlessness. "You guys were, uh, taking so long that I went for a little walk."

The women seem unsettled that Puck left without telling someone. Even Robyn, the devious little snake, fuels the suspicion. "You went for a walk . . . behind the yoga studio?"

"Yeah," Puck says, disappointed that they didn't concoct a better excuse in the moment because now they have to commit to this one. "I wanted to see what was back there."

Robyn is throwing them off their A-game, and for what? Revenge? Of course a shuddering orgasm wouldn't make her forget about the icebreaker changeup. This girl seems perfectly capable of hating them and hate-fucking them at the same time. And yet, in a way that scares them, Puck wishes that the pleasure they've been sharing with Robyn in private could start to bleed into public, too. What is she like, Puck wonders, outside of these sexual games they've been playing? Do they even have time to find out?

"So, what was back there then?" Mia asks.

"Oh, you know . . . a dumpster," Puck says, then decides they need to get the heat off them fast before someone starts poking more holes in their cover story. "Did you all have good showers?"

This feeble attempt at a diversion is met with excruciating silence.

It's Robyn who responds.

"Mine wasn't hot enough," she says, because of course she can't help it. Puck would be tempted to tell her to go fuck herself—except they've taken care of that already.

Chapter 13

Many women who look like Mia make for nightmarish drunks. Millions of petite blondes have demons living inside them who only need to taste the unholy combination of vodka and cranberry in order to emerge. But Mia has always been adorably sentimental when alcohol is in her system, and tonight is no exception.

In the limo back to the hotel, Mia went a little too hard on the champagne, on top of the drinks she had at the tapas bar, so she spent the whole ride telling everyone how much she appreciated them. By the time the car pulled up beneath the Athenian portico, it was clear she wouldn't be able to get up to her room unassisted. In a somewhat surprising gesture of trust, Robyn asked Puck to "help Mia upstairs, please." It's a role that would have naturally fallen to them back in the day, but now it has to be delegated.

Even as they tend to Mia now, Puck is thinking about how often they used to provide this support unbidden, and about what changed. Was it just the distance? Damon? Something else? And why did Mia drink so much on the way back? Was she rattled by what happened on the bus ride, suppressing it all day until she got in the car home? She's not so far gone that she can't walk, but Puck takes her hand in the elevator anyway to keep her steady.

"Did you have . . . funds today, Buck?" Mia slurs.

"Funds?" Puck asks.

"Fun!" Mia shouts, almost earsplittingly loud in the confined space, and then giggles at herself.

"Yes, I had a lot of fun," Puck tells her, slowly, like they're responding to a child, wondering whether Mia would even remember it tomorrow if they told her about showering with Robyn after hot yoga.

"Good, I wanted you to have fun," Mia says, her eyes welling up. "I just . . . I just . . . I miss you a lot, you know? Like *a lot*."

Puck isn't sure how to respond to this sudden sincerity. There's almost no point putting extra care into their words given Mia's current state, but they want nothing more than to match her earnestness with their own. They miss Mia, too. Like, a lot. They wish they could have lived two lives after college: one in Atlanta climbing the ranks at work, and one up in New York being a stabilizing influence on Mia. A little human cloning would've been all they needed to preserve their best friendship—and maybe the turbulence in Mia's love life could have been averted, too. Puck was always a load-bearing beam for her relationship with Zander, and look at what's happening in their absence: a doomed wedding with a heartbroken ex and a new set of friends who don't seem to know the real her.

"Fourth floor" is all Puck ends up saying, right before the elevator doors slide open. "This is us, honey."

They tug Mia into the hallway, which amuses her. "Weeee!"

She careens out of the elevator. OK, maybe Mia is drunker than she seemed at first. And Puck is realizing they're not sure where she sleeps. The sign at the elevator bank has two arrows pointing in opposite directions: To the left is 400–450, to the right 450–499.

"What's your room number, Mia?" Puck asks her. But instead of responding, Mia pulls them toward a random chair by a side table in the elevator bank, sits down a little too fast for Puck's liking, and starts to laugh.

"You're not going to leave it, Puck," she says, then catches her mistake. "*Be*-lieve it."

"Believe what?"

"My room number," Mia says, switching on a dime from uncontrollable laughing to faux solemnity. "It's so creepy. It's 468"—and then she adds a ghastly "Oooooh" for effect.

She pauses as though waiting for Puck to react. Are those numbers supposed to mean something? They're even, but that's all that comes to mind.

"I'm lost," Puck admits, deciding that if they're going to wait for Mia to sober up some more, they might as well sit down on the carpet.

"It's Zan's old dorm number," Mia gravely intones. "Room 468."

That's all the assurance Puck needs to know they're on the right track. Her recall, all these years later, of the placard on the door of Zander's dorm is telling. Her bringing it up now, two days from walking down the aisle with another man? It's damning for Damon.

"Really? That's wild," Puck says flatly, not really selling it, but knowing they don't have to bother with the correct tone right now. The information is useful, but the coincidence itself isn't all that interesting.

And then Mia starts to weep. "He'll be OK, Puck?" she asks, tears dribbling onto her chin. "Zander? You think he'll be OK?"

If Puck were feeling mischievous, they'd tug on Mia's heartstrings a little, appealing to the misplaced guilt just below the surface. They'd tell her that Zander might fall apart without her, that he could relapse and lose his job and end up working in fast food before too long. But there are still rules of engagement that Puck has to abide by—a Geneva convention for stopping weddings that forbids them from stooping quite that low—and besides, Mia is already doing their work for them. She's still crying in the chair, and Puck softens at the sight.

"He's already OK, Mia," Puck assures her. "Zander's doing really good. I've been talking with him a lot these past couple days. He's been promoted at the restaurant twice, and he's so proud of being sober. He wants to open his own place one day if things keep going well."

Even though Puck is telling the truth for once, Mia doesn't like the answer. She loses control, dropping her face into her hands and sobbing even harder. "Why . . . *why* couldn't he have been doing good with me?" she chokes out.

Puck's heart sinks. They know they're answering more for their own benefit than for Mia's at this point—in the morning, this entire conversation will probably be a blur for her. But she wants Zander, that's for certain. And he *can* be "doing good" with her, if Mia can just do one brave thing—once she's back in her right mind. But pointless though it may be, Puck is willing to hear themself talk for a bit, if only to pass the time while Mia takes a breather.

"I think sometimes people need to lose everything in order to fix their lives," Puck says, shifting out of a cross-legged position and pulling their knees toward their chest. "You wouldn't believe how many people who come on *Homewreckers* didn't give a fuck about their partners until they got cheated on. Once everything's ruined, they suddenly become invested in making it work again."

Puck looks up to check on Mia before staring back down at the crimson carpet. "People like Zander have to assess the wreckage of their actions before they can rebuild," they continue. "It's just how he is, Mia."

"Rock bottom," Mia says, nodding, which suggests she's talked with him at least a bit about AA. Have they had conversations here that Puck hasn't witnessed firsthand? If so, good. They need as much tailwind as they can get headed into tomorrow.

"Rock bottom," Puck repeats, like they're confirming to a child that she pronounced a word correctly.

"He had a cute bottom, too, Puck," Mia says, chuckling as she wipes away her tears, the emotional shifts happening so fast now, they're starting to give Puck a headache.

Puck allows themself one guilty pleasure of a pointed statement, Geneva convention be damned: "He *still* has a cute bottom, Mia. It's almost enough to make me glad skinny jeans came back."

Mia laughs again, but this time her eyes start closing as she does, and while she's thin as a rail and Puck would like to think they have strong arms, they definitely can't hoist an unconscious woman down this eternal hallway to Room 468. "No, no, come on," they say, pushing up off the floor and grabbing Mia by her shoulders. "Let's go to bed, sleepyhead."

Mia jolts back awake, looking at Puck with a trusting gaze that stings because of how long it's been since they've seen it, but also because they have to keep operating behind her back for her own good.

"And Damon and *Lena*?" Mia asks, her mind leaping between subjects. "What the fuck?"

Mia's in no state to be a reliable source but Puck can't resist a little recon.

"Yeah, what did he say about that?"

Mia's speech is broken but Puck tries to follow the through line: "He called me at the shopping place. The barricade?"

"Arcade," Puck says, helping her find the word.

"He said it was so long"—Mia swallows down what sounds like a particularly perilous burp—"ago. Didn't think it mattered. Awkward enough with Zan here. Two exes is too many, isn't it?"

This girl needs to sleep. But file this under the reasons this whole ceremony needs to go up in smoke: Two days before the wedding, Mia still doesn't know key parts of her fiancé's backstory, Damon's insecure about one of his oldest friendships, and neither of them are being fully honest with each other.

Puck kneels down, drapes one of Mia's arms around their shoulder, and stands her up, walking her down the hall until she gains her own momentum. Bit by bit, they work their way to Room 468.

"OK, where's your key card?" Puck asks when they finally reach her door.

"Dress . . . pocket," Mia says. "I love that this dress has sprockets."

It's the sort of banal observation that Puck might lovingly make fun of at a different time—the verbal equivalent of someone hanging wall art in their vacation home that says "Life's a Beach." But Mia's feeling too tender now. Instead, they pull the key card out of her front pocket and open the door.

Puck wordlessly goes through the same routine they did countless times back at Emory: They walk Mia over to the bed, help her undress, then bring over a pair of makeup wipes to clean her face, taking extra care to remove every last atom of eyeliner from her lids. There's an intimacy to the ritual that harkens back to a better time in their friendship. Mia stays silent, but coos with delight when Puck brings over an enormous pajama shirt from the dresser to pull over her head.

"So comfy," she says, and Puck just smiles ruefully, laying her back down before they get up to fetch some water for her nightstand.

If only they had been here for her. If only Mia could listen to reason. But, God, she's always been so bad at taking advice.

When they return with a full glass, Mia looks up with big needy eyes. "Tuck me in, Puck?" And she laughs at the internal rhyme. "Tuck Puck, Puck tuck."

Puck leans down to pull the covers up to Mia's chin and she takes advantage of the proximity to plant a big kiss on their cheek.

"I love you, Puck," Mia says, but it doesn't sound like something Puck is hearing in the present; no, it sounds far away, like an echo from a life that is no longer their own.

Love. When is the last time they heard that word used in a real way, not as a cudgel hurled between oiled-up twentysomethings on a game show? When was the last time someone said it to Puck and they truly felt it, all four letters of it? It didn't always feel good, Puck remembers. Sometimes love in its early stages felt like pain, a yawning void in the middle of you demanding to be fed. In theory, the direction is supposed to reverse at some point, the love giving as much as it takes. But Puck doubts they've made it that far—and wonders whether they ever will. Something has gone wrong in their life, they suspect, now that an expression of affection so freely given between friends sounds like an alien language. But that won't stop them from returning Mia's gesture—and meaning it.

"I love you, too, Mia," Puck says, kissing her on the cheek before leaving the room, looking forward to the quiet contemplation of their walk back to 444.

But what they find outside instead is Damon, who's making a habit out of startling Puck in hallways. He looks tired, but clear-eyed. Apparently, the men didn't go quite as hard in Asheville as the women did, or at least Damon kept his wits about him. Phil is probably blacked out somewhere.

"Hey, how was boys' night?" they ask. "Did you all do body shots off some strippers?"

"No," Damon says, too fast, like he's guilty of something, even though Puck knows from Robyn's itinerary that the guys went to a virtual reality bar—a rare concession in Mia's anti-gaming policy. The only skin the groomsmen saw tonight was computer-generated.

"Relax, I was joking," Puck assures him.

"Oh, I know," Damon says, then changes the subject, skipping straight past the pleasantries. "I was just coming by to check on her. How is she?"

"Drunk," Puck reports. "But she'll live, Dr. McLeod."

The genuine anguish on his face suggests he's in no mood for jokes. This is not Damon McLeod, SVP of something or other in the family business. This is a boy who's out of his depth.

"No, I mean . . ." Damon starts to say, trailing off, then starting over. "Look, Puck, I know we haven't talked much since college, but you know her really well. Maybe better than anyone. Is she doing OK? I'm worried about her."

Puck could twist the knife and tell him what Mia said about Zander. But they shouldn't right now; they'd rather Damon *see* incontrovertible proof than hear it secondhand. Indeed, so far, this is reading to Puck like one of those situations where they should just keep a *Homewreckers* contestant talking until a useful nugget comes spilling out. There's a reason therapists ask so many goddamn questions and provide so few answers.

"What do you mean?" Puck asks with as much earnestness as they can muster.

Damon looks past their head, like he can't make eye contact with Puck if he's going to say this. "I don't know. I think she's happy with me, but it's still so hard to believe this is happening. You remember what it was like back at Emory, right?"

"You mean when you were eating Chex Mix with chopsticks so that you could keep your controllers clean?" Puck asks. "Yes, I do."

"That's very specific," Damon says with a laugh that papers over how offended he might actually be. "But right. And Mia has always been, well, Mia."

"You're worried she's still out of your league?" Puck asks him. "Don't tell me your brother's toast on the bus got to you. He's an asshole, Damon, no offense."

Secretly, of course, they hope what Peter said has been nagging at him all night, but they can pretend to be on his team for another minute. Damon deserves happiness too, just not at

Mia's expense. He also needs help getting back to the person he used to be, before his brother and family and the entire infrastructure of American capitalism corrupted him.

"Yeah, I guess it got me thinking," Damon says, scratching the back of his head, where his cowlick used to stick straight up in college. Surely Damon can't be happy with his own transformation from soft trust fund gamer boy to food processing junior executive. Everyone seems to get more honest late at night, when they're drunk either from liquor or exhaustion, and it's telling that Damon is feeling all this now. Puck can afford to press a button—gently at first.

"Well, I wouldn't be hung up on the past," Puck says. "I mean, look at you now. You're dressed like you make your deckhands fight each other for sport."

Damon looks down at his shirt and his loafers, then back up at Puck, his expression serious. "This isn't really me, Puck. You know that, right? We're just not in college anymore. I can't wear a Charmander shirt to my bachelor party."

But why not? Puck wonders. What is it about heterosexuality that turns people who have all sorts of lovable quirks, hobbies, and interests into mindless fish swimming down the river of mainstream culture? Damon was never Puck's favorite of the group, but damn it, he used to *like* things. Now he's just another guppy riding the current.

"Lena had no problem with you being a nerd, apparently," Puck points out, trying to sound playful while still searching for information about the short-lived relationship.

Damon looks uncomfortable with the subject, stammering through his response. "We were kids when we dated, Puck," he says. "Besides, she's dressing differently now too. Did you confront her about that?"

"No, because she's not dressing for an imaginary golf course," Puck says.

"I'm . . . figuring it out!" Damon protests, and it's clear Puck has hit a nerve. He takes a breath to regain his composure. "I'm blending in, I guess."

"There seems to be a lot of that going around," Puck says, almost involuntarily.

Damon cocks his head. "What's that supposed to mean?"

But Puck doesn't have energy left to respond. They can't open the dam now because too much will come flooding out. Mia is trying to act like a McLeod, Robyn is trying to look straight, Zander is trying to pretend he's OK with all of this, Lena wants to act like she's moved on, and Damon is even more insecure than Puck suspected. Can anyone here be fucking *real*?

Instead, Puck says, "I left Mia sleeping on her stomach with a glass of water on the nightstand," injecting a tone of finality into their voice. "I'd check on her in an hour to make sure she hasn't thrown up."

They walk past Damon down the hall. He has his own issues to figure out, but it's hard to have endless patience for a man whose own self-discovery requires abducting Puck's best friend into an empty world of plenty. He could have sorted out his masculinity without derailing everyone else's lives to bear witness to it. In about five years, maybe less, he will realize he'd still prefer doing *Zelda* cosplay to being a power player in the chicken world. Or maybe he'll abnegate everything that once made him *him* in exchange for a bigger office in the C-suite, cementing his own misery. Whatever internal crisis he's having will resolve itself one way or the other; and no matter what, he'll be set for life.

But Mia isn't marrying the Damon he used to be, and she's clearly not thinking about the Damon he might become. No, she's marrying *current* Damon, thinking he's a late-bloomer who finally grew up, not a boy trying to prove he's a man when it's perfectly fine for someone to be a boy if he could only care less about what the world thinks of him. Puck has half a mind to turn around, say "Fuck the plan," and unload on Damon to try to jolt him out of his pursuit of an impossible and unfulfilling ideal.

But when they turn the corner that leads to their room, they see Robyn standing outside their door again. She taps her wrist where a watch would be. *Jesus.* Can't Puck get any rest tonight?

Chapter 14

Robyn doesn't issue any commands or orders after Puck ushers her into their room, first taking care to ensure that no heads are poking out of open doors. After surviving the shower sex unscathed, they'd hate to be discovered in the hotel hallway. No, instead of saying something surly or intimidatingly sexy, Robyn kicks off her shoes, walks over to Puck's bed, and crawls under the covers, still in her clothes.

"I'm so tired," she sighs. "Can I sleep here tonight?"

It's a retroactive request, given that Robyn is already pulling the down comforter up to her chin—and a surprising one. Puck was prepared to perform if Robyn were in her usual mood. Babysitting a drunk Mia wore them out, but they've managed under worse conditions before, stifling yawns between thrusts until their duties were fulfilled. But Robyn's apparently not interested in any exertions. Is she going soft on them already? Does Puck hope she might be? When was the last time they cuddled someone without fucking them first?

But the truth is they're too tired to search the memory bank for that answer right now. Looking at Robyn curled up in bed, eyes already closed, Puck can see beyond all their charged quips for the first time: She is gorgeous and she is warm and that's all they really need tonight. They unlace their Docs, leave their pants on the floor, and climb into bed in just their band tee. Even though Robyn has a few inches on them, they barnacle onto her back, making themself the biggest spoon they can be, wrapping an arm around her waist. Robyn grabs Puck's hand and pulls it tight toward her belly, like she's latching a seat belt.

All she says is "Mmm," already fading into unconsciousness.

Puck smells her hair. It smells like bergamot, lavender, and honeysuckle—and Puck can admit that a woman as complicated as Robyn *does* deserve to have three aromas at once. She's gay but looks straight, she hate-fucks them but also randomly wants to snuggle, she's annoyed anytime Puck slightly tweaks a wedding plan, and yet the second she crosses the threshold of Room 444, all is forgotten. But Puck supposes she doesn't have to make sense, the same way a Dalí painting can be riddled with internal contradictions but still be beautiful.

There's a sorrow Puck feels at night sometimes, or maybe it's always there and it just gets heavier when they finally stop moving. Whether it's hanging out with Zander or sharing a drink with Mia at the hotel bar, there have been flashes at this wedding of a time before Puck let *Homewreckers* consume their life—memories now buried under years of work. The show can't be all there is, can it? And yet it's all they have.

Tonight, though, Puck has something else: a sphinxlike woman in their bed, her breathing slowing, her intoxicating perfume lulling them into slumber. The morning birds will wake them both. But for now, Puck wishes they could stay like this forever and let the outside world move on. Maybe the sorrow that comes with stillness wouldn't be so bad if they could hold on to someone.

Thursday

Chapter 15

Puck can't remember the last time they enjoyed a meal this lazily. Most of the crafty they eat on set gets rapidly shoveled into their face in spare moments, and when they get home, they typically pop a frozen dinner in the microwave, not because they can't afford to eat better, but because they don't really care to. Why waste twice as much time on an only slightly better outcome when you're eating alone anyway?

But sitting here on a checkered blanket with a view of the mountains, eating a dainty sandwich quarter every few minutes until they reach an ideal level of fullness, Puck understands why some people take their time. The Athenian catering staff are making the rounds with carafes of lemonade, ice water, and sweet tea, refilling glasses upon request. Not a single cloud has obscured the sunshine all afternoon. Robyn probably ordered the weather to cooperate for this group picnic and the sky obeyed.

Last night with her was *different*. Robyn stirred a little bit in the night, and for a sleepy half-hour that felt like a dream, they idly talked about the day trip to Asheville and the post-yoga sex until they drifted back off again.

"Am I doing a good job?" was the last thing Robyn asked, and Puck felt a twinge in their heart at the fact that she cares so much about a wedding that they feel certain will unravel within the next forty-eight hours. Still, they told her that she was the best maid of honor anyone could ever want, but her breathing had already deepened again, so Puck wasn't sure she heard the assurance.

She had already left when Puck woke up—presumably to set up this picnic. And she has indeed done a good job. "This was a fantastic idea" they tell her now, toying with the idea of being nice to her in public and hoping she returns the favor. She's sitting beside them on a blanket they're sharing with Francis and Willa, and it's the closest the two of them have come to acknowledging that they're even on remotely friendly terms. "It was your idea, right?"

"Yeah, I read an article about wedding picnics on Brides.com," Robyn says, selecting a shortbread cookie from the tiered tray on the center of their blanket. "It just seemed really *Mia*, you know? Casual but still upscale. Elegant, yet approachable."

As much as it might pain them, Puck is realizing that Robyn really has gotten to know Mia well in a short amount of time. There are aspects of the itinerary Puck doesn't agree with, and seem to have been designed to appeal solely to the McLeods, but this picnic is perfectly tailored to the bride's sensibilities, just with a bottomless budget.

Across the sprawling meadow in front of the Athenian, the family and friends of the couple are spread out playing lawn darts, enjoying cocktails, or simply lying in the sunshine. Most of the wedding party has set up blankets along the edge of the forest encircling the Athenian so they can enjoy a bit of shade as needed. Puck spots Phil downing his third mint julep—and yes, they've been counting—while Mia and Damon pop grapes and figs in each other's mouths like decadent Greek aristocrats. The mood is high, and it's all Robyn's doing.

All the more reason why she can't know what Puck has in store for today—their most devious plan yet, and one they've been plotting like it's an elaborate bank heist this entire time. If Robyn knew how much *Ocean's Eleven*–style advance planning had gone into this scheme, she might be impressed—if she wouldn't be so outraged at its purpose.

On Tuesday morning, before the spa day began, Puck found a map of the Athenian grounds in the lobby and walked the entire property. Their interest was piqued by a short path through the forest that led to a fishing pond where a single bench looked out over the water—the perfect place for a certain former couple to reconnect.

After their makeout session with Robyn was so rudely interrupted in the sauna later that afternoon, they snatched Mia's phone out of a spa locker, used the code they still remembered from college to unlock it, and copied the phone numbers of everyone in the wedding party. And later that night, after Robyn left and Puck recovered from being a writhing mess on the floor, they wrote out a series of riddles about different landmarks on the Athenian property.

Then, on Wednesday morning, they called a still-sleepy Ron to ask for Nick's number. He was confused why Puck wanted to talk to the new PA while they were on vacation, but he gave it out anyway.

"So, you're breaking up a wedding?" Nick said, when Puck walked him through what needed to happen.

"Don't get too excited," they cautioned. "My telling you this doesn't make us friends."

"No, but maybe you owe me a favor," Nick said, commendably deciding to play his hand. "This is pretty complicated, and I'm going to have to hijack our SMS system to do it."

Puck had to promise Nick that he could shadow them for the rest of the season to secure his cooperation.

And now all Puck needs to do is send one text to set this whole thing in motion. In another world—one where Puck wasn't waylaid by Robyn every spare moment—there might be a plan B to fall back on if this one didn't work. But today there is only plan A. This is their big chance to ensure the permanent outcome that began as a brainstorm on a piece of stationery.

While Robyn is busy talking with Francis, Puck pulls their phone out of their pocket and texts Nick: *Ready?*

The response comes almost immediately: *Yes.*

He's on top of it. He must really want the quid pro quo Puck promised.

OK, go. Puck texts back, and then they quickly return their phone to their pocket so they can act surprised when Nick sends a dozen messages at once from the system they use to text the *Homewreckers* contestants' burner phones. Moments later, the bridesmaids and groomsmen are checking their buzzing, dinging, and vibrating devices.

"What is this?" Willa asks, reading the first text to herself.

Unsurprisingly, Robyn looks angry as she scrutinizes the contents of her screen.

"You guys, come over here!" Damon shouts, and the members of the wedding party dutifully get up off their respective blankets to congregate around him and Mia.

"Did you all get this too?" Mia asks, once everyone is assembled.

"Yes," Anya confirms, as the others nod.

"I thought it was a scam, so I already deleted it," Peter says.

Robyn seems disturbed that something is happening she didn't account for in advance—and after how sweet she was last night, Puck allows themself to feel a little bit guilty about it. It's a shame that saving Mia from years of hurt means ruining Robyn's rigorous planning, but it has to be done.

"This wasn't on the itinerary," Robyn says, looking toward Mia as though she's hoping the bride will kibosh this whole thing.

That look doesn't stop Mia from turning back to her phone screen and reading aloud to the group in her best teacher voice: "Welcome to the Athenian's signature scavenger hunt experience, handcrafted for your wedding party. In a moment, each of you will receive an individual riddle leading you to your next clue. If you follow your chosen path, you'll find a prize waiting for you at the end, just as Mia and Damon have found their own prize: true love."

Lena instinctively *aww*s at a line that made Puck queasy when they wrote it on Tuesday night.

Mia continues: "It's vital for the experience that you each keep your riddles private. Please use the attached map as a guide. When you reach your clue, reply with a picture of it to receive your next riddle. Happy hunting, everyone!—The Athenian."

Robyn looks up from her phone, on which she's been reading along, and announces, "I'm going to find someone from the hotel staff to ask about this."

Dappled in sunshine, surrounded by her friends, Mia is too happy to be bothered by her maid of honor's anxiety. "Don't worry about it, Robyn. The hotel is doing something creative for us. It's fine, I promise."

"Yeah, it's the *Athenian*," Peter says, with all the self-awareness, or lack thereof, of someone whose family stays in five-star resorts like they're Holiday Inns. "They think of everything here."

"Yeah, and at least I finally get to play a game!" Damon says, which momentarily puts Mia on the defensive in front of the group.

"Hey, I didn't say you *can't* play video games, just that you can't do it all night, every night," she says, trying to make the comment come across as teasing but unable to disguise the judgment laced through it.

"OK, OK, that's enough, you two," Phil says, looking a little too wobbly on his feet to excel at a scavenger hunt, but no less enthusiastic for it. "Let's get ready for our riddles. I want to finish first."

"You usually do," Willa quips, and that gets everyone to laugh, defusing any of the lingering tension between Mia and Damon.

"It doesn't sound like a competition anyway," Lena weighs in. "More like we're working together . . . separately." Puck can always count on Lena to try to keep the peace—and her participation trophy attitude will ultimately help the plan. Puck doesn't need people rushing through their clues.

But Puck should also say something to the group—before Nick sends the next text—in order to maintain their cover. They look down at the map of the Athenian on their phone. "Wow, did you know there's a stone labyrinth in the botanical garden? This place really *does* have everything," they observe, doing their best to sound like they're learning new information.

"I did, actually," Robyn says.

Then the first wave of individualized riddles hit everyone's phones. The non-Emory set has been given a series of clues leading them to the west of the hotel. Willa's first riddle, for example, says, "I hope you are having an a-maze-ing time at the picnic," which wasn't Puck's finest work, but they had to create flowcharts for twelve different people, so they can be forgiven for some laziness. Francis is getting sent to the greenhouse while Tom is going to the astrolabe and Anya visits the statue garden, and so on and so on.

The Emory crew, meanwhile, have received more detailed and deliberate instructions. More specifically, Mia and Zander were sent two different riddles that lead to the same place. Mia's says, "This is the perfect place to pond-er," and Zander's says, "Don't bother fishing for another clue until you've found this one," both of which, of course, should send them to the "fishing pond," clearly labeled as such on the map.

As for themself, Puck instructed Nick to send them a set of riddles that they already have photos for, so they can keep up appearances in the rare event anyone wants to compare notes afterward. That should give them all the freedom they need to spy on Mia and Zander.

The wedding party consult their first riddles, and one by one, some of them exclaim "Oh!" in recognition and head off, while others begin power-walking toward their respective goals.

"What does yours say?" Puck asks Robyn, mostly to test how seriously she's taking the exercise.

"I'm not showing you!" she says, which is reassuring. It doesn't seem like she's going to sabotage this activity after all, but probably only because of Mia's endorsement. Robyn dutifully heads off toward the Athenian's oldest elm tree, immediately solving her clue, as Puck predicted she would.

Puck waits until Mia and Zander head off down the forest footpath, the bride-to-be leaving shortly before her ex. And then, once the rest of the group has dispersed, Puck darts into the trees, quietly working their way toward a group of boulders along the edge of the pond where they should be able to hide within earshot of the bench. For now, Puck is willing to risk peeking around the side of the largest rock, but once Mia and Zander arrive, they will have to mostly rely on audio surveillance.

Mia gets to the bench first, but instead of whipping out her phone and snapping a picture of the pond right away, she takes a seat to soak in the scenery. *Good.* Puck wants her to settle in. Zander follows about thirty seconds later. Hearing his footsteps approach, Mia turns around and calls out, "You must have the wrong clue. The pond was mine!"

"I don't think so!" In a few short seconds, Zander closes the distance between them and sits down next to Mia with a brazenness that Puck finds encouraging. "Look," he tells her, holding out his phone, "mine is about 'fishing' for answers. There's only one way to interpret that."

"It could mean the restaurant," Mia says. "The Court, on the sixth floor."

"It's not the restaurant, Mia. We're at a picnic—all of the clues are going to be outside."

"You don't know that!"

A bit of inane bickering has always been healthy for Mia and Zander. It keeps the pipes clean. But Puck doesn't want them to waste valuable seconds arguing over a scavenger hunt they made only as a pretense to put these two in exactly this position: alone, together, with no one—that they know of—listening.

"What does yours say?" Zander asks.

"'This is the perfect place to *pond*-er,'" Mia recites.

"Well, that's pretty unambiguous. What if we both snap pictures of the water and see what the hotel says?" Zander proposes.

At that, Puck realizes they should duck back behind the boulder in case they're spotted. And if they *do* hear a shutter noise or two go off, they've got a contingency plan. Nick will text both of them saying that the location of their next riddle is currently occupied, and that they should stand by. But instead, Puck hears Mia suggest, "How about we just sit here for a minute? It's kind of nice to get away from all the commotion."

Zander, though, apparently isn't interested in peace. "Why'd you invite me, Mia?" he asks, blunt and unsparing.

He's going straight there. *Good.*

"Because I care about you," she answers right away, but it sounds forced, like Mia has practiced saying it aloud to convince herself it was the reason. "And so does Damon."

"If you care about me," Zander rebuts, "inviting me is probably the *opposite* of what you should do."

"Do you not want to be here?" Mia sounds genuinely anguished.

"Not to watch you get married to *him*. You know that Damon used to jack off exclusively to anime women? Fuck, Mia, he's my friend, or I thought he was. But we used to make fun of him between us, remember?"

"He was a kid, Zan," Mia says, more pleading than scolding now, like it's important to her that he understands why she's doing this. "We all were. People change. You of all people should believe that."

Puck would prefer if this conversation didn't get so cutting quite so fast, but it makes sense that it might. These sound like the kinds of things they've needed to say to each other but couldn't among the group: For Mia, being direct with Zander might have felt like betraying Damon, and Zander has probably just been too fucking bitter and hurt to vocalize any of his feelings until now. But if Puck knows anything from their time at Emory, it's that the chemistry between these two should help them power through a heart-to-heart, even if they skip a few steps. They'll be pawing at each other before long, Puck is certain.

"I do believe that," Zander says. "I *have* to believe it. But I don't believe that you're into him. I'm sorry, but I don't."

Puck peeks between the rocks and sees Zander's palms falling onto his knees in exasperation.

"You don't think I'm into him, or you don't think I'm over *you*?" Mia asks.

Zander's answer comes immediately: "Both."

Zander is the sort of man who can make something true by saying it with enough confidence, which must only make it more infuriating for Mia when he's actually right. "You don't get to say that to me after what you put me through," she says.

"Tell me I'm wrong then," Zander fires back, without acknowledgment.

"You're not even going to say you're sorry?"

"I'm sorrier than I can possibly say, Mia," Zander says, his tone softening. "I want to spend *months* saying sorry if I can. But I'm about to lose the opportunity."

Puck risks a peek around the side of the rock now that it seems like Mia and Zander are fully engrossed in this conversation. The former couple are completely focused on each other now, maintaining unbroken eye contact.

"Then why did you waste the time you had with me?" Mia asks, and she no longer sounds accusatory but mournful instead. "Why is it only now that I'm marrying Damon that you get sober?"

"I got sober before you got with Damon," Zander protests. "Look, Mia, we can talk in circles all day, but there's only one way to solve this. Tell me you're over me, that you love him more than you ever loved me, and I'll drop it, I promise."

His tone is authoritative but solicitous. He's looking directly at her, completely unafraid even though he's holding his heart out to be broken. Even from a distance, it looks like Mia is having difficulty maintaining her composure.

"I can't do that," she finally says, tearing her eyes away from him.

"Why not?"

They still need some time to cook, but this exchange is heading in the right direction. If Puck had to guess, they'll be kissing each other in a few minutes. Puck slides back down behind the boulder, pulls out their phone, and sends Nick a text: *Give Damon the fishing clue.* If everything has gone according to plan, the groom should currently be in the rose garden, which places him about a minute out from the pond.

Done, Nick texts back.

"You don't get to force everyone else to go back in time just because you have regrets, Zan," Mia is now saying, as Puck tunes back in to the conversation.

"I don't *want* to go back in time," Zander says, a decade's worth of passion packed into every single word. "I only came to this wedding because I want you *now*. I want you *tomorrow*. I want you *always*."

Goddamn. Puck swoons at that, and they're not even within ten feet of Zander. They can only imagine the effect those declarations might have on a straight woman sitting right next to him. Fuck it, they don't want to imagine: They peek around the boulder again and see Mia, overcome with emotion, reaching out and grabbing hold of Zander's hand. *Success.* Now Damon needs to arrive, hopefully just as the affection ratchets up even further. Wherever he is, he needs to walk faster. "Why couldn't you tell me this before, Zan?" Mia says. "The wedding . . ."

"Doesn't have to happen," Zander finishes. "You have free will, Mia. You have maybe the *most* free will out of anyone I've ever known. You're a force. You're fucking uncontainable. Those people out on their stupid fucking picnic blankets eating their stupid fucking canapés don't know that, but they can find out."

Damon should be here by now—at least within sight. Mia is holding on to both of Zander's hands now, and while it's not a kiss, this would be incriminating enough on its own. There would be no way for Damon to forget how bad this looks. Where is he?

Puck looks down at their phone. Nothing from Nick. They send him a text: *Anything from Damon?*

He just sent me a picture of a fish painting in what looks like the hotel restaurant, Nick replies.

Goddamn it, Puck thought Damon was good at games. Why would he think that "fishing" referred to the Court?

If Mia and Zander send pond pics, tell them to wait where they are, they text Nick.

And then they're off through the woods, trying to salvage their best hope.

Chapter 16

Puck bursts out of the forest and races toward the hotel, determined to drag Damon over to the fishing pond by his ears if they have to. At this rate, with the way that conversation was going, he might find Zander proposing to Mia.

"Hey, I thought it wasn't a competition?!" Robyn shouts after Puck as they dodge an attendant carrying a tray of strawberry tarts. But they're already halfway to the front entrance by the time they register that Robyn even saw them, which they hope doesn't arouse suspicion. It's too late now.

Seconds later, they're tapping their foot on the elevator ride up to the Court. Their annoyance hasn't abated at all. The map Nick sent Damon clearly labeled the body of water "FISHING POND" and there were no indoor locations listed. Sure, Damon probably got into Emory because the deans wanted his family to donate enough money for them to build a seventh library, but he's not stupid, is he?

The elevator door slides open to the sixth floor, directly into an unmanned host station and waiting area. Beyond it is a nearly empty restaurant, which makes sense. The McLeods have rented out the whole place, and almost all of the guests, save for a few who preferred to dine indoors, are out at the picnic right now. There's no sign of Damon but Puck does see a painting of a freshly caught trout on the wall. He must have been here recently, right? Except—

"It's called the yellow-rumped warbler," Lena is saying, from somewhere on the other side of a partition, deeper in the restaurant.

Who is she talking to? Puck slips past the host station and tiptoes toward the sound of Lena's voice, grabbing a seat at a table close by, but still out of view.

"And that's your favorite bird?" another voice says.

It's Damon. *What the hell?* Are *neither* of them doing the scavenger hunt? Puck didn't think Lena would ignore clearly laid-out rules—and Damon was supposed to be out by the pond five minutes ago, watching his fiancée hold hands—or worse—with her incredibly hot ex-boyfriend. *D 8 Z and M.* It's the only surefire way to sink this ship, but is it already too late? How long can Nick hold Mia and Zander out there?

"Yes," Lena confirms. "I had to think about it for a second, but yes."

"And is it rare or something?"

"No, it's one of the most common warblers."

"Right, right," Damon teases her. "I was about to say, most of the warblers I see out in the wild have yellow rumps. I'm always looking at yellow bird butts."

Lena lets out an unguarded laugh, which sends an unexpected pang through Puck's heart. It's rare to hear her sound so joyful. Lena's work always seemed so serious whenever she posted about it on social media, full of dire warnings about ecosystem collapse. It never occurred to Puck, maybe because they never got to know her well enough, that the girl might also just think that birds are really cool.

"Now let me ask *you* a question," Lena says. "What's your favorite video game?"

"I haven't been playing much lately," Damon says, and while he doesn't name Mia, the implication is clear.

"Yeah, I know, but you've got to have a favorite. Even an old one," Lena presses, but then, her conscience clearly getting the better of her, she adds, "But if you don't want to say . . ."

Is this what their short-lived relationship was like? Did they get to just be kids together? Lena always acted so mature, with such a developed sense of justice, but maybe there was an innocence she only felt safe to indulge around him, once he finally gave her a chance. And then she gave up that intimacy willingly to protect her feelings, even though it was probably the last thing she wanted to do.

Puck is trying so hard to picture how it all worked between Damon and Lena that they don't spot the server heading straight toward their clandestine position. *Fuck.* They've got about five seconds to decide whether they want to let the short-lived lovers keep talking—which could open up a new, last-minute pathway for ending the wedding—or reveal themself and hope that Mia and Zander can still be caught. But by the time the server reaches Puck's table and apologizes for not catching them at the host station, they panic. Maybe Damon and Lena should keep going, after all. In any event, Puck needs to remain incognito for now.

They make their voice as unrecognizably high as possible, accessing an octave they've ignored for years. "Can I just have a water?"

"Sure thing, sweetie," she says. "I'll be right back with that."

"*Elden Ring*?" Lena is asking after the server leaves Puck's table.

"That's my favorite these days. I was getting really into it before I got so . . . busy," Damon says, choosing his words with care. "I've put about nine hundred hours into it."

"Isn't that one really hard?" Lena says. "This guy at work was telling me about it."

Puck has got to hand it to Lena: She's very good at playing dumb when she wants to. The old Lena knew everything about Damon McLeod. Puck wouldn't be surprised if she had played a thousand hours of *Elden Ring* herself just to walk in his virtual shoes.

"I think that's why I like it," Damon says. "You know, a lot of things about being a McLeod were straightforward. I never had to worry about school or getting a job. So I think the challenge of *Elden Ring* is really compelling. I can fight the same boss for hours, make these tiny incremental improvements, and then finally, somewhere along the way, I become good enough to beat the game."

"Just like life," Lena says, and Puck can't tell whether she's agreeing with his metaphor to appeal to him or she's actually earnest enough to believe it.

"Well, kind of," Damon says with a laugh. "I mean the first time I played the game, I used the Blasphemous Blade, which is kind of a broken weapon. But now I'm beating the whole game with a basic longsword." After a pause, he adds, "Don't tell Mia how much I'm playing, though."

Puck now wishes they *had* cut this short, because Damon waxing philosophical about video game design is quite boring.

The server returns with a glass of ice water and Puck squeaks out a "Thank you."

"Did you want anything else, honey?" the server asks.

"No, that's all," Puck says, aware of how strange it is to come all the way up to the Court for tap water, but they're past the point of caring. With a shrug and a very Southern "Holler if you need me," the server leaves again.

"So what makes the Blasphemous Blade so strong?" Lena asks, and Puck knows they can't take much more of this. Is there still time to get Damon down to the pond?

"Oh, it has a special attack that knocks over most enemies, deals fire damage, *and* gives you your health back," Damon says.

"Wow," Lena says, and it doesn't sound like she's faking it at all. Either she's genuinely interested in a video-game sword or she can feel Damon's excitement vibrating through her like a tuning fork.

"Yeah, it's pretty busted," Damon says, before developing some self-awareness about the length of his soliloquizing. "But wait, let's go back to your birds. You said my mom gave your nonprofit how much money again?"

"Three million," Lena confirms.

Puck hears Damon laugh, but it's a surprised laugh. "Wow," he says. "I mean, she can afford it, for sure, but she almost never gives money to charity directly. They do most stuff through the foundation. She must have really liked you."

"I don't know about that," Lena says, but Damon's too enthusiastic to let her self-pity breathe.

"Can you buy the warblers some pants with that money or do they want to show off their yellow rumps?" *This* is the kid from college: earnest, guileless, unafraid to be nerdy.

"It'd be hard for a bird to wear pants," Lena muses. "They don't exactly have waists."

And this is how the relationship must have worked, if only for three months: Lena's literalness making a perfect foil for Damon's goofiness, her compassion creating space for him to be silly without feeling judged. If there's anyone who can pull Damon out of his keto bubble and restore him to who he used to be, it might just be Lena, who loved him before he ever changed, and who can apparently still draw out the sensitivity and humor Puck believed was gone. At their core, Damon and Lena are both people seeking permission to be themselves, and who only seem able to show who they really are in secret.

Should Puck have pivoted after what they heard on the party bus? Were Damon and Lena the move all along? Puck starts to map it out again in their head: *D + L*? No, Mia and Zander were—*are*—still the safer bet. And there's no time to redraw the play anyway.

The conversation is interrupted by footsteps. It's the server again, but this time carrying a plate that Puck realizes is destined for Damon and Lena's table.

"Your tofu bánh mì, miss," the server says, setting the plate down.

What? They're having a full sit-down lunch?

"You know, after this," Damon says, as Puck hears Lena bite into the sandwich, "I can talk to my mom about making the donation a recurring thing."

Will Lena take the bait? It would mean getting to interact more with Damon, but it would also be an ethical shortcut—and Lena's a fan of doing things through the proper channels.

"That's very sweet of you, Damon," she says, after she swallows. "But I'd like to earn it."

And just as impulsively as Puck decided *not* to interrupt Damon and Lena, they change course, standing up, walking past the partition, and pretending like they just got to the Court. Damon's far from getting back together with Lena, while Zander and Mia are probably on page 150 of the Kama Sutra out in the forest by now.

"Hey, Damon! Hey, Lena!" they say, acting surprised to see them. "Did you come up here because of the painting too? Apparently that's not the clue."

"Oh, right," Damon looks down at his phone, disappointed that his furtive chat with Lena has been interrupted, and perhaps still residually upset with Puck over last night's conversation. "The scavenger hunt."

"Yeah, aren't you playing?" Puck asks, internally fuming.

"Oh, Lena's phone died at the picnic," Damon explains, "so I told her to tag along with me. And then she was hungry, and there weren't great vegan options at the picnic, so when we came up for the painting, I ordered her something."

Damon doting on Lena would be great news if it wasn't too little, too late.

"To go, I hope?" Puck asks, trying to move it along. "We should probably finish this thing."

"Right, yes, to go," Lena lies, gesturing toward the server, making the shape of a box with her hands.

But just as the server scurries off to fetch a container, they feel their phone vibrate in their pocket. It's a text from Nick. *I tried to keep them there, but they both started texting me new photos,* he says. *I think they thought the system was broken.*

"Is that your next clue?" Damon asks as Puck stares at their phone.

"Uh, yeah," Puck lies, firing off a quick text: *How long ago?*

Mia is packing up her sandwich, taking one more bite so she can save an even half.

Pretty soon after your last text to me.

Fuck. That wouldn't have been very long—and Mia and Zander used to make it last once they got started. Did Mia start to feel guilty, or did Zander lay it on too heavy? Either way, it doesn't sound promising. All this effort—their most multi-pronged and important plot yet—has probably gone to waste.

Do you want me to keep going? Nick again.

There's nothing Puck wants to do less, now that it all seems incredibly futile, than to walk through the rest of this fake scavenger hunt, pointlessly traipsing around the grounds of the resort.

Yes, but make it short, Puck texts Nick back.

Thwarted, defeated, and humiliated, they leave the Court with Damon and Lena and sleepwalk through the rest of the steps, texting their obligatory preloaded pictures at regular intervals. As planned, the hunt eventually leads the entire wedding party back together by the fountain in the lobby. Mia and Zander don't look in any way rumpled. All their phones ding at once, but Puck is feeling too down to even bother pretending to look at the message. It says: "Your reward for completing this scavenger hunt is the friendship you have all found with each other."

The group groans.

"What a bummer," Peter says.

Yes, Puck has to admit, it was a bummer—several days' worth with nothing to show for it.

Chapter 17

It's easy for Puck to forget about their failed plan when they're fucking Robyn into oblivion. But that's part of the problem. Some of their most valuable plotting and scheming time has been eaten up by this unexpected variable in the equation. All of those letters on the notepad in their nightstand should have had a "minus R" appended to them. She's a sexy variable, but still. The wedding timeline turned out to be more condensed than it originally sounded. A week isn't actually a lot of time when Robyn's incredibly anal itinerary is detailed down to the second, including afternoon breaks for rest and relaxation—one of which she is now using to accept all but the last inch of Puck's dildo while on her hands and knees.

"Harder," Robyn is ordering, probably already calculating in her head when she needs to finish to begin preparing for the rehearsal dinner.

But Puck is the one who's truly preoccupied. On the eve of this union, they feel no closer to preventing it than they were on Monday—all foreplay with no climax. A quick moment of Mia and Zander holding hands was nothing; Puck has experienced more intimate and meaningful skin-to-skin contact while accepting change from a barista. To really end this, Puck thinks, as they grind their hips into Robyn, they still need something tangible. A bona fide event. Something neither Mia nor Damon could wave away. They could have made it happen by now if Robyn weren't showing up at their room during every break she gets—and yet Puck has wanted her to be here, too. It's too much to handle at one time.

"Keep going," Robyn whines as Puck's pace slows.

Puck makes a conscious effort to thrust at a faster rhythm, pulling themself into Robyn while keeping a firm grip on her hips. They tell themself they can still get this done, but they aren't sure anymore whether the "this" they're thinking about is bringing Robyn to orgasm or breaking up a wedding. What is Mia doing tonight anyway? The day's itinerary, freshly printed off that morning, is still lying on Puck's nightstand—and if they scooch their knees forward just a little bit they can make out the last few lines. As they do, Robyn makes a startled but not entirely displeased noise.

"Ooooh," she moans. "*Now* we're getting somewhere."

What does it say at the bottom of the page?

9:30–10 p.m.—The bride, the mother of the bride, and the mother of the groom gather briefly in the Grove.

What the hell is *that*? Some kind of eleventh-hour intergenerational bequeathal of maternal counsel? A final word between Mia and her mom, they'd understand, but Mrs. McLeod, too? Mia probably has about as much in common with a woman that rich as she does with a platypus. Still, Puck can use this: It means Mia will be somewhere alone after everyone else has likely gone back to their room.

"Hey, where are you?" Robyn asks, jarring Puck back to reality. Their cadence has slowed to a crawl, and Robyn is not happy about it, but she also sounds . . . concerned? Yes, there's no mistaking the gentle note in her voice.

"I'm just trying to mix it up," Puck offers a half-hearted excuse, quickening their pace again.

"Don't overthink it, Puck," Robyn says. "Just fuck me."

Puck obeys. They drain all thought from their mind and focus on matching their pace to the rhythm of Robyn's moans. And as they do, they feel like they're reaching out toward some sort of enlightenment, grasping at a truth they've ignored this whole time: *Don't overthink it.* Puck's mistake this week was thinking that they needed to play four-dimensional chess. They got too excited about throwing Lena into the mix, especially after they discovered she was no longer dressing like a Greenpeace activist. And they thought that Damon had to literally *see* evidence of an indiscretion for this thing to be over. *Homewreckers* has made them cocky, more interested in pulling off an elaborate Rube Goldberg–style scheme than they are in plain old efficacy. The failed picnic game is proof of that. But there's no Ron to impress here: This plan can just be one step: "M + Z." They need to go back to basics: Just fuck Robyn, and just fuck up the wedding.

Somehow Puck manages to arrive at this conclusion at the exact same second that Robyn's hands dig into the mattress for stability as she comes.

"It's simple, see?" Robyn teases them afterward, turning around to face Puck, her typically pin-straight hair adorably mussed up.

"It is," Puck agrees. "A lot simpler than it looks."

Chapter 18

This shouldn't have to be so suspenseful. As Puck slinks through the Athenian hallways, paranoid they'll run into Zander even though they gave him a five-minute head start to get downstairs, they think back to the croquet match. Should they have paired Mia with Zander that first day? Their regrets and second-guesses could fill a book at this point: They could have asked an even more provocative question on the party bus. They could have sent Damon a different clue that said, "Go to the fishing pond, you big dum-dum." The plan could have just been a single step this whole time: Get the two hot people to make out as quickly as possible, subtlety be damned.

But Puck also wants to give themself credit: This Hail Mary pass would have no chance of working if they hadn't run good plays up to this point. And tonight can still work, with enough luck.

At 9:55 p.m., Puck texted Zander saying that they were in bed with an upset stomach, asking if he wouldn't mind grabbing them a club soda from the bar. If all goes well, he should be arriving downstairs just as Mrs. McLeod and the mother of the bride are wrapping up with Mia, and she probably won't be able to resist saying hello to Zander, if the pond is precedent.

The stairs are safer than the elevator, Puck decides, though either way there's a chance of collision. God, this is so much more slapdash than *Homewreckers*, but then again, they're flying solo here, all while sleeping with the enemy and taking long absences from the front lines. And just like *Homewreckers*, so long as it works, they can still take full credit for victory. No one has to know how much went wrong along the way. Not that they'll ever tell anyone about this. No, this secret goes to Mia's grave. Or Puck's. Whichever gets dug first.

They tiptoe out of the stairwell toward the Grove, carefully scanning for familiar faces, but as they hoped, the place is deserted: Everyone is already preparing for their beauty sleep. And there's no sign of the moms, which means they must have obeyed Robyn's cutoff time to the second, but Mia is nowhere to be found, either. Only a handful of hotel employees remain, picking at various tasks: swapping out the flowers on the lobby tables, polishing the marble floor, emptying the water dispenser next to the check-in desk—all the little odds and ends that add up to make the Athenian feel like a pristine oasis. If Puck hadn't been so stressed this past week, they could have tried to actually appreciate some of this luxury; as it stands, the hotel has felt like the *Homewreckers* set, just with nicer furnishings and a lot more walking in between.

At the sound of Zander's voice, Puck creeps carefully toward the row of indoor topiaries cordoning the Grove off from their side of the Athenian lobby. As expected, he's at the bar, presumably ordering Puck's drink. They check their phone: 10:02 p.m., almost exactly when they wanted him to arrive. But where is Mia? Did she already go upstairs? Does Puck need to text her and ask *her* to get them a club soda, too, and then apologize for sending both of them to do the same thing? How should they salvage this?

"Zan?" Puck hears Mia call out from the other side of the lobby.

Phew. Mia's steps quicken when she notices where her ex is standing—and even peering through the bushes, Puck clocks the look of concern on her face.

"You're not drinking, are you?" she asks.

Zander turns to face her, seemingly wounded by the accusation. "You really think I'd slip that easy?"

"No, I just—"

The bartender returns with a glass, a pair of lime wedges floating atop the ice. "Your club soda, sir."

"It's for Puck," Zander reveals. "They said their stomach is doing cartwheels."

"Sorry, I just got worried," Mia says, quieter now that she's close to him. "I've just been so happy all week that you've stopped drinking, you know? I'm really glad we got to talk more today." She casts a sideways glance at a stool, as though suggesting to Zander that she might want to continue that conversation. Puck doesn't make a peep, but internally, their heart is shouting, *Yes, yes, yes!* They don't know what became of their talk by the pond, but it doesn't matter, because whatever happened, Mia is conflicted enough now to resume it.

"That's not how I think of it," Zander says, somewhat cryptically, picking up on Mia's cue and sliding a stool out for her.

"Huh?" Mia asks as she takes the seat.

"That I 'stopped drinking,'" he says. "Yes, that's literally what happened, but that's not how I want to remember that milestone. It's not when I *stopped*, it's when I *started*. It's when the rest of my life began."

"That's such an accomplishment, Zan," Mia says, and Puck can understand why she'd be impressed. In college, liquor evaporated the second Zander got within a few feet of it—and Mia could certainly keep up, too.

"Some people can never go near a bar again, and there are still some nights when I know I shouldn't," he says. "But I've got so much going for me right now that, if anything, I feel addicted to the things sobriety is unlocking for me. Turns out sous viding lamb chops is a lot easier when you're not loaded."

There's a pause as Mia waves away the approaching bartender, who dutifully retreats to the back of the house. "And if the restaurant goes away?" she asks him.

Mia is worried about Zander, which means she's invested. Puck spots a familiar smile on his face at the question: It's the smile that means Mia has found the crux of a matter—her superpower as a friend, and, presumably, as a partner. She's talking to him like old times, but their mouths need to do more than just talk sometime soon.

"Yeah, I've been speaking to my sponsor about that," Zander replies, a little wistfully. "He warned me that if I pin my sobriety to success, to something external, it increases the risk of a relapse. It has to be internal"—he pauses to tap an index finger against his chest, and Mia follows the motion—"I have to change here, too."

"And are you? You know, changing . . . *there*?" She reaches out a finger to tap Zander's chest and Puck has to resist cheering from the topiary at the intimacy of the touch. Mia is teetering dangerously close to the edge now.

Before he speaks, Zander swivels his stool directly toward Mia, obscuring his face from Puck's view, but they can tell from his first word that something inside him is melting.

"Yeah, I think I am," he says, in a hushed tone. "Because even if everything crumbles and I'm right back to some prep station, chopping scallions for two hours a day, I won't ever forget how this feels."

"How *what* feels?" Mia asks, her voice breaking, and she's just fishing now, but Puck can't blame her.

"Sitting here," Zander says. "Talking with you."

Mia smiles, but almost simultaneously, Puck spots the telltale glisten of a tear in her eye. The former lovers are talking so quietly now, almost whispering, that Puck has to hold their breath to avoid detection. "Why wasn't this enough for you before, Zander?" Mia asks, pleading, the question scratching her throat on its way out. "Remember when we went up to that cabin in Vermont and got snowed in? You said it was so nice to just talk, and to not be able to drink even if you wanted to?"

"We did a lot of stuff in that cabin," Zander says, and Mia shoves him, playfully, but with an edge to it, and almost forcefully enough to knock him off balance.

"Be serious, Zan," she says.

The old Zander would keep joking. But this Zander isn't afraid to look inward. "Mia, I tried to say this earlier, but I can't tell you how sorry I am for hurting you," he says, his voice throaty. "By the time I realized the full force of what I had done, and how terrible I was to you, you were somewhere else. I wanted to make amends—I *need* to make amends—but I thought you might think I was just trying to win you back. Or that . . . *he* would see it that way anyway. And I do want you, but even if I didn't, I would still want to make it right."

It occurs to Puck that their club soda is going flat on the bar by now. If their stomach were actually in knots, they'd be pissed about the delay. But this is good. The more time Zander and Mia spend together, the more likely it'll end with their tongues down each other's throats. They have enough faith left in their chemistry for that—though they don't love Damon being invoked in this conversation, if not by name.

"I wish you had stopped drinking earlier" is all Mia says.

There's a pause. Puck stops breathing for a few seconds, even through their nose. Zander could probably julienne the tension in the air.

"I wish I had too," he says, sounding almost hoarse now, choking out the words. "Every. Single. Fucking. Day. But it had to be for me. I loved you then, and fuck it, Mia, I love you now, even if you're marrying someone else tomorrow. Because when I say that I never want to forget how *this* feels, I mean how it feels for me to even be able to *say* how I feel. I didn't have that when we were together, but I have it now, and I never want to let it go."

Puck still can't see Zander's face, but those gleams of moisture in the corners of Mia's eyes have become full-on waterfalls now. She leans toward Zander, placing her hands on his shoulders for stability as she slides to the edge of her seat. And then she's kissing him, not how Puck used to see her make out with him in their dorm room in college, all sloppy horniness with no precision, but tenderly and purposefully, like she doesn't just want to kiss him, but that she wants him to *be* kissed—to really feel the fullness of her feelings for him.

"I don't want you to let it go, either," she says, when she finally pulls away. Zander stands up, but not to walk away; instead, he steps closer and pulls her into a heaving embrace.

This is the moment when Puck would turn to Ron with that knowing "I told you so" grin, but as it stands, all they have is the satisfaction of knowing their friend is being pulled back from the brink of a bad decision. And this *has* to be enough. There's no way she can marry Damon now. This scene, even viewed from cracks between shrubbery, has an air of finality to it: This is how it was always supposed to end. Which only makes it more distressing for that profound correctness to be interrupted by a ding. Puck's. Fucking. Cell phone.

How could they have forgotten to put it on silent?

"Was that your phone?" Mia asks Zander, ending the embrace and suddenly looking very guilty.

"No, I thought it was yours," he says, and then they both start to look around the empty lobby with guilty faces, sending Puck scurrying away in a flash.

"I better get this up to Puck anyway" is the last thing they hear Zander say as they dash into the elevator bank. That must mean he didn't spot them, right? But if they want to keep it that way, they have to get upstairs *fast*—and not by the route Zander will take.

Only behind the door to the stairwell does Puck take half a second to check their phone. It's Lena: *Hey Puck, Robyn is up here looking for you. She says she needs to chat about your suit for tomorrow but doesn't have your number. Is it cool if I connect you two?*

Always the ethicist, Lena *had* to check first instead of giving Robyn the fucking phone number. Now Puck has to beat

Zander to their room, accept a club soda from him, and field Robyn's apparent booty call, all within the next ten minutes. But this is exactly the kind of high-pressure situation Puck was built for. They shift into their highest *Homewreckers* gear.

First, they somehow draft a text back to Lena while taking the stairs two at a time: *Tell her to come to my room in 15*. They fire it off before they've even reached the second floor. Then, they gun it up the rest of the stairs, breaking into a sweat by the third landing, but a little clamminess will help with their excuse. They're supposed to look nauseous, right? Puck hopes they've timed this right so that Robyn doesn't arrive before Zander has left their room; someone as fastidious as she is might interpret fifteen minutes as five.

Bursting out onto the fourth-floor landing, Puck hears the elevator counter ding in advance of the doors opening. *Zander*. They break into a sprint, whipping around the corner just before they hear the elevator open in the distance behind them. Mercifully, they can use this next stretch to try to catch their breath. It's not like Zander's going to run the club soda down the hall.

But they still need to make it to Room 444 free and clear. Each door they pass is agony. Robyn, or another member of the wedding party, could poke their head out at any minute, and Zander's not far enough behind that he wouldn't overhear Puck being up and about—in which case, why would he have had to fetch club soda for them?

Finally, Puck reaches their room. They let the door close onto the security latch behind them, take a deep breath, then basically leap under the covers, rumpling them up for effect as they prepare to win the Academy Award for best portrayal of a person with a mild illness.

Ten seconds later, there's a knock at the door. *Phew.*

"Zan, is that you?" Puck croaks, but their heart is still racing from the thin margin of error. "Come in."

Zander walks in with the now-flat glass of club soda. Puck can still spot a bit of Mia's lipstick on his chin.

"One club soda," Zander announces as he sets the glass down on the coaster waiting on Puck's nightstand.

"You're a lifesaver," they say, throwing in a groan for good measure. "I hope it wasn't too much trouble."

"It wasn't," Zander says with a smile. "I really needed the walk."

Chapter 19

The last thing Puck wants to do after another long night of strenuous extracurricular activity with Robyn is leave their room, especially when they're still recovering from their close call with Zander. Robyn showed up two minutes after Zander left, which means the two of them probably barely missed each other in the hallway—a possibility Puck has spent the last two hours retroactively worrying about, even though it's already been averted, the adrenaline lingering in their body long after it served its purpose. So when Robyn suggests venturing out onto the back lawn of the Athenian sometime after her third or fourth orgasm of the night—they've lost count—Puck's first reaction is to whine.

"What do I have to do to tire you out?" they ask in mock exasperation. "Run you around on a leash?"

"Couldn't hurt," Robyn quips without a moment's hesitation. "But my bite is worse than my bark, unfortunately."

"Don't worry, I'm an experienced handler," Puck says, not nearly as quickly, but still trying to participate despite their tiredness.

"Good."

Even though it was mere days ago, Puck can't remember what it was like to think Robyn was some normative straight girl. It feels like one minute she was yelling at them about the rules of croquet, and the next she was here, completely naked, loose strands of hair matted against her sweaty forehead, casually firing off kinky repartee. But that's not the only way Puck has misjudged her. Her shell, once so prickly, was hiding a surprisingly tender freak beneath it the entire time. When she showed up at Puck's room a couple of hours ago, the first thing she said was "Where were you? I missed you," and her tone suggested she didn't just mean the sex, though it certainly wasn't off the table. Could this *thing* they've so quickly built together—Puck doesn't even know how to describe it—ever survive outside of the Athenian?

Puck catches themself assuming that Robyn would even want that. The subject of what happens after the wedding has loomed at the edges of their postcoital conversations. Earlier tonight, Robyn asked Puck to give them an "oral tour" of their studio apartment, and they managed to resist the obvious double entendre long enough to tell her about the little balcony overlooking the square, the built-in bookshelf where Puck keeps the Emmy they stole from Ron's house, and the ficus that will never die, no matter how infrequently it gets watered. As they idly run a finger from Robyn's sternum down to her belly button, Puck tries to imagine this tornado of a woman there, in their home. She wouldn't have asked if she couldn't foresee visiting one day, right?

But that would mean eventually telling Mia about all this. And besides, when the wedding is canceled, will Robyn feel bad about *this* being where she met Puck? Surely any minute now she's going to get an emergency text from Mia, summoning the bridesmaids to battle stations. That'd hardly be an auspicious start to a real relationship, if Puck is even ready for that. Their life back in Atlanta doesn't have much room for lazy coffee dates or strolling through Piedmont Park on Sunday afternoons. And they certainly don't want to do barre, though maybe they should try it if Robyn still has this much energy after her body has already been pushed to the limit for hours on end.

"Why do you want to go outside at two in the morning?" Puck asks her, bracing themself for the excursion.

"Perseids."

The word doesn't mean anything. "Did I fuck you so hard you forgot English?"

Robyn sits up on the bed, gathering the down comforter around herself. "There's a meteor shower and it's a clear night. C'mon, we're already awake."

Stargazing feels like such an adolescent activity compared to what they were just doing, but Robyn's enthusiasm is endearing. This must be what Mia was drawn to: not her particularities or her persnicketiness, but the sheer joy she can feel. In a world full of people who act like it's uncool to enjoy the things they enjoy, Robyn pursues what she desires, and is pleased when she gets it. Cats don't feel guilty when they sneak a lick of ice cream off the counter, and why should they? No excuse Puck can come up with to remain in bed—like the fact that they'd need to put on clothes, or the lateness of the hour, or their fear of getting eaten by coyotes—can stand up to the beautiful simplicity of Robyn's want.

"I'm surprised this didn't make it onto your very detailed wedding itinerary," they tell her. "'Two a.m. Purr-Seeds. Dress code: Jammies.'"

Puck is joking, of course, but Robyn answers seriously anyway. "I thought about it," she says. "But I figured keeping everyone up late the night before the wedding was a bad idea. The bride can't have bags under her eyes when she walks down the aisle."

Puck leaves aside the fact that Mia could stay awake for an entire week and still look as fresh as a rose. Because the truth is they wouldn't want to see anyone else right now. Only Robyn. This strange beauty in their bed. Especially if this is the last night they get to spend with her. They surprise themself by kissing her on the forehead before standing up to pull on a pair of pants and an undershirt.

"Well, are you coming?" they ask after getting dressed, turning to find Robyn still clinging to the comforter, regarding them with a kindness that hits places inside Puck that haven't been touched in years. But just as quickly as Puck notices the expression, it shifts.

"I just did," Robyn smirks. "A bunch."

"That was too obvious," Puck deadpans. "You should be embarrassed."

"You should be embarrassed for not knowing what the Perseids are. I thought you were gay."

Only then does Robyn leave the bed to put her yoga pants back on along with one of Puck's oversize pajama tees.

Puck thinks about the compassion they saw in Robyn's eyes as they walk down the halls of the Athenian. It's been a while since someone caught feelings for them, but it's been even longer since Puck wanted to reciprocate them. Love isn't like riding a bike. It's more like trying to do long division after leaving grade school; one day, with no warning, you completely forget the order of operations. Through all these years on *Homewreckers*, and during their handful of ill-fated relationships, Puck has struggled to understand why companionship even matters. If they can derive purpose from work and pleasure from the bar, do they really need someone for the moments in between? For the sad weekday takeout meals and the Target runs and all the myriad errands that make up a modern life? Previously, whenever Puck has plugged an imaginary girlfriend into those scenarios, it's never felt right. But now, as they slip out the back exit of the lobby with Robyn, they visualize this particular woman in all of those moments and something feels . . . *different*. The humdrum would be less humdrum. The cold noodles would taste better. All that upkeep would maybe mean something. It would be for a world in which Robyn could be this excited by the prospect of lights streaking through the night sky.

It was so easy for Puck to kiss Robyn in the sauna that first day, and almost easier to fuck her. But they feel their heart thump against their ribs as they grab Robyn's hand and walk deeper into the darkness. She doesn't pull away, but there's some awkwardness as Puck tries to remember whether they like to interlace digits or clasp palms. Fumbling for the right position, they scan Robyn's face for a reaction and detect what could be a small smile, but without the benefit of moonlight, it's hard to tell.

"Here, let's lie down," Robyn says, picking a seemingly arbitrary spot on the grass.

Is she *that* eager to stop holding hands? Did Puck make things too tender too soon? That hasn't been a problem of theirs for years. The excitement of feeling like a lovesick teenager may not be worth all this anxiety. They exhale as they sit next to Robyn, trying to calm down, and then recline all the way, feeling blades of grass brush against their scalp. The sensation brings them back to buzzing their head during senior year at Emory. It was Mia who ran the clippers for them. She was obsessed with petting Puck's "fuzz" for weeks afterward, always bordering on being *too* supportive of them, if anything. Even some queer kids at Emory asked Puck if they were really sure they wanted to chop all their hair off, but all Mia said was "That's cool," followed quickly by "Can I do it?" Puck hopes that what they've done this week has been enough to rescue that version of Mia. It must be.

For now, they can relax. The summer air is thick and warm, even more so than a typical August, like a weighted blanket on Puck's chest. "What exactly am I looking for now?" they ask Robyn after a minute of staring at nothing but a few familiar constellations: the Big Dipper, Leo, and is that Cassiopeia, too?

"Just wait," Robyn says. "You have to let your eyes adjust first."

"I was promised meteors."

"How can you be such a patient lover but such an impatient everything else?"

Puck is startled by the flutter they feel in their chest at Robyn using a variant of *that* word. But they try not to let their excitement show. It is, in fact, a good question—one Puck struggles to answer even after turning it around in their head for a silent moment.

"I guess I spend most of my time making things happen," they finally tell her. "So it's hard for me to sit around and *wait* for things to happen."

"At your job, you mean?" Robyn asks. "*Homewreckers*?"

It's been hard for Puck to keep their hands off Robyn long enough for them to get into the weeds of their profession, but she knows as much as anyone else at this wedding about what they do—and that includes the Emory crew.

"Yeah," Puck responds, and as they do, a new tier of dimmer stars come into focus, a hundred dots of light they couldn't notice until their pupils had dilated more. "Every day, I have to make sure people get into some sort of trouble."

"And they wouldn't get into trouble without you?"

"Not enough for the show to be worth watching," Puck says, repeating the same line they've always used when asked why reality shows need producers. For the first time in a while, though, they wonder whether they should interrogate their own pat answer. *Why* do they do what they do? And why do people like to watch it? So many things have become axiomatic to Puck over the years they've spent throwing themself into this work: Drama is millennia older than Shakespeare, as they like to pontificate, and it serves a vital function in human society, even if it takes new, sometimes trashy forms. Maybe *90 Day Fiancé* isn't *The Iliad*, and yet it kind of *is*. But none of that argumentation feels like it matters out here with Robyn.

"Well, I certainly couldn't do what you do," Robyn says, then quickly points at a spot in the night sky. "Oh! There!"

It's already too late to follow whatever meteor Robyn just noticed. And Puck is too busy swallowing down the offense of her remark. Why couldn't Robyn do what they do? She certainly seems to be organized enough to be a producer. So, is she just like Samantha, then? Does she have qualms about how Puck earns a paycheck? Puck has gotten good about not caring when queer people judge them, but this? This actually stings, as much as Puck wishes it didn't.

"Why not?" they prod. "If your wedding planning is anything to go by, I think you'd be better at my job than I am."

"The wedding is me using my powers for good . . ." Robyn says, trailing off at the end as she realizes how that observation could be interpreted. So it *is* the reason Puck suspected: moral condemnation, as though everyone else who works in marketing or banking or whatever Robyn's desk job entails is so pure.

"Oh, and I'm using my powers for evil?" Puck's question comes out just on the wrong side of the thin line between wounded and defensive.

"No, no, no, I don't mean it like that," Robyn says in a surprising moment of contrition. "I just mean it would stress me out."

"But don't you thrive on that stuff? You gave people fridge magnets of the bachelorette party pics, for God's sake. I'm not sure how that's even possible. Do you have a 3D printer in your room? And why don't we ever fuck in *your* room, anyway?"

Puck is trying to cover up how hurt they sound with a flurry of jokes. But none of them appear to have any effect. In fact, Robyn stays silent long enough that Puck turns away from the sky to make sure she's awake. Her eyes are open, but she doesn't seem like she's tracking meteors anymore—more like her gaze is glued to some imaginary point in the middle distance.

"I know we tease each other a lot, and we've been having fun, but can I tell you something real?" she asks, still looking up.

Puck immediately answers "yes," curious about what could have precipitated such a long pause. Robyn remains a mystery even after all the intimate things they've done together. But maybe the bedroom is where she feels strong, and this is where she can actually take off her armor.

"I've battled with OCD my entire life, in case it wasn't obvious," she says. "The way I am about the wedding? It's not some quirk; it's clinical."

Puck hates that they have to stifle the immediate urge to banter—to say something like "I just chalked it up to maid of honor syndrome." Compassion used to come more readily to them, and they do feel it for Robyn now, but it's unsettling that it's not their first instinct. Have they spent too long thinking about how to turn people's vulnerabilities into entertainment for them to be able to just . . . listen? *Homewreckers has* changed them, they're realizing, and in ways that require active effort to counteract.

"I used to think that if things didn't go a certain way, or follow a certain track, that something terrible would happen to me or the people I love," Robyn continues. "Like if I took the 'wrong' road home from work, I thought I'd get in a car accident and die—or kill somebody. A kid, even. Sometimes the anxiety would get so overpowering that I'd pull over and wait hours for the traffic to stop and the roads to empty before driving home."

"Jesus," Puck utters involuntarily.

"I tried Jesus," Robyn says. "And then exercise. And then staying home all the time after my job went fully remote. The only thing that helped was a ton of therapy."

Robyn has always seemed so, well, *unstoppable* is the word that comes to mind. It's hard for Puck to picture her feeling overwhelmed by anything, even though they know it's possible, even though they know brains love to misbehave. "How did the therapy help?" Puck prompts, before finding the tact to add, "If you feel comfortable sharing . . ."

"Not in the way I thought it would," Robyn says. "I thought she'd help me figure out how to get rid of those thoughts, but instead, she told me I'd probably never stop thinking that way, at least not entirely."

Puck catches their first meteor streaking across the sky, tracing a bright line at the edge of their vision, but now is not the time to point it out. Something much more beautiful is happening beside them: a night-blooming flower, opening up. Puck realizes how rare it must be for Robyn to really talk to someone. This whole time, beneath all her bluster, she's been dealing with a deep wound. Of course she has. Everyone is, whether or not they show it.

Robyn inhales sharply, then lets out the breath, before continuing, her eyes still fixed on a spot somewhere between earth and heaven. "She told me to accept the outcome I was dreading instead of trying to outthink it. Turns out you're a lot less worried about trying not to die if you tell yourself you're *absolutely* going to die, if that makes any sense."

Puck tries to decipher the strategy. "So you're walking around all the time telling yourself that terrible things are definitely going to happen?"

"Yeah, I guess I am," Robyn responds, a hitch catching in her throat as she admits it. "But it's better than believing I can prevent those things with sheer willpower, you know? The fear is easier to deal with if you don't try to stop yourself from feeling it in the first place."

It's hard for Puck to imagine someone with so much drive having airplane crashes and brain-eating bacteria playing in her mind on a constant loop—not because they doubt it happens, but because it seems so cosmically unfair that it does. Puck doesn't enjoy life's pleasures half as much as Robyn seems to, so wouldn't it be better for the universe to saddle *them* with all that anxiety instead? Let Robyn watch the stars without worrying about one falling on her head. If Puck were to be as honest as Robyn is being right now, they'd have to admit that they, too, are white-knuckling life. They're trying to stay one step ahead of that nagging, unresolved feeling that they never really grew up. That *Homewreckers* froze their development at "hot masc on campus" and they haven't learned how to move past it. That they're too scared of what life might look like outside of an all-consuming routine of work and play that leaves little room for introspection.

What would it feel like to say some of that to Robyn now? Puck opens their mouth, searching for the words, then they think twice. Holding hands was hard enough.

By morning, the wedding will be called off, Puck is sure. That kiss Mia and Zander shared at the bar, however brief, is not the kind that can be easily forgotten. Then, after the dust settles, Puck can pick up their friendship with Mia again. They'll try to be more caring, and less of a work drone. They'll make plans to visit Mia wherever she decides to move. They'll be an ear for her as she recovers from the shock of all this. Things will get better, starting tomorrow, Puck assures themself, but only half believing their own promise. Fifty, friendless, and alone still feels like their most likely future. But what if Robyn were in that future instead? What if they could be who she needed them to be? Picking up twice as much toilet paper on the way home from work wouldn't be so bad if every so often, even just a couple times a year, there were moments like this: feeling absolute trust from someone who doesn't easily give it out. Puck reaches out to take Robyn's hand again and squeezes it, not caring anymore about how needy it makes them feel. Goddamn it, they like this girl.

"I'm so sorry, Robyn" is all Puck manages to say.

"There's nothing to be sorry about," she says. "I just wanted you to know why I'm like . . . *this*."

But as they notice another brilliant vertex of light cut across the sky, a distressing thought occurs to Puck. One they almost don't want to vocalize. "Do you feel that way about the wedding?" they ask. "Like if it doesn't go well, something bad will happen?"

The possibility puts them in a terrible position. So far, Robyn has likely been operating under the assumption that Puck doesn't approve of Damon, and is just *very* indelicate about it. But Puck wasn't counting on actually caring about her grand aspirations for a picture-perfect "Appalachian luxury chic experience" wedding, as they once heard her refer to it. Robyn would be livid if she knew anything about Puck's plan, and after what she shared tonight, they don't want to devastate her.

"No, it's not like that," Robyn clarifies. "I have a good handle on my management strategies. I just meant that I still know how to pay attention to little details, without all the catastrophic thinking. Like I said, using my powers for good."

"For Mia," Puck says, the guilt like acid in their throat.

"For Mia."

Puck focuses on the feeling of Robyn's palm in their own. On the incredibly basic but unimaginably powerful gesture of giving another person your hand. They lean over and kiss Robyn on the cheek, unsure what to say and feeling a creeping uncertainty about what they have already done. But it's too late now.

"For the record, I take back what I said about the Emory crew," Robyn says. "You're not *all* bad."

She's referring to the group as a whole, but Puck can't help but feel like the statement is just about them. *They're* not all bad, right? They hope not.

Puck lies with Robyn on the lawn for another hour, still watching the sky at first. But then, as the novelty of watching rocks sear through the atmosphere starts to wear off, Puck's gaze returns to earth. Now that their eyes have fully adjusted, and thousands more stars have come into focus, the rounded mountains surrounding the Athenian look like gently arcing swatches of darkness cut out of an otherwise dazzling canvas of light. It's as though the peaks don't want to encroach on the night sky, clinging low to the ground not because of how eroded they've become over an eon, but out of respect for the display above. They're merely a frame for the picture, and they know it. It is ennobling to call them mountains when the Appalachians could easily be mistaken for hills.

Maybe falling for someone is less like long division, Puck decides, and more like respecting these ancient, fading peaks: You feel something for someone that you call "love" until it becomes true.

Friday

Chapter 20

It feels pointless to get ready for a wedding you are sure will be—or has already been—canceled, but Puck doesn't have much to do this morning. After quickly getting dressed, they spend five minutes adjusting their tie, daubing some lotion on their face, and polishing a bit of scuff off their Docs. Best to look like they're still expecting everything to proceed as normal, even though they know exactly what they'll find when they walk into Mia's room: the bride in tears, maybe with her mom or a few bridesmaids providing comfort.

Some feigned shock will be necessary. Mentally, Puck practices saying "What happened?" a few times as they walk down the hall to Room 468. But does that sound too presumptuous? Perhaps it's better to keep it even more open-ended: "What's wrong?" Puck is settling on the latter response when they push open the door, only to be greeted by an angry shout.

"Hey!" It's Anya's voice, followed a moment later by, "Oh, sorry, Puck, I thought you were one of the groomsmen, with the suit and all."

They don't have time to process the comment because what they see past Anya is even more troublesome: Mia in her glam chair, surrounded by an entire pit crew of attendants who have laid out an array of mysterious elixirs and potions on the antique wooden vanity. One of them, a woman in a mustard-colored stylist's apron, is putting a topcoat on the bride's nails, while another gets back to working a curling iron after picking a stray speck of dandruff off Mia's updo. The bridesmaids—except Robyn and Willa, who are nowhere to be found—are all hard at work perfecting their own physical forms, primping and tweezing and brushing. Mia's makeup looks done already, save for a few final flourishes. How can she *still* be doing this?

Mia and Zander made out. They held each other while sobbing. Puck watched it all happen. Do the McLeods have her brainwashed? Puck knows how to produce half-drunk *Homewreckers* girls, but they don't have cult deprogramming expertise—and that's apparently what it will take to get Mia to do the right thing.

Puck's goal was to end this wedding and now not only is their best friend headed toward a bad marriage, but she also has to keep a secret every day until it ends: She was intimate with her ex on the eve of her wedding. It'll only be a matter of time before Zander lets something slip out of jealousy or spite—or until Mia gets a guilty conscience and tells Damon herself. After that, she'll be divorced, unemployed, and broke, forced to escape from Raleigh on her own steam. How can she not be worried about that likelihood? Puck walks over to the glam chair to get a closer look at her.

"You look gorgeous, Mia," they say, tempering their shock, but it's more than an obligatory compliment. She does look stunning. If Mia really can't find it in herself to be gay, then she at least needs to be saved from the worst heterosexual fate imaginable.

"And you're looking handsome, if that's an acceptable adjective to use," Mia says, looking up from the chair, her face frozen in place. "Sorry, I shouldn't smile while the makeup finishes setting."

"That's fine," Puck says. "I promise to only say extremely serious things. We can talk about global famine. Is Lena here? She'd be great for that."

"Hey!" Lena shouts from her makeshift perch by a floor-length mirror.

Mia stifles a laugh. "Puck, I'm serious. These pictures last forever."

Forever. It's a tough word to swallow. Even after last night, Mia has somehow deluded herself into thinking it's her and Damon for the long haul. What good was all of that plotting and maneuvering if Puck has ended up right back here, put in a situation where they might just have to say directly: "Don't do this. You're making a mistake"? Should they just say *that*? There aren't many options left. But maybe they can make one last oblique attempt to reach her.

"Hey, I was looking for you last night," Puck says. "After your drinks with the moms. Did they give you the birds and the bees talk?"

Mia scolds Puck once again. "No jokes, Puck, remember?" The nail technician sets a small space-age-looking machine on the shelf of the vanity and gently moves Mia's hand inside of it. "I was with Willa last night. She wanted to modify her bridesmaid dress, and I had to talk her out of it."

"Not fashionable enough for her?"

"Something about the lines being all wrong."

It's an elaborate lie, which means Mia must feel some shame about what she did with Zander. But Puck isn't sure what to do from here. Their scribbled memo isn't useful anymore. The only thing left to do is improvise. A glance around the room reveals Lena struggling with an eyelash curler at one mirror, while Anya applies a lint roller to a particularly troublesome section of her hem. Robyn is probably off somewhere making sure each flower has the appropriate number of petals—a thought that makes Puck feel more affection toward her than anything else, now that they know what they know.

Puck decides the best thing they can do is vamp for more time. "And how are *my* lines?"

"You're pulling off the lilac suit," Mia says. "And the pocket square kind of makes you look like a sports commentator. Are you leaving *Homewreckers* for ESPN?"

"Hey, you said no jokes!" Puck retorts.

"Only applies to you, I'm afraid," Mia says, looking down at the blue light coming from the contraption her hand is caught in. "I'm the one in the chair."

Typically, an idea would have come to Puck by now. But they still have nothing. At a certain point, if no one intervenes, Mia will get married just so all this beautification doesn't go to waste. In the straight woman cultural imaginary, unfortunately, some pictures *are* worth a bad marriage.

Puck sits down in the armchair opposite Mia, digging in for a tense interaction. They're going to have to be delicate about this, but at some point the gloves might need to come off. "How are you feeling?" they ask, softening their voice to send a message: *It's me, your old friend, and I want to level with you.*

"Good," Mia says, recognizing the tone, but there's a forced quality to her answer. "I mean, I'm nervous, but that's normal, right?"

It's a question that's not really a question—and Puck needs to thread the needle with their response. "Don't ask *me* that! I think anyone who legally commits to someone for the rest of their life *should* feel anxious about it!"

"So, in other words, it's normal," Mia clarifies.

"I mean, sure, but you love him." Puck offers the false assurance to try to avoid this becoming an overt argument even as the conversation takes a more combative tilt. "And this is what people do when they love someone." Come to think of it, maybe Mia just needs someone to play chicken with her: double down on the idea of her marrying Damon until it starts to scare her as much as it should. So Puck keeps going: "Ten years from now, when you're picking up little Samuel and Stacy McLeod up from soccer practice and coming home to your mansion, it'll seem silly to you that you ever had butterflies in your stomach," they say, closely scanning Mia's frozen face for anything that might betray her true feelings.

And there it is: the slightest wince, and not just at the mild rudeness. "I don't think I want to live in a house. Damon's parents' place feels so big and lonely now that it's just the two of them. I'd rather get a condo downtown. A loft, maybe."

Good. Puck's getting somewhere. Unlike Mia's airbrushed skin, there are some cracks here that Puck can claw their fingers into and spread open, so long as these girls stay out of it. Thankfully, they all seem preoccupied with their beauty regimens.

"You haven't talked about where you're going to live yet?" Puck asks, genuinely alarmed at the revelation, not even needing to play up their concern for effect.

Mia pauses while the hairstylist puts away the curling iron and produces another ominous-looking instrument Puck can't identify. God, this process is medieval. Even before coming out as nonbinary, they never bothered to learn about beauty. Having messy, air-dried hair and nothing on their face except ChapStick has never stopped Puck from being desired in queer circles—and now they don't even have the hair anymore.

"Oh, no, we have talked about it," Mia clarifies. "I think we're going to get a little pied-à-terre in Raleigh and then a house out in Governors Club. That way Damon can have the kind of space he's used to and I can still pop downtown for the things I want to do."

Puck doesn't know the Triangle super well, but they definitely don't like the sound of "Governors Club." It conjures up the image of a neighborhood where an angry posse of Nextdoor moms whip themselves into a paranoid frenzy over the sight of a squirrel breaking into a bird feeder. And Puck *definitely* isn't happy to hear that Mia and Damon are already thinking about living separately. If they were a queer polyamorous couple—or even any other straight couple except a horribly mismatched rebound—Puck might support the arrangement. But as it stands, it's the reddest of flags. Is that why Mia hasn't stopped this yet—because she'd rather slowly slip out of the marriage than deal with the discomfort of preventing it?

"Just be careful, Mia," Puck says, trying to disguise their warning as a joke. "Big and Carrie had a pied-à-terre and then he died on his Peloton, remember?"

It's not that funny an observation, even Puck has to admit, so Mia has no trouble avoiding laughter this time. "I didn't think you watched *Sex and the City*," she replies, accepting another dusting of powder on her face. "You're a film bro. I'd expect a David Fincher reference from you. Something about the house in *Gone Girl*."

Puck is impressed with Mia's knowledge of Fincher's filmography—but they have a vague recollection of Zander showing her *Se7en* in college.

"You made me watch *Sex and the City*!" Puck playfully protests. "We binged it over two weekends in our dorm when you found out I hadn't seen it, remember? The theme song is playing on a loop somewhere in the back of my brain."

"Yes, but that was the *original*," Mia clarifies. "Big dies in the *reboot*. Which means you kept watching."

"Guilty," Puck admits, and they feel a certain surrender at the word. This conversation is already reaching a dead end. For some reason Puck can't understand, Mia is determined to go through with this, even after everything. The only thing they feel like they can do now is—

A shout from across the room. "Get away from her!" Robyn is standing in the open door, green eyes glowering.

Puck's heart plummets as Robyn races toward them, mascara-streaked tears running down her face, with a small square of paper clutched in her hand. Even Mia furrows her brow against her better judgment as her crew of helpers swivel to face the disruption.

"Robyn?" Mia asks, puzzled. "What's going on?"

"What's going on is that your 'friend' has been planning to sabotage this wedding all week," Robyn says, as Puck stands up to intervene.

"Robyn, I—"

But she won't look at them. All the intimacy of the night before has vanished.

"Don't talk to me," Robyn fumes. "Talk to Mia. Explain this"—and at that, she produces Puck's memo. Mia pulls her hand out of the manicure machine to accept the paper, and she reads aloud, more frown lines forming on her face.

"'M plus Z, D eight Z and M, use L . . .' Puck, what is this?"

"It's your initials, Mia," Robyn says, wiping away her own tears, even as she scowls. "It's the Emory crew. 'Mia plus Zander, Damon *something something* Zander and Mia, use Lena.' I found it in their nightstand."

"Wait, what were you doing in Puck's nightstand?" Mia asks.

Puck notices that Lena and Anya have dropped everything they're doing to watch this scene play out. Willa has arrived too, her dress missing a shoulder strap, which means Mia wasn't entirely lying about trying to talk her out of the alteration, but that's not important now. She's standing in the doorframe, eyes agog, unsure whether she should enter.

"I was fucking them, OK?!" Robyn shouts. "A fucking mistake, *obviously*."

And that elicits a gasp not just from Mia, but from the nail tech, who doesn't even know any of these people.

"You were sleeping together and didn't tell me?" Mia asks, momentarily forgetting about the incriminating piece of paper in her hand. The question is directed at Robyn, but Puck decides to answer first—anything to lower the temperature.

"It wasn't serious," they say, and that gets Robyn to look at them, though they immediately wish she didn't. Her beautiful face is distorted with hurt and anger. Puck thinks back to what Robyn said last night, about once worrying that everything would fall apart if things didn't go exactly as planned. Puck has made those fears come to fruition.

"It wasn't *serious*?" Robyn repeats, and Puck wishes they could retract their words. Downplaying it was all instinct; they wanted to try to address the memo *before* the hidden tryst, one thing at a time. But before they can offer context, Mia speaks again.

"Puck, what does this mean? 'M plus Z'? Were you trying to get me and Zander back together?"

"They were," Robyn answers, before Puck can come up with a believable lie. "All week I've been ignoring it, but they haven't been acting right. The way they changed my icebreaker on the bus? The random scavenger hunt no one at the Athenian even knew about? After I found that paper, I ran a search for the phone number those texts came from. It matches leaks from *Homewreckers* contestants that got posted to Reddit."

Fuck those fucking Redditors. Puck needs their obsessiveness for the show to stay in the cultural conversation, but truly, they all need something better to do with their time. They've ruined everything.

"And Zander said last night that he was coming down to the bar to get a fizzy water for Puck . . ." Mia says, putting it together.

Alarm replaces anger on Robyn's face. "Wait, you saw *Zander* last night? Did something happen?"

But instead of answering, Mia just starts to cry.

"Please don't, sweetie, I already did your lashes," the makeup girl cautions, but the bride has reached her limit.

"Don't tell me what to do!" she shouts. "I'm sick of people telling me what to fucking do!"

"Mia, I'm—" Puck says, trying to wedge a word into the conversation.

"You're leaving, is what you are," Mia says, collecting herself and speaking with a terrifying clarity as she folds the piece of paper in half and tears it along the seam.

"No, wait, Mia, we need to talk," Puck says desperately, looking back and forth between Mia and Robyn, neither of whom will meet their gaze. Lena is crying out of sympathy. Anya and Willa, meanwhile, appear close to whipping out pitchforks and marching Puck out of the hotel.

As Puck looks at Mia in her tear-ruined wedding makeup, they can finally see the disaster this was always destined to be. They were so certain they wouldn't be discovered that they never even considered how much pain it would cause if the scheme came to light. They felt free to use all their usual tricks. At times, it was even fun. But this is no longer fun. Was it *ever*?

Puck isn't clear anymore on what they were hoping to accomplish here—or why they felt the need to do it so intensely. This is big. This is elemental. This is unforgivable. And there's no rewind button. This can't be tweaked in an editing bay.

"You've said enough, or too little, I can't tell which," Mia says, her voice sounding far away. "And my head hurts."

"I didn't want it to happen like this," Puck says, feeling their own tears coming now.

"*Oh*?" Mia asks, finally looking at them through streaks of mascara, some kind of pin jostling out of her hair, updo coming loose in the process. "How *did* you want it to happen? And why did you think that even mattered at *my* wedding?"

Puck wants to answer, even though they know they shouldn't, but they can see the bridesmaids shifting closer, instinctively forming a protective circle around Mia. Some gendered groupthink has a social purpose, Puck realizes, and right now, they are on the wrong side of it.

"I shouldn't have done it," Puck says, feeling the inadequacy of that admission in real time. "I'm sorry. It was wrong."

"You think?!" Robyn shouts.

"This isn't TV, Puck," Mia says. "This is my life."

"I know it's your life," Puck says, seeing an opening they probably shouldn't take, and plowing straight through it anyway, "and that's exactly why I wanted to help. This is a big thing you're doing, and . . . and . . ."

"*Yes*?!" Mia prompts, angrily.

"And you're not going to be happy with Damon."

They regret it immediately.

Mia's seething. The bridesmaids tighten their circle around her. "And you're not going to be happy, period. Because you don't have anything going for yourself besides your stupid show. All you've ever done is watch *us*, Puck. Your life is empty."

Puck can't bear to hear their deepest insecurity come from someone else's lips, let alone Mia's. It hits a place so fragile and so deep inside them, all they can do is lash out.

"At least I've never cheated on my fiancé at my wedding!" they shout. "At least I've never compromised who I am for a family of billionaires! At least I'm *myself,* Mia! Can you say the same? Was breaking Zander's heart really worth selling your soul?"

They feel the cruelty of what they're saying the second they finish, and they're just as shocked by it as the women are. Mia stands up, signaling that the conversation is over. And the look on her face isn't shock anymore, or anger, or even pain. It's pity.

"Is your heart really so hollow that you needed to play with mine?" she asks.

The question slices Puck down the middle, and a million inarticulable feelings pour out of them at once. But as they open their mouth to say something, anything, to redeem themself, they take stock of the facial expressions of everyone in the suite. Lena is sobbing. Willa looks even scarier than normal. Anya seems ready to throw hands. And Robyn? Her eyes are angry, but her lips trembling. Why did Puck say their relationship didn't mean anything? It did. More than they ever got the chance to say, or even realized until now. Why did they do any of this? It was just a wedding. People marry the wrong person every day, hell, every *hour*. There's no way to explain themself. They swallow their words down instead.

"I think you should go, Puck," Willa says, taking position at Mia's flank now. "We'll take care of this."

Puck turns to Robyn and mouths another woefully insufficient "I'm sorry."

"Don't worry about me," Robyn says, her voice flat and unforgiving. "Like you said, it wasn't serious."

Chapter 21

The worst part of fleeing the Athenian in disgrace is still having to wait for the valet to fetch your wheels. It's so humiliating that Puck wants to march off to whatever hidden dirt lot all the cars are kept in themself and hot-wire their own ride. But instead, they stand at the top of the front stairs, in shock, waiting for some kid who probably can't even legally rent a car to bring back their Subaru.

Life's little mundanities, it turns out, don't come to a halt when you've fucked up in the worst way imaginable. Puck still had to pack their bags, bring their key card to the front desk, and say that their stay was "great, thanks" in an extended stupor, all before they could stand here on the edge of escaping this horror show of their own creation. Thirteen years of friendship with Mia are over in a flash. Their reputation with anyone who cares about them—or used to—is in tatters. And then there's Robyn. Losing her shouldn't hurt most of all because Puck has only known her for a week, but it does. Last night, Puck felt uncertain whether Robyn could fit in to their routines at home; now, facing the prospect of an entire life without ever seeing her again feels impossible.

Puck wants to lie down and curl up into a ball right here and let everyone coming and going step over them. But they only need to keep it together long enough to climb into the privacy of their car, which will ideally happen before—

"Puck? What are you doing here? Are you leaving?"

It's Zander, in his suit and bow tie, appearing from the sliding doors behind Puck. The only comfort is that he looks just as gutted as Puck does, and they can't blame him. How do you go from having your ex kiss you like she's trying to suck out your soul to watching her marry your friend the next morning? Maybe it's because they've spent the last hour in pained silence as they packed and checked out, or maybe it's seeing Zander so downtrodden too, but Puck can't hold it together anymore. They all but fall into Zander for a hug.

"I fucked up, Zan," they say, letting out a sob into his chest.

"Back up . . . what's going on?" Zander asks, wrapping his arms around them and giving them an extremely gender-affirming pat on the back. Even in crisis, he can make Puck feel seen for exactly who they are. But wait: Does he not know yet?

They linger for a moment before letting the hug end, accepting that Zander is going to see them cry, as if they have any choice at this point. "I lied to everyone, Zan. Including you."

"Hey, it's OK," he says. "I don't know what happened but let's talk it out. I'm leaving too, OK?"

That's when Puck notices the rolling suitcase behind Zander, aluminum handle extended. Has he been too busy packing to hear? Puck had assumed that everyone in the wedding party would have caught wind of what happened by now, but Robyn might have instituted a strict lockdown. If anyone could keep word from getting out, it'd be her.

"You're leaving?" Puck asks him.

"Yeah, I, uh, kissed Mia last night," he says, looking at Puck, expecting shock and getting none. "Then this morning," he continues, "when I found her and asked if she still wanted to go through with this, she just cried and ran away. So I figured it'd be better for everyone if I wasn't here. Why are *you* out here?"

Puck realizes this is the first time they'll say it aloud, and it feels shameful to even form the words in their mind. If they had just looked in a mirror earlier this week and recited the plan to themself, maybe they would have realized how wild it sounded, and then they could have prevented all this unnecessary anguish. But instead they have to tell Zander everything while daubing the tears from their eyes.

"I already know that you kissed Mia, Zan, because I made it happen. I've been planning *all* of this."

Zander looks confused, taking a step backward while he reassesses what's happening. "*I'm* the one who kissed her. What do you mean you 'made it happen'?"

"I mean I'm the reason you happened to find Mia alone in the Grove when I asked you to fetch me a club soda. I'm the reason you both ended up at the pond. I'm the reason you got to talk to her so much this week," Puck says. "You think Damon just conveniently wasn't around? It was me, the producer, *producing*. I distracted him, with Lena's whole glow-up situation."

"Dude, that's kind of messed up," Zander says, understating things but thankfully not rebuking Puck as forcefully as all the bridesmaids just did upstairs. "Did you make Lena hot, too? How long have you been working on this?"

"No, no," Puck clarifies. "Her makeover wasn't me. I just saw the potential there."

Zander lets out a long whistle. "So you've been engineering everything?"

"Yes."

"That day in the lobby with the cucumber water?"

"Yes."

"And the game on the bus."

"I can't take full credit, but yes."

"The scavenger hunt?"

"That was me."

"Christ, Puck, did you forget you weren't at work?"

It's a fair question. For Puck, *Homewreckers* has felt like serving in the military: Even when you're on leave, you're still technically in it. They never understood how other people their age could just "clock out." Puck can never *forget* they aren't at work because work is an extension of who they are and what they do: not just understanding what makes people tick but actually *making* them tick. But can that really be who Puck *is*? What kind of inner purpose requires betraying your friends?

"I guess so," Puck finally responds, giving up on thinking about it. They're well past their limit on looking inward, and suffering the consequences for it.

Zander shakes his head disapprovingly. "Why'd you do it, dude?" he asks.

Puck wishes they had a good answer. When the idea first occurred to them it seemed a bit devious but ultimately beneficial. But it was never even *that,* was it? Something as simple as staging the croquet teams was still a bridge too far. At some point, securing the outcome *they* wanted became more important than their friends' feelings, even as they learned about their post-college lives in more depth than they ever had before.

What's wrong with Puck that they could hear these people in some of their most private moments and still decide that the plan was the most important thing? Has *Homewreckers* really made them blind to the impact of their actions? Maybe if they had been forced to follow one cast for seven years, and witnessed the repercussions of the show beyond a few heated reunion episodes, they'd have behaved differently—but even then, Puck's not so sure, and that's cause for concern.

"I don't know, Zan," they say, unable to express any of that just yet. "I guess I just thought she was making a mistake."

"I did too, but I didn't fake an entire scavenger hunt," he says. "How did you even *do* that?"

"Friend at work."

Zander sighs, his mood visibly shifting into some sort of nihilistic bemusement, the disappointment he feels toward Puck seemingly blunted by a fresh wave of his own heartache. "Well, fuck, man. And they all found out?"

They nod.

"I mean, Puck, what you did was wrong. Like, really wrong. And they can be mad at you—hell, I could be mad at you if I wanted to be. But you didn't make her kiss me. You didn't shove our heads together. Unless you had some kind of wire-and-pulley system I wasn't seeing."

He's offering a way out of the shame, and Puck wishes they could take it. But they can't. Everything that was said to them upstairs, as much as it hurt, needs time to sink in. It would be so easy to blame everyone else for what they did this week, even though Puck crafted all the conditions for them to do it. Then they could return to *Homewreckers* with a clear conscience believing that their old friends had overreacted to some mild antics. But the truth is they didn't cross a line; they leaped straight over it. They were so busy trying to ensure everyone made the "right" choices this week because they didn't want to examine their own: the choice to value work above all else, the choice to sleep their way through all of Feeld instead of looking for someone to love, the choice to derive meaning in life from emotionally devastating other people, all for an Emmy that isn't even theirs. At least, Mia, Zander, and the rest of them were trying to build something, even if they were failing along the way. What has Puck been working toward? Record-breaking ratings? They've been afraid to grow up and they made it everyone else's problem. So, no, they can't take the escape hatch.

"I appreciate what you're trying to do," Puck says. "But frankly, I deserve to be run out of town by an angry mob. I'm just lucky they're not tarring and feathering me."

"Well, at least everyone will know why *you* left," Zander says. He runs a hand through his hair, trying to pass it off as an idle gesture, but Puck can see the agony painted across his sweet face.

"I'm sorry, Zan," they tell him, but no words will ever suffice for what he must be going through.

Zander shakes his head. "You know, I talk a lot about AA," he says. "But my parents also started going to Al-Anon, and you know what they teach you there?"

Just yesterday, Puck would have been tired of more sober-speak, but now they feel lucky Zander is even talking to them. "What?"

"You can't control someone else's addiction."

Puck doesn't agree with what Mia is doing but they resent the comparison. "Are you saying that Mia is *addicted* to Damon?"

"I'm saying you're addicted to controlling people," Zander replies.

Puck feels the comment land in their gut. It's heavy—the sort of observation that will take months to digest. And it's a reminder that Zander is indeed chewing on what Puck did, even if he isn't going to consign them to pariah status quite yet.

"I really do regret what I did, Zan," they say, and it's true, though they don't want to admit how deeply his words have cut them. They thought they were mostly intervening because Mia was making a critical error, but by the end, they had convinced themself they were acting on his behalf, too. They've seen this past week how much he's changed. He deserves to be with someone he loves as much as Mia—but apparently that won't actually *be* Mia, who is presumably getting her makeup redone right now.

"You know, Puck, if I had wanted you to be my wingman, I would have asked," Zander says, speaking earnestly now, man to man. Then, a flash of recognition. "You were working me from the very beginning, weren't you? What did you say to me that first day over breakfast? *You're here, right?* Something like that."

"I swear I hadn't started plotting yet," Puck says, then catches themself. "But it was right after that."

"Well, you shouldn't have encouraged me. It's clear she wants him now."

Zander turns around, pretending to look back into the hotel through the sliding doors, but it's obvious he's just hiding his face.

"Oh, Zan," Puck says.

They wish they had the moral standing to comfort him, because right now he's experiencing the rawest, simplest, and most brutal feeling of all: rejection. It's a punch to the throat that robs you of the breath you'd spend on anything else. Zander has been in love with Mia since they were practically kids and now he probably still has the taste of her on his lips as he flees her wedding. Out of instinct, Puck opens their mouth again to attempt a reassuring word, or to try to cheer him up with a joke. They could say something true but ill-timed, like a reminder that he's definitely the "hottest guy on the J train." That his future wife will probably suck his dick every night because she'll never have to order DoorDash again. But before they can add that to the hundreds of other mistakes they've already made, the valet pulls up in Puck's stuttering Subaru.

"That's you," Zander says, turning back around, eyes wet, and it reads like a command to leave.

But it's also an accidental description of Puck. This fucking car *is* them: It's broken, and it doesn't know when to quit. Without a hug, only a bleary-eyed look from Zander, they get in and drive. The cabin gets overwhelmingly hot on sweltering days like this, but they keep driving. They stop at a Waffle House for the world's saddest patty melt, and then they drive. They sit in a park somewhere in North Georgia and cry and drive some more. And finally, when they're too tired, too weepy, and too sweaty to keep going, they pull off at a motel to sleep.

It's the world's shittiest roadside inn with a sign that still advertises rooms with Jacuzzis and HBO. It's exactly what they deserve tonight.

Saturday

Chapter 22

A knock on the door in a place like this can never be good.

Unless it's someone coming to fix the room's sputtering AC, in which case hallelujah. Puck had just decided to fetch some ice from the machine outside, but they'll accept a mechanic instead. Puck opens the door, bucket in hand, wearing nothing but a tank top and pajama shorts, only to find Mia looking just as slovenly in the kind of sweatshirt that girls only put on in times of extreme duress: *Break glass in case of emergency*, except instead of a fire ax, it's an Emory Eagles softball hoodie with a decade's worth of sad nap slobber baked into it. Her hair is frizzy, and bent in odd places where yesterday's hairspray must still be doing its work. She's not crying now, but she has been doing some borderline seismic sobbing recently, judging from the lines on her face.

"Fuck," Puck utters, without thinking. Her being here can only mean one thing.

"You couldn't find a nicer place to hide?" Mia asks, casting a look of disapproval over Puck's shoulder into the motel room, likely imagining what sorts of horrors a black light might reveal if she were to shine it on the sheets.

"How did you—" Puck stammers.

"Find My Friends," Mia explains. "You set it to 'indefinitely' the last time you came to New York."

Puck thought a lot about that visit on the drive: Mia was at the end of her rope with Zander. Even though she loved her kids at P.S. 178, she was applying for private school jobs so they could afford to survive yet another rent increase. Puck was stressed about leaving *Homewreckers* behind, even for a long weekend. The pair took a subway ride out to Brighton Beach that Saturday and ended up at some random retro roast beef restaurant where they ate a plate of cheese fries. Puck and Mia laughed about how all that time at Emory they wanted to get out of the bubble, and now that they were well "outside the perimeter," they missed *this*: friendship, food, spontaneity, no high stakes or crushing responsibilities. But Puck forgot about the joy of that impromptu meal the second they got back to set in Atlanta.

"Well, yeah, it's a small step down from the Athenian," Puck says, shuffling their feet, unsure what Mia's intentions are.

The wedding has been called off. That much is obvious. But why would she follow them here? To make it extra clear that Puck's meddling was unforgivable? To go scorched earth? Mia has never been an angry person in their decade plus of friendship, but after the scene at the wedding, Puck doesn't know what to expect anymore. They feel like they've locked eyes with a stray dog in an alleyway and need to figure out whether they're in any danger. And they deserve to get bit, don't they?

"Good thing I'm just passing through, then," Mia says. "My mom and I are caravaning down to her place in Atlanta, but when I saw where you were . . ."

Puck risks completing the thought. "You just had to make a pit stop at the E-Z Inn, huh?"

Mia doesn't crack a smile and, in truth, Puck wouldn't want her to. "What happened with the wedding?" they ask, before awkwardly pivoting: "I mean, I'm so sorry, Mia."

But Mia doesn't look like she wants to address it in a doorframe.

"Can you make me a drink after you get your ice?" she asks instead, sniffling, then pointing at the empty bucket.

It's a hopeful indicator. Mia is probably still going to cut Puck out of her life forever, but they can at least be civilized about ending things.

"A French 75, I'm guessing?" Puck quips, realizing from the scolding look that appears on Mia's face that it's much too soon for a joke like that. They'll have to break the tension another way.

"What do you even have in there?" Mia probes, wrinkling her nose at the sight of the cheap bedding and the boxy TV/VCR combo on a faux-wood console with peeling laminate. "Besides bedbugs."

Puck takes a quick mental inventory of what they have remaining in the QuikTrip bag on the nightstand: some Ritz crackers, a half-eaten pack of beef jerky, and a few energy drinks that they bought for the drive.

"I only have tap water and Monster," Puck offers. What a menu, and judging from the condition of this motel, only one of those two options is likely to be lead-free.

For half a second, Puck spots the corners of Mia's mouth being tempted to turn up into a smile—and based on the brief look they exchange, they both know why. Back at Emory, Monster was Mia's hangover cure du jour. She hated the taste of it, but she spent many a Saturday afternoon lying on a blanket on the floor, lights off, slurping down that ungodly mix of caffeine and sugar in an attempt to rally for another night out while Puck read poems aloud for the ambience. As miserable as those days were, there was something perfect about them, too: Puck holding Mia's hair back for her in the bathroom with one hand, reading from an Emily Brontë collection with the other. "The night of storms has past / the sunshine bright and clear." It was sacred and profane, what could happen in a room alone with someone who really saw you. And now Puck has broken that bond for good. Brontë would have something to say about that, too: "Now trust a heart that trusts in you."

"Well, if I'm going to have Monster, I'll *definitely* need ice," Mia says, and walks past Puck into the room. There's no avoiding a big talk now, and although they might dread it, Puck needs it to happen, too. They need to hear it all out loud again: That they try to fill an absence in themself by interfering with other people's lives. That they may have discovered early on that they were gay, and then nonbinary, but that they never really found out who they were after that, not really. That they have always been nothing but a puppeteer. Maybe if Mia says all that again, louder this time, it will finally make them change for good. Puck can leave this motel with the condemnation tattooed on their skin and try to become somebody at long last. They'll take up ceramics or something. Isn't that what people do? They work and then they try to shape something: a mug, a poem, a relationship?

They let Mia disappear into the room behind them and walk past the parked cars, toward the buzzing of the vending machines at the back of the motel. Is this the last hour they'll ever spend together? They wouldn't blame Mia if she wanted to cut all remaining ties and run far away. She could start all over in L.A. and talk about her exes and old friends like they're unspecified villains in some tragic backstory.

The sound of ice crashing into the bucket only underscores the harsh reality of that possibility: Mia being gone for good. Puck has barely made any new friends while working on *Homewreckers*. They didn't realize until this week just how much they relied on the thought of the Emory crew simply being there, even when they didn't talk to them frequently at all. They were a backstop against the threat of an entirely solitary life. And now Puck will have to . . . what? Start over? Go to dinners with Ron and a bunch of glassy-eyed network execs? Get after-work beers with the PAs? No, even pottery would be better than that.

And in another timeline where Puck didn't ruin everything, they could try to pick things up with Robyn. She's so much more than the workout girlie Puck thought she was at first blush; she has a ferocity that has helped her survive having a brain that betrays her every second she's awake. There are flames in her heart that Puck wants to fan in their direction, too. They want the courage to open up to her the way she opened up to them two nights ago. But that possibility is foreclosed now too.

Puck takes a deep breath as they reopen the door to their room, bracing themself to look in the eyes of their best—and probably soon to be former—friend.

"Do you want green or blue?" Mia asks from the foot of Puck's bed, holding up both options.

"I'll do green," Puck says, walking over and accepting the can with all the humility of accepting a peace offering, though there's nothing conciliatory about Mia's expression. "It really tastes like *green*, you know?"

Puck is only cracking wise out of discomfort, and Mia is not amused. She remains eerily quiet as Puck rinses out two glasses, scoops some ice from the bucket, and pours out the neon-colored liquid. For a moment, they consider sitting next to Mia on the bed but decide to adopt a cross-legged position on the floor in front of her instead. If they're going to take a badly deserved tongue-lashing, they shouldn't be eye level. Mia inhales sharply as Puck's butt touches down on a carpet that probably hasn't been steam cleaned since the seventies.

"Puck, really?" she says, unsettled.

"I'll shower," Puck shrugs. "I tried taking one last night but the water has a *very* fine line between freezing and scalding so I gave up."

They're biding time at this point, making chitchat in an attempt to delay their own execution. Small talk about plumbing is better than the obvious topic. But Mia is ready to talk.

"I called it off," Mia says. "Someone probably told you by now, though."

Puck's phone hasn't made a peep since they left the Athenian, with the exception of a text from Nick asking: *Mission accomplished?* They deleted it as soon as it appeared on their screen.

"I assumed when you showed up," Puck clarifies. "No one has said anything to me."

"Phil heard all the shouting, and even though Robyn tried to get everything back on track, I knew I had to tell Damon—and you know what he said?"

Mia waits for Puck to respond before continuing.

"What?" Puck is picturing Damon in tears, his vision of graduating into manhood shattered.

"That he was *relieved*." She takes a sip of the blue concoction in her glass. "That he could tell my heart was somewhere else but he didn't want it to be true, and he was too afraid to ask me if it was. He said he felt like he was dreaming, and that as much as it hurt, he was glad I brought him back to reality."

Jesus, Puck really underestimated him, didn't they? Lena called him "nurturing" and Mia called him "sweet" and neither, apparently, was lying. Puck even saw glimmers of Damon's softer side in the Court that day, but they ignored them.

"Mia, I'm so sorry I ruined your wedding," they say once there's enough silence to squeeze in the apology. Whatever else Mia wants to get off her chest, Puck needs to lead with as direct and forthright a mea culpa as possible.

But Mia has more to say. It sounds as though she spent much of her drive rehearsing it. "Yesterday, I felt like I didn't want to see you again, Puck. Not ever. But then this morning, I realized I wasn't crying half as much over Damon or even Zander as I was about you," she says, flatly. "Marrying Damon would have been wrong. Eventually I would have realized I had lost myself. You were right about that."

There is no joy in hearing this. Not anymore. It's clear from her voice, drained of its usual singsongy lilt, that Mia's not here to praise Puck's acumen in matters of the heart.

"Mia, I'm really—" they start to say, ready to skip to the groveling part, but she cuts them off.

"What you did was wrong, though," she continues. "It was *my* life to ruin, Puck, not yours. You've always wanted to protect me, but sometimes being someone's friend means letting them make their own mistakes."

"Even if it means letting you become someone you're not?" Puck can't help themself. Some piece of them still genuinely wants to know where the line is.

"I'm a person, Puck. Not your doll," Mia says. "If I wanted to marry Damon, I would have done it. You wouldn't have to like it."

"I know, I know, and—"

"Friends are honest with each other. You made it clear how you felt at the hotel bar that first day, but everything after that should have been my choice, not yours," and then Mia finally starts to lose her cool, some passion reentering her voice. "Like, Jesus Christ, Puck, you had a *diagram*! That's crazy! Even *you* have to know that's crazy, right?"

Puck can't maintain eye contact with Mia anymore. They look down at the dirty thin-pile carpet instead, wondering if it was ever another color before it became a dingy brown. They wish they could dissolve into it, becoming just another layer of grime in decades of accrued sediment. "I wanted you to be happy, but I went about it in the wrong way," Puck says, but even then, they still feel like they're still defending themself too much. "In an *inexcusable* way," they add.

"If you felt so strongly about it," Mia says, making a face at the sip of energy drink she has just finished swallowing, "why didn't you just level with me, instead of talking in riddles and playing literal games?"

"And you would have taken that well?" Puck stares into the green abyss of their glass, still afraid to meet Mia's gaze.

"I don't know!" she shouts. "Maybe I wouldn't have taken it great! But it would have been a hell of a lot better than where we ended up! Never in a million years did I think inviting you to my wedding would end in us sitting in some shitty fucking motel drinking fucking Monster. I'm trying to get somewhere in my life, Puck, and you're, well, stuck."

Stuck. The word hits them square in the chest. After graduation, Puck had started to pity Mia instead of envying her aura of beautiful ease. She was barely getting by in New York, while Puck got a plum promotion at *Homewreckers*. Zander's drinking turned her home life into chaos while Puck enjoyed the comforts of living alone on an ample salary. But at least Mia *lived.* The last decade of Puck's time could only be summarized as a series of escalating job titles; Mia had peaks and valleys, rapids and eddies. She reached into the core of things that Puck would never—and maybe *will* never—experience: love and loathing, desperation and longing, need and loss. Was Mia the one pitying *Puck* all this time?

And was their invite to the wedding ever in question? God, Puck realizes with a wallop, of course it was. They had always assumed that there was a shared approach to friendship among the Emory crew—that they could not talk for months, even years, and pick things right back up where they left off. But Mia has been moving in real time while Puck has been frozen in place. It would have stung if Mia had decided not to invite them, but Puck wouldn't have been able to blame her, either. How was Mia supposed to know that Puck still considered her their best friend without the evidence to back it up? That visit to New York was three years ago now. If future anthropologists found their phones, they might assume Mia and Puck were acquaintances at best.

"You're right," Puck says, trying to stop the emotion welling in their throat before giving up on containing it. "Mia, God, I'm so sorry. I messed it all up. Your wedding, our friendship, everything. I've just been fucking working this whole time, you know? I think maybe I never grew up, and I've just been hiding from the world on that stupid show. And then I took it all out on you."

"Well, I'm glad you're having some big realizations," Mia says, finishing off the rest of her glass and standing up. She's leaving already? Puck needs at least another hour to beg for forgiveness. They've hardly begun to dissect how pathetic they feel.

"Please don't go," they say, but Mia is already walking toward the exit. Puck stands up to follow her, taking a few short steps, but Mia pivots in place just before reaching the door. No anger remains in her eyes, only disappointment. "I didn't come here to help you learn how to be a person, Puck. That's your job. I came here to make sure you knew how badly you fucked up."

"I do, I really do," Puck says.

"Do you, though? Because you didn't just break my heart. You broke Robyn's, too."

It's hard to believe given the last image Puck has in their head of Robyn is of her trembling and irate, refusing to look at them. Hell, Puck figured by now she was probably burning them in effigy, igniting an enormous wicker person on the Athenian lawn. But heartbreak? Puck can't deny they shared something with her—something that felt forgotten, familiar, and brand new all at once. Mia's right: They are missing some essential piece of being human, but the sensations they experienced stargazing with Robyn are good leads to follow to get back on track. Puck brushes away their tears.

"What do you mean I broke her heart?" Puck asks.

"I think she was falling in love with you, you fucking idiot," Mia says, then pauses, choking down an unexpected sob, like she can't bear what she wants to say next.

"Mia—"

"You're so incredible, Puck. That's what hurts so much about this. I really love you. I always have. For a second during sophomore year, you even made me wonder whether I *was* gay. And your show isn't stupid. I've watched every single episode, even in the years you didn't call me at all. I've been telling everyone I meet in Raleigh that my 'best friend' works on it. Except at some point that started to feel like a lie. Because my best friend can't just be some cool person I knew in college who doesn't talk to me anymore, you know? A best friend has to actually *care*."

Puck sits down on the edge of the bed, bowled over by the force of their own shame.

"What can I do?" they plead. "What can I do to not lose you?"

But they can tell from the hardening of Mia's expression that she's done all the emotional work she was willing to do on this detour. She's actually going to leave now—and it's going to be even more torturous to know that she'll be back in her childhood bedroom for a while, just across I-20 from Puck's place in Decatur.

"I get to decide when to forgive you," Mia says, shoving her hands in the pouch of her hoodie, car keys jingling softly as her fingers find them. "*If* I forgive you. It'll take a long time to trust you again. For all I know, another notepad is going to turn up showing that you planned for us to meet in this motel all along."

"I'm not that smart," Puck protests.

"Clearly," Mia responds, not missing her chance at the dig. "But you can do one thing for me."

"What?"

Puck would do anything: They'd do a thousand jumping jacks, even in this heat. They'd quit their job. They'd lick the yellowed, smoke-stained plastic blinds blocking the sun from entering this god-awful motel room.

"Don't make the same mistake with her that you did with me."

She's talking about Robyn again. But how could Puck make the same mistake with her? Ruin Robyn's wedding? She's not getting married to anyone.

Mia notices the confusion on Puck's face, the slightest smirk breaking out on her face. "You really *aren't* as smart as you think you are, huh?" she says. "Be honest with her, Puck. I tried to tell you how sweet she was at the start, but you didn't listen, did you?"

"No," Puck says, knowing the question is rhetorical but answering anyway, if only to say one more word before Mia walks away, probably for good.

"She's been through a lot, and she really cares about people," Mia continues. "And though I can't imagine why, after everything you did, she cares about you. She deserves to know the Puck I once did."

Mia turns away. She opens the door, walks out, and lets it swing shut behind her. But the last words she said are still in the room, finding new ways to be devastating.

Two Weeks Later

Chapter 23

For the first time Puck can remember, they're having trouble keeping the names of all the *Homewreckers* contestants straight. It took a long time to acquire the skill, with plenty of ad hoc mnemonic devices invented along the way: *Rebecca Smith looks like a lesbian. Well, the book* Rebecca *was famously queer and Smith is full of lesbians, so Rebecca Smith.* That one turned out to be true, oddly enough. Rebecca came out shortly after her season aired—the first of a surprising number of *Homewreckers* women with wandering boyfriends who turned out to be disciples of Sappho anyway.

Now, though, as Puck stands in the video village, they're having trouble remembering whether Micah's girlfriend is named Alexa or Allegra. Virtual assistant or allergy medication? It doesn't matter what she's called; Puck just has to send this woman off somewhere so they can talk to Jess Sandusky alone.

"Micah's over at the gazebo," Puck tells Alexallegra, then adds, "He was looking for you, I think."

It's the slyest thing Puck has done since coming back to work, and it doesn't feel great. Micah is not, in fact, at the gazebo. Ron has asked Puck to get Micah and Jess alone so they can deepen a connection that has apparently been rekindled since "Massage Gate," as everyone on set was calling it by the time Puck got back to work. Today should be easy, almost automatic: Send the devoted girlfriend on a wild-goose chase, have Nick install Micah in a spare bedroom, and then covertly deliver mistress Jess to Micah, all wrapped up in a bow. Bad decisions will predictably ensue—and the cameras will catch it all.

But this morning, Mia's words have been echoing in Puck's mind: "I'm a person, not your doll."

As few brain cells as some of these contestants have, they are still indeed people—even Micah's girlfriend, whose name, Puck confirms with a glance down at their face sheet, is in fact Alexa. The girl dutifully scurries off through the back garden toward the gazebo, blissfully unaware of Puck's lies. Toward the end of a season, many contestants inevitably realize the producers are not their friends, but Alexa has remained reliably gullible, which is why today's shooting schedule has "Micah–Jess love scene" written in ink: They can bank on this one. It'll be simple to produce, and it will deliver exactly what the audience wants. The millions of women who watch *Homewreckers* will *tsk* at Micah and say, "Once a cheater, always a cheater." Biases need confirmation, and it's always been Puck's duty to shore up those assumptions. Except that bargain has felt more Faustian these past two weeks than ever before.

Nick, who has turned out to be quite the career climber, is already back from setting Micah up in the mansion, eager to collect on Puck's offer to shadow them. "Should I get Jess on the walkie now?" he asks.

Some part of Puck hears Nick ask the question. But the idea of hailing Jess on the walkie makes them think about the one girl they actually want to call.

In the two weeks since getting back home, they've done almost nothing but think about the things they wish they could say to Robyn, most of them beginning with some inadequate version of "I'm sorry": *I'm sorry I ruined your best friend's wedding. I'm sorry I was jealous that your best friend used to be my best friend. I'm sorry I lied, deceived, and manipulated everyone around me, thinking I was helping them when actually I was just assuaging my own loneliness with a false sense of control.* But the longer that litany of self-flagellations went on, the more certain Puck became that Robyn could never—and probably should never—forgive them. Not that this has stopped Puck from rehearsing their countless apologies out loud while anxiously cleaning their bathroom, which only made them think about the amazing shower sex they had; while watering their dying plants, which made them think about the terrible and extremely gay joke they made about the rubber plant in their room at the Athenian ("I hardly know 'er!"); and while microwaving frozen tortellini, which made them wish they could be eating bacon-wrapped dates with Robyn at the Iberian Pig.

They debated texting Mia to ask when—or even if—they should reach out. Why would she say what she said back at the motel if there was no possibility of reconciliation with Robyn? But there are a million things Puck needs to say to Mia before they can ask for her advice.

"Puck?" Nick prompts, wrenching them back to the harsh reality of the *Homewreckers* set, where they have to boss people around whose names they'll flush from their mind in a week. "You wanted to talk to Jess, right?"

"Uh, yes," they finally confirm. "Let's do it."

Nick turns to mutter into the walkie, leaving Puck with their thoughts again. It's a characteristically hot Atlanta day, but they wish it were even hotter so their brain could cease to function. Anything to melt away the image of Robyn's face when she came into the bridal suite carrying that cursed piece of paper. Mia said that Robyn deserves to know the Puck that *she* once did. But who even was that, really? At some point, the scrappy, headstrong young queer they once were became nothing but a manager with a hollow life. That entire week at the Athenian, they turned up their nose at their friends for unblinkingly following the social order, when they've been down here enforcing it all along, making sure that the *Homewreckers* contestants step in perfect time with heterosexuality's most expected beats.

Puck looks across the lawn to the back patio door of the house. What's taking so long for Jess to get sent outside? When a request comes from Puck, delays aren't acceptable—or usual. But when the door swings open, it's not Jess who emerges from it. Is that? No. It couldn't be. And yet it is: Robyn with a "y" is storming toward them, trailed closely by the set security guard.

"Hey!" he's feebly shouting, unable to keep up with her pace. He might as well be trying to stop a tsunami with a feather.

When Robyn wants to find someone, she'll find them, whether it's inside a hotel spa or on the set of a reality show hundreds of miles away. But how? Even though the filming location has been posted online countless times over the years, the home is fenced in, and the security at the gate is top-tier. Did Robyn hop the fence? How many fucking barre classes has this woman taken? Puck is frozen to the spot as Robyn stomps off the back deck onto the grass and barrels straight toward them.

"Do you know her?" Nick jokingly asks, with all the bravado of a man in his twenties, registering Robyn more as a spectacle than a serious threat.

"We just met," Puck says, and the statement feels as emotionally false as it is factually true. But Puck has learned more about themself, and about love, in the last few weeks than in the last decade. For starters, they've learned that they became an asshole sometime between graduation and now. They've learned that friendships aren't save states in one of Damon's video games that you can simply reload. And most of all, they've learned that it's still possible to feel a sort of totalizing infatuation with someone—the kind of crush that tempts you to shred up your life and start over. Because as terrified as they are of Robyn charging toward them, Puck mostly feels thrilled to be anywhere near her again.

"Were you ever going to call me?!" Robyn shouts, dangerously close now.

"Is this like your ex or something?" Nick asks, and even he seems nervous, getting a crash course in the intensity of dyke drama. But before Puck can answer him, Robyn is standing in front of them, wearing a form-fitting black shirt and matching leggings, like some kind of sexy burglar. Did she seriously pick out a "break onto the *Homewreckers* set" outfit for this confrontation? That'd be hot if it weren't also unnerving.

"Robyn, I'm at work," Puck says, dumbly, as though that wouldn't have already occurred to her, and as though it would make a difference. In the corner of their vision, they spot the other producers, and yes, Jess Sandusky, gathering at a distance to watch this scene unfold. Even Ron is walking over to find out what's going on.

"Can we not do this here?" Puck begs her.

"Do what?" Robyn asks.

"I don't know . . ." Puck mutters, suddenly finding the grass very interesting. "*This*?"

Nick pretends like his walkie made a noise and retreats into the forming crowd. The freckle-faced security guard has apparently given up entirely now that he sees Robyn and Puck talking, safely assured that she's not going to shoot anyone. He too joins the gawkers on the periphery. Even amid the intense awkwardness, the irony of it isn't lost on Puck: After so many years of producing the show, they have finally *become* the show. The homewrecker-in-chief is now the ignominious star of a *Homewreckers* scene.

"I think this is the perfect place to talk about the wedding, actually," Robyn says. "Isn't breaking people up what you do here?"

Puck needs this conversation to move somewhere else, and fast. There are things they need to say to Robyn that ideally should not be overheard by their boss, or all of the colleagues who—until now, at least—saw Puck as some kind of demigod, capable of bending reality itself to their whims. But Mia didn't get the luxury of having her dreams shattered in private, Puck reminds themself. And all these now-gawking contestants, from the very first person Puck ever produced all the way down to Jess Fucking Sandusky, have had their heartbreak repackaged as amusement for the masses. If there was ever a time to stop and let karma punch them in the face, it might as well be now—when the woman they want so badly is standing in front of them, much sooner than they expected her, but still invigoratingly present nonetheless.

"Of course I wanted to call you," Puck says, trying to keep their voice low. "There's so much I've wanted to say to you, but I didn't know how."

Robyn doesn't bother controlling her own volume. "And you didn't want to ask Mia about me?"

"She and I aren't exactly on speaking terms right now," Puck whispers. "And I don't blame her."

"I don't either," Robyn says, still refusing to match Puck's hushed tone.

This conversation is confusing for Puck, on multiple levels. Does Robyn want to mortify them at their workplace or is she simply hurt they haven't called her? Is this supposed to be a relitigation of the wedding from start to finish or does Robyn want Puck to profess their love for her? Puck only knows one thing: They can't lose their only chance at starting over with Robyn. She stormed onto the *Homewreckers* set, and she could storm off it, too.

"All I've done since I left the Athenian is think about what I would say to you," Puck confesses, letting their voice get louder now.

"So what was the plan, then?" Robyn asks, unmoved by the admission. "Because it looks like you hooked up with me, broke up my best friend's wedding, and then disappeared. You didn't think you owed me anything afterward?"

Even the whispers among the crew stop at that. This is juicier drama than they've filmed so far this season—and it's happening inside their own ranks, which only makes it even more scandalous. If Puck were over there with the crew, they'd be training a half-dozen cameras on this scene, making sure every boom mic operator was limbered up and ready to track the action. But standing where they are, all Puck feels is deep regret.

"I owe you *everything*," they say, feeling their heart pounding as they say it, and finding that suddenly all of the things they rehearsed in the mirror are gone. "I feel like I was asleep until you walked into that sauna. You're like . . . the world's sexiest alarm clock."

"Sexy alarm clock?" Robyn balks. "*That's* what you wanted to say to me?"

Puck takes a breath. Despite the cascading series of epiphanies they've had these past few days, there's no point pretending like they're already completely reformed. The kind of changes they need to make will take months, if not years, to take hold. But Mia's advice at the motel was to "be honest," and that's exactly what they need to do right now.

"Look, Robyn, I'm not a good person," they begin, not caring who overhears them now. "I'm not going to become a saint overnight. But you see that girl over there?"—they pause to point at Jess Sandusky, who seems alarmed to be mentioned in the middle of this argument, but also delighted to see her tormentor thrust into an unflattering spotlight—"I'm supposed to tell her to go to an upstairs bedroom in the house where another girl's boyfriend is waiting for her. Then I'm supposed to get them to have sex with each other, or at least go to second base, on camera—the more pixelated things have to be, the better. And then I'm supposed to make sure the girlfriend walks in on them. And then everyone will watch it, and talk about it online, and I'll get another few years of doing exactly *this*, which isn't great, but it's not bad, either. I have a nice apartment and a beat-up car, and I might actually get to retire one day, which is saying something. But I would quit right now if it meant we could go on one date. Maybe to a coffee shop, and we can see if they have a job application while we're at it, because that's about the only place I'll be qualified to work in Atlanta outside a reality TV set. You could turn down a second date and it would still be worth it. I would give up everything for a shot at something with you, even if I ended up with nothing. And I don't deserve that shot. But I have to ask for it."

Robyn looks overwhelmed, but whether that's good or bad, Puck can't tell. The crew has fallen completely quiet. Even if Puck doesn't actually resign, Ron may fire them for saying all this in front of the crew. In the kayfabe of reality TV, no one's supposed to admit how unethical it all is. Jess certainly looks alarmed to learn about the grand plans the show had in store for her. But Puck doesn't care anymore. They only care about trying to get back to the feeling of lying with Robyn on the Athenian lawn, looking up at the stars, feeling their soul expand into the sky. That's worth this immense embarrassment. That's worth living on a barista's wages. That's worth figuring life out anew.

After a painful silence, and her face moving through seven different emotions in a row, Robyn finally speaks. "And what would you order?"

"What?"

"At the coffee shop. On this hypothetical date you're taking me on."

Puck just bared their soul and Robyn wants to talk about the menu at Dancing Goats?

"I guess I'd get a latte?" they say, unsure where this is going, but taking heart at the change in tone. "Maybe a mocha if I'm feeling fancy."

"And what would *I* order?" Robyn asks. Is that corner of her mouth threatening to turn into a smile? Would she really be so quick to forgive?

Puck considers Robyn's question for a moment, trying their best to pretend like they don't have an audience. "You'd probably have some sort of strawberry matcha with the most nonsensical milk substitute," they say. "Like milk made from pine cones or something, because you have to be so specific about everything."

Robyn is grinning in earnest now, but over her shoulder, Puck notices the *Homewreckers* crew looking confused by what's happening. Eyes are wandering, walkies are pinging, some light conversation is resuming, and Puck can't even blame anyone. This is precisely the kind of goopy queer nonsense straight people could never follow. Hell, Puck barely understands what's going on. Robyn hasn't accepted their apology, but it also feels like accepting a proposal is not entirely outside the realm of possibility, either? They're already mentally preparing for a trip to Home Depot to copy their apartment key.

"Well, *I* think you wouldn't get a latte," Robyn says, taking a step toward them. "You'd get a black coffee because you'd think it would impress me, but secretly you'd want some sugar."

The gayest part of Puck wants to say that Robyn could be their sugar, but they remember that they are still at work—or are they? Didn't they just put in their verbal notice in front of Ron and all these witnesses? Perhaps Puck *should* use the line, just to spite them. All their coworkers were clearly hungry for some real-life drama; let them choke on some unfiltered queer sweetness.

"Should we leave . . . right now?" Puck asks, returning Robyn's smile, not caring how goofy they look.

Robyn came all the way here for *them*. But there's still an aching beneath the obvious affection in Robyn's eyes. Some parts of her heart must be healing more slowly than others.

"I don't want you to quit your job, you little gay loser," she says. "I just didn't want you to come back here and pretend like what happened between us didn't happen. This is hard. I'm still so mad at you. But you don't get to cut and run."

"I never want to run from you again," Puck says, giving in to the cringe now. It might just be their imagination but they think they hear one of the camera guys audibly groan at that, but honestly, who gives a fuck anymore?

Robyn is crying a little now, but she's also moving temptingly closer to Puck. "I didn't come all this way *not* to kiss you, you know?" she says.

"But if I kiss you, we can't talk anymore," Puck says.

"Exactly."

And as their lips meet, it's Nick the PA who lets out the loudest cheer.

One Year Later

Chapter 24

A year ago, holding Puck at gunpoint would have been the only way to get them back to a wedding in North Carolina. But they never could have guessed that Lena and Damon would rekindle their brief relationship—and they *especially* couldn't have guessed that they'd get married so soon.

Puck was stunned to get the invite in the mail, but when they saw the location, they knew it was real. Only Lena and Damon would have an *Elden Ring*–themed wedding in a bird sanctuary—the perfect fusion of both of their interests. But the reality of it was difficult to accept: The envelope was addressed to both Puck and Robyn.

"One of these days you're going to have to accept that people are starting to move on from what happened," their girlfriend assured them over dinner, but it was still hard to believe.

Puck called the couple later that night to thank them for the unexpected invite, but also to reassure them they'd understand being omitted from the guest list. If they were only being invited out of obligation, they wanted Robyn to be able to attend solo. They had spent months making amends over phone, email, and text—and with everyone except Mia, they'd reached some kind of new normal. But no one was going to be able to pretend like last year's disaster was just a dream, and Puck didn't want their presence to be a sore spot.

"Well, I hate that people got hurt, but I can't imagine where I'd be if you hadn't sent us on that scavenger hunt," Lena had assured them.

Damon had significantly less emotional insight to offer when he took over the phone. "Listen, Puck, there's a character in *Elden Ring* named Marika. She's a queen but she's also technically the same person as her consort Radagon, a female half and a male half making up one super-powerful being. Anyway, I was thinking that's who you could come as for the wedding."

"Wait, which one?" Puck asked him. "Radagon or Marika?"

"Both, that's the whole point," he said, and then proceeded to launch into a lore dump that ate up the rest of the call.

Puck was so delighted to hear Damon back to his old ways that they didn't care about being typecast as the video game's resident nonbinary character. And after they spent some time on the *Elden Ring* fan wiki, they realized they could absolutely pull the look off with the right red wig.

As Puck pulls up to the valet outside the Wing Wildlife Reserve, they're slightly less embarrassed at the thought of handing over their keys to somebody else than they were last year. Robyn made them take the car to the dealer shortly after she moved in. "If you're going to be a stereotype, you at least have to make sure your Subaru isn't a death trap," she'd said, and Puck reluctantly took a half-day at work to get it fixed at long last.

But they are definitely embarrassed to step out of their car in nothing but a gray vest and tattered waistcloth, carrying a hammer they spray-painted gold on the balcony last night.

Their butt-length wig gets tangled in their seat belt as they try to unlock it.

"Sorry, just give me a second," they tell the waiting valet.

"Take your time, man, I've seen everything by now," he says, chuckling.

Robyn, of course, had no trouble getting out of the car despite wearing a winged golden helm that obscures much of her vision. Puck can hear her laughing as they finally free their synthetic hair from the buckle and step outside. "Isn't your character supposed to be a more formidable foe than that?" she teases them. "Radagon, undone by a seat belt."

"And what are you supposed to be again?" Puck calls out over the top of the car. "Some lady with smelly feet?"

"I'm Malenia, Goddess of Rot, of course," she says—and Puck feels a genuine pang of affection remembering how Robyn, who has never played a video game outside of *Mario Kart*, spent an entire weekend researching *Elden Ring* lore to pick the perfect costume, even ordering a custom piece of fake armor to complete the look.

"Well, excuse me, Rot Goddess," Puck says, producing a crumpled-up twenty-dollar bill from their wallet for the valet. "Take good care of her," they instruct the kid, repeating the same tired joke from last year.

"Do you always have to do that?" Robyn asks as she sidles up next to them.

"What? It's a fine piece of machinery!" Puck protests.

The valet interjects. "You take good care of *her*, dude," he says with a tilt of his head toward Robyn, before getting in the car and driving away.

They intend to. Puck knows this first year with Robyn, in many ways, is still a honeymoon. But it's also been full of hard conversations and gradual improvements. Puck is playing catch-up with someone who cracked the code on adulthood years before they did, but they plan to look after Robyn for as long as they can possibly keep up with her. She has helped Puck process their remorse over last year's wedding snafu, encouraging them to be gentle with themself without dodging accountability, either.

As the Subaru vanishes down the dirt road, Puck hears a familiar voice.

"Puck!"

Mia is dressed in an enormous white sorcerer's hat with a matching robe, her hair temporarily dyed light blue—or at least Puck hopes it's temporary. They have no idea who she's supposed to be, but frankly, Puck doesn't care. She looks impossibly gorgeous.

"Mia!" Puck calls back.

Puck still doesn't fully know where they stand with Mia—and it's awkward that they'll have to figure it out while dressed so ridiculously. Puck broke the ice three months after that day in the motel with a niche Libra meme about panda bears sent over an Instagram DM. After Mia heart-reacted to that one, Puck ventured into more earnest territory, sending a long message reflecting on their actions but making it clear they didn't expect forgiveness yet, or even ever. Mia said she still needed some time, but eventually started texting them again.

Zander was much faster to forgive, telling Puck they acted like "a dumbass," and then going right back to the tenor of their normal comms, occasionally sharing movie thoughts. He was especially psyched when the next Nolan film turned out to be an adaptation of *The Odyssey*, and not the helicopter cop movie it was briefly rumored to be.

Though Mia's not quite back to normal yet, Puck is overjoyed to hear her even utter their name out loud after what happened last year. They hurry over to Mia and bundle her up in a hug, careful not to muss up her costume.

"Thanks for not hating me," is what Puck settles on as a greeting, but then they quickly add, "I mean, I hope you don't hate me. Do you hate me?"

"I don't hate you," Mia says, squeezing Puck back. "It's really good to see you. Or whoever you're supposed to be. Do you understand any of this?" She gestures at the other guests walking through the row of ivy-covered arches that presumably lead to the bird sanctuary, all of them wearing various configurations of robes and armor, some carrying prop swords, others adjusting odd headwear.

"I'm not sure I want to," Puck responds—and that earns a gorgeous tinkling laugh from Mia that sends a jolt of hope through their heart. But once Robyn joins them, so does Puck's guilt. The last time all three of them were together, it was *Mia* who was happily partnered, and now, in addition to ending that relationship, Puck has stolen Robyn away to Atlanta, too.

Mia went back to Raleigh shortly after calling off the wedding, which surprised Puck. But in their intermittent text exchange, she explained that she'd wanted a change of scenery anyway, even before dating Damon, and she managed to secure a private teaching job that allowed her to afford her own place. Robyn remained in close contact with her, modeling the sort of friendship maintenance that Puck should have been doing all this time: long phone calls, gifts, even the occasional letter. Although it's been difficult, Puck has tried to respect that their own relationship with Mia has been moving in a different lane than Robyn's, and at a slower speed.

But standing here now, Puck is coming face-to-face with all these weird, complicated, and intersecting feelings. Luckily, Mia cuts straight through the awkwardness, wrapping Robyn up in an easy embrace. When they eventually disentangle, after almost a full minute of swapping stories and complimenting each other's costumes, it seems as though it's Robyn's turn to feel bad. Puck notices her clocking the envy on their face and she wraps her arm around their shoulder in response. The affectionate gesture is appreciated, even if it's accompanied by yet another reminder that Robyn is taller than them, which they have equally complicated gendered feelings about. But those can be sorted out another time. This reunion is more than enough discomfort for one afternoon.

"I'll let you two catch up, Pucky," Robyn says, using a recent pet name that's in dire need of workshopping. "I'm going to go find my Raleigh friends." Then, with her typical alacrity, she heads off through the trellises, leaving Mia and Puck alone.

"Drink?" Puck asks, unsure what else to say.

"Drink," Mia confirms. "C'mon, the bar's this way."

Puck follows Mia down a side path through the woods, the birdsong above them the only soundtrack as they leave the din of the arriving guests behind. After a minute of walking, the trees give way to a large greenhouse still being set up for the evening reception. Through the windows, Puck can see helpers moving many of the planters to the side to make way for extra seating. It's two thirty p.m.—hours before the reception—but the bar inside is open and serving. Puck will need some liquid courage to get through this conversation.

"What can I get you, ladies?" the bartender asks as they take two open stools, and while Puck has gotten used to letting casual misgendering brush off them, it's Mia who intervenes.

"There's only one lady here," she says, hitting the right balance of letting the bartender know he messed up but without inviting further questions.

"I'm sorry, of course," he stammers.

"Thank you," Puck mouths to Mia, genuinely moved.

"Let's try that again," the bartender says, lingering on the faux pas when he should just move on. "What can I get you *both*?"

Does he want a gold medal? "I'll take a French 75," Puck says, with a wink at Mia. "Empress."

"Excellent choice, *sir*," the bartender says, and Puck decides to take it. His heart is in the right place. "And for you, miss?"

"Just a Diet Coke for me, thanks," Mia says, which piques Puck's curiosity. She's never been one to turn down a cocktail. She's not pregnant, is she? Mia removes her enormous wizard hat and sets it down on the seat next to her. She still looks silly, her hair the color of Crest toothpaste, but seeing more of her face helps Puck take her more seriously.

"I can downgrade to a ginger ale or something," they offer, feeling just as self-conscious about their order as they are about their own outfit. "If you're not feeling a boozy vibe."

"No, it's just . . ." Mia says, then pauses. "Zan passed the two-year mark. He doesn't mind if I drink, but I kind of like being his sober buddy."

"Zander?"

Well, well, well. Puck got the sense that Zander hadn't been telling them everything over text. When Puck last asked him what he was up to, he wrote back something like "Busy. Working six shifts a week," and left it at that. It's all coming together now.

"At first I didn't tell you because I was still mad at you for ruining my wedding," Mia explains. "Then I didn't tell you because I was mad that you were right about me and Zander. And then I didn't tell you because it had been so long that I was worried you'd be mad at *me* for not telling you sooner."

The old Puck would have felt triumphant about this. But now they just feel remorse over all the time their misdeeds have cost them, for this strange temporal gap in their friendship with Mia. Because even if Mia and Zan *hadn't* ended up together, that would have been fine, too. Puck has had to accept that even if everyone technically made their own choices back at the Athenian, and even if they were motivated in large part by their friends' happiness, trying to tip the scales was still wrong. They are learning to let people make their own choices, even on *Homewreckers,* where the contestants are more than happy to generate their own drama if they simply outline a few paths and ask them to pick one. Multiple choice is still producing, it's just more hands-off—a happy medium that allows Puck to live with themself. If there's a heaven, they're pretty sure they're still disqualified from entry, but they can at least aim for purgatory. And as it turns out, most of the *Homewreckers* cast *wants* to get into trouble; they don't need as much pushing as Puck once assumed.

"Mad at you? In what world could *I* ever be mad at *you*?" they ask Mia. "After what I did last year?"

"You don't need to punish yourself forever, Puck," Mia says, pausing to acknowledge the bartender as he delivers the drinks, placing a slice of lime onto the rim of her Diet Coke with an exaggerated flourish before attending to some other early arrivals at at the bar who are wearing elaborately embroidered red cloaks. God, everyone really went all out on the theme, didn't they?

"What if I want to punish myself forever?" Puck asks Mia.

But she won't have it. "Puck, stop, you've been too hard on yourself for months now."

"How do you know I've . . ." Puck starts to ask, but they don't need to finish.

"Robyn," Mia interrupts. "She says that you ask her how I'm doing almost every day."

It's no surprise that Robyn sees through Puck so easily. She has had X-ray vision for their bullshit from the very beginning, and if anything, it's only gotten more penetrating since they started living together. But Puck has a high enough regard for their own intuition that they're still a little mortified. Robyn has been keeping a secret from them for months, hasn't she? She must know about Zander.

"You've told her," they surmise.

"Yes, but don't be mad at her. She said it was killing her to not be able to tell you."

"Why does everyone think I'm going to be mad at them?!" Puck shouts, which doesn't help their case. "I'm a good Puck now! An honest Puck! I don't bite!"

"I know a few Emory girls who would dispute the biting part," Mia quips.

For a second, her fizzing Diet Coke is the only sound between them. Puck wants to trade their French 75, which they ordered mostly as a bit, for a soda so they can also stand in solidarity with Mia's . . . boyfriend? Partner? What exactly are they to each other now?

"So how long have you been dating?" Puck asks, taking a sip of their drink but then remembering they should clarify. "This time around, I mean."

"Promise not to be mad?" Mia asks, and Puck rolls their eyes at that—but she is, of course, joking, as she confirms with a cheeky smile before continuing. "Zander called me right after I left your dumpy motel room that day and he got on the first flight to Atlanta. He said he had a lot of regrets in his life but kissing me at my own wedding wasn't one of them. We had sex that night."

If Puck hadn't already swallowed, they would spit purple gin all over the bar. "You *what*?!"

"I mean, we're all adults here, right?"

They've been dating again this *entire* time? Next Mia is going to reveal that *she* and Zander are the ones getting married this week. It's almost like the Emory crew has laid a trap to try to get Puck to feel justified about what they did, even though they've spent a year repenting for it. Puck *was* right about everything, and yet so wrong at the same time, and while that might seem puzzling, they know now that intent and action are not the same. Actually confusing is how Zander managed to keep the resurrection of his relationship a secret for so long.

Just as Puck is trying to unravel that mystery, an enormous wolf walking on two legs comes up behind Mia and wraps her up in a hug from behind.

"Who's an adult?" the wolf man asks.

"Certainly not you," she says, turning to greet Zander.

Removing the heavy faux-fur mask from his head, a sweaty Zander grins at Puck like he hasn't been hiding the biggest development in his life from them for the last year and change. "What's up, bro?" he says, addressing Puck, but his attention is divided. "Hey, Mia, is this Diet Coke? I'm sweltering in this costume."

She nods and he reaches over her to pick up the glass, gulping half of it down in one draught.

"Hey, that's mine!" Mia scolds him.

"Is there anything better than a cold Diet Coke, Puck?" Zander says, like he's reading ad copy. "Everyone in AA talks about a Higher Power, but I think men became gods when we created aspartame."

"OK, I'm cutting you off," Mia interrupts, grabbing the glass back from him. "You've had too many of these."

"And what are you supposed to be?" Puck asks, taking in Zander's glorified fursuit top to bottom.

"I'm Blaidd, the Half-Wolf," he says, like it's obvious, then points down at Mia. "I'm the loyal companion to Ranni the Witch here."

"Is that who I am, baby?" Mia asks.

"Yes, and I'll always protect you," Zander jokes.

Puck is glad to see them getting along but they would prefer the wolf-man acknowledge the elephant in the room. "So, uh, it kind of seems like you two are already married?" they prod.

"Look, we're sorry we didn't tell you, Puck," Zander says. "The truth is I *have* been really busy working. I'm opening a place in Durham. Breakfast sandwiches for Duke students. I can charge twenty bucks for a fresh bagel with a Kraft single and some bacon. Trying to save money for the *real* restaurant. And I've been busy in . . . other ways, too."

Even dressed like this—or is it because they're dressed like this?—Mia and Zander are still the hottest couple Puck has ever seen. The dirty joke only elicits a shove from Mia, who clearly isn't ready to let the conversation venture into banter territory just yet. She looks at Puck—and Puck feels like she's *really* looking at them again, for the first time in years.

"I forgave you a long time ago, Puck," she says. "After I heard how happy you were making Robyn, I knew you had changed."

They reach out to grab Mia's hand on the bar and clasp it tight. "I'm trying, Mia, I really am."

"You don't need to beat yourself up anymore, OK?" Mia assures them. "Zander and I? We owe the rest of our lives to you."

"You owe it to Robyn," Puck says through their tears. "I messed everything up, and she's the one who fixed it."

Mia squeezes Puck's hand back. "My dear Puck," she says, "I think maybe we fixed each other."

Acknowledgments

The first reader of this book, Ana Osorno, made me a mug that says "Proud Puck Apologist" and what did she get in return? A cruel dig at her ceramics hobby, delivered from the perspective of this book's protagonist. I *certainly* don't share Puck's opinions about pottery, a perfectly valid way to spend one's time. Really, doesn't the world need more bowls that are also kind of plates but mostly bowls? Sure they're unstackable and you have to hand-wash them, but they're also always blue-green for some reason! And there aren't enough of them in circulation, so the lesbian artisans who churn them out and foist them upon their friends are performing a valuable service. In seriousness, Ana, you saved this book. Your early feedback helped me immensely when I was losing faith in the premise. I'm a proud Ana apologist.

Other early readers include Brittany Harrington, Kate Compton, Amalie MacGowan, and Sharon McIlvain, all of whom offered incisive notes and provided free therapy. You are all geniuses. You are all beautiful. And how is that fair, really? Thank you for your crucial notes and reassurances. This is the novel that was read by the most people before release and I hope it worked. Otherwise, I want everyone to know who they can blame. It was all Brittany's fault.

ACKNOWLEDGMENTS

Thank you to my guardian angel Leila Campoli, to Alli Dyer at Temple Hill Entertainment, and to my editor Caolinn Douglas. If I ran the Pearly Gates, everyone who worked at Zando Projects would get VIP entry. Because of them, I've been able to spend the last five years dreaming up silly stories about queer people who are all sad in slightly different ways. Writing *Patricia Wants to Cuddle, Roland Rogers Isn't Dead Yet,* and *Puck* in rapid succession has been the highlight of my life.

And finally, thank you to all the hot nonbinary people who are mean to me. Please keep it coming. Everyone else needs to step it up.